THE KEY TO THE UNIVERSE

PATRICK SCALISI

OWL HOLLOW PRESS

Owl Hollow Press, LLC, Springville, UT 84663

The Key to the Universe

Library of Congress Cataloging-in-Publication Data
The Key to the Universe / P. Scalisi. — First edition.

Summary:
When the mythical Key to the Universe lands in his antique shop, Abe Titterman's enemies will go to any lengths to get their hands on the artifact that could potentially unlock the very meaning of existence.

ISBN 978-1-945654-29-9 (paperback)
ISBN 978-1-945654-30-5 (e-book)
LCCN TBD

Cover Design: Eugenia Hryshanina

*To my own Pop-pop, Pasquale Scirocco, whose adventures
included smuggling a monkey aboard his US Navy vessel,
having his appendix out in the middle of the Pacific Ocean,
and helping to shape four wonderful grandchildren.*

PART ONE

PROLOGUE

I t was early morning, and already the large foyer of the Halloran Estate on Mars was a flurry of activity.

Porters with wrist-mounted holographic displays and tablet pads directed dozens of people throughout the massive house. The clamor of indistinct conversation was everywhere: Now that Minnie Halloran had passed away, who was to receive the fine china set she had used to entertain the Warden of Delta Proxima? Or the original Picasso she had inherited from her father? Or the vintage starship parked in the garage? The greed in the air was thick, like fog on the terraformed lakes made by Minnie's intergalactic company.

Gabriella Rossi stood apart from it all as she took a moment to examine her appearance in a compact makeup mirror. The small, round reflection showed a woman of stout build with a plump face and brown hair shot through with gray that had been pulled into a severe bun. Gabriella was aware, as she dabbed her face with powder, that people saw her as an overbearing aunt. This was a perception she didn't mind; it disarmed her adversaries and distracted from her true nature.

Satisfied that age lines and crow's feet had been sufficiently diminished, Gabriella replaced the compact in her purse and entered the foyer, trying not to gawk at the grand staircase that could accommodate fifteen people shoulder to shoulder. Hoverlamps floated everywhere, casting far too much light on what should have been a grandiose space, decked with tapestries and statues from a dozen alien worlds. The glaring brightness reached into every shadowed alcove and high-ceiling corner to reveal the dust and cobwebs that had accumulated in the week since the massive cleaning staff had been let go. Rumor was that Minnie's reclusive son Peter had wanted nothing to do with the ancestral home except to put it on the market.

A representative from the solar system's prestigious Winkroot Law Firm stood at a podium just inside the entryway. Wearing a patterned, high-neck suit buttoned to the bottom of his chin and clutching a computer pad in one hand, the lawyer tapped out a few commands on his screen before looking up at Gabriella's arrival.

"Ah, Missus Rossi, we've been expecting you," said the lawyer in the same appeasing tone that he likely used with judges and clients alike. "Your representative has already begun sorting your inheritance, though it is legally required that you sign in receipt of the goods offered."

"I understand," Gabriella said.

The lawyer looked down at the computer pad and tapped the screen again. He began to read, "'To Gabriella Rossi, in appreciation for services rendered, I leave the contents of Vault Seven.'" He then turned the computer pad around and offered it to Gabriella along with a stylus. "In accordance with Solar Funerary Code 37.A, it is required that you sign here, and here, and here, please."

She did so, wondering how many times the lawyer had repeated *that* phrase today.

Taking the pad and stylus back, the lawyer waved to one of the firm's junior associates and said to Gabriella, "One of our junior associates will show you the way."

Gabriella had sent Michael Conti ahead to begin sorting the vault. She didn't know the full extent of what Minnie had left to her and didn't want to be bothered with antique chandeliers or book cases. Only one item interested her, and getting it had required *years* of effort—years of making sure that Minnie Halloran could never refuse Gabriella's request. With any luck, this acquisition would satisfy the powers that be and allow Gabriella to retire; running the Martian Mafia was a game for the young.

From the main foyer, the Winkroot junior associate led Gabriella past the library (Minnie had collected *actual* books) before coming to a staircase near the kitchen and dining room. Sounds from above faded away as they descended to the second sublevel.

At the bottom of the stairs, they came to a solid metal door nearly eight feet high. The junior associate kneaded the skin on the underside of his wrist and waved it in front of the security device next to the door. The crest of the Winkroot Law Firm appeared on the display screen. With a silence and smoothness that belied its size, the door slid into a wall recess, allowing entry.

"That's an interesting trick," Gabriella said to the junior associate.

The man pulled back the sleeve of his suit jacket; the skin just below his wrist pulsed with a single circular light.

"Genetically coded security protocols," the junior associate explained. "Ensures we offer the finest service to our clients. Every third-year associate is implanted with one. Sometimes they require a little massage to get the blood flowing."

Out of politeness, the lawyer indicated that Gabriella precede him into the vault. The air inside was stale and sterile, indicative of a highly controlled environment. Metal doors were set along both sides of a narrow corridor, the stone walls and ceiling in between reinforced with additional bands of metal. Each door bore a small brass number at eye level that increased as they walked down the hall. When they came to door number seven, the junior associate repeated the security procedure and waited in the hall as Gabriella stepped inside.

Michael was there, bent over a wooden crate and sifting through impact-resistant filler up to his elbows. He looked up when Gabriella entered the vault, withdrew his arms and stood at attention like a Solar Marine. It was then that Gabriella realized that this was *not* Michael Conti, but his brother, Anthony.

Gabriella looked around the small rectangular room, which had riveted walls and a single light strip in the ceiling. There was nowhere for another person to hide.

"Anthony, where is your brother?" she asked slowly as a sense of dread filled her chest. Anthony Conti was good for certain jobs—usually those that required fists instead of brains.

"Mikey's sick, Mama," Anthony said without moving from his rigid stance. "Been throwing up all night. I think he got the fungus flu."

Gabriella struggled to keep her outward appearance neutral and scanned the room again, this time taking note of its actual contents. There were crates and metal boxes, along with some items draped in white storage linen. *More of Minnie's treasures and artifacts*, Gabriella thought. *Stuff she could never find room to display.* To the right was a small safe set within the wall, its square door closed tight.

Gabriella allowed some of the dread to leave her body.

"How long have you been here?" she asked. "And for the love of all things sacred, Anthony, there's no need to stand like that."

Anthony relaxed a bit and smiled a near-idiotic grin. "Been here all morning, Mama. I did exactly what you asked."

"And what was that?" Gabriella said, gracing him with a small smile of her own.

"Yep, I did just what Mikey told me: the stuff in the safe got donated, and the rest is being sorted."

Gabriella's head whipped toward the wall safe. "Say that again," she ordered in a low, menacing tone.

THE KEY TO THE UNIVERSE · 13

Anthony's smile disappeared. "The stuff in the safe got donated?" he said, his inflection rising at the end of the statement. "And the rest is being sorted?"

Gabriella didn't say anything in response. Removing her purse from the crook of her arm, she held it in one hand while searching its contents with the other. Seconds later, she withdrew a small pistol, a LAS-er Derringer 2 model that was fashionable among protection-minded ladies. Gabriella turned a toggle on the gun, pointed it at Anthony, and blinked once as she shot him square in the chest. Her expression never changed as Anthony disintegrated into a small pile of dust with barely a surprised whimper.

Gabriella replaced the gun and stepped outside the vault to where the junior associate still waited.

"Part of the contents of this vault was inadvertently donated," Gabriella said to the lawyer. "Where did it go?"

The junior associate removed a palm-sized computer pad from his pocket and tapped the screen. After a moment, he said, "Your authorized representative had the items sent to a store called Intergalactic Curios on Phobos approximately one hour ago."

Gabriella nodded. "Have my driver ready to leave," she said. "I can find my own way back upstairs."

The lawyer looked up briefly from his pad. "And your authorized representative, ma'am?"

"He won't be joining me," she replied, and strode toward the vault exit.

CHAPTER ONE

There was no use arguing with a robot.

Quinn Titterman knew this, but he kept running through the bot's operational files in the hope that something—*anything!*—would get it running again.

Command: Sort

Response: File not found

Command: Inventory intake

Response: Unable to process your request

Command: Reboot

Response: An unknown error occurred

Quinn groaned. It was no use. To try and debate a robot's logic was worse than talking to a brick wall. At least the wall would have the courtesy to keep its mouth shut.

Morning was generally a quiet time at Intergalactic Curios, when Quinn—usually the first to rise—could get started on the day's work. There was, after all, always something to do. As one of the most prestigious antique shops in the inner solar system, Intergalactic Curios was known for light-years around for the quality and selection of its goods. In Quinn's opinion, there was no better way to spend school break than by handling some of the most sought-after antiquities in all of creation.

Of course, it didn't hurt that the shop was a curiosity all its own. Owned and operated by Quinn's great-grandfather, Abe Titterman, Intergalactic Curios was the only manmade structure on the fourteen-mile-long Martian moon of Phobos. Quinn's ancestor, Isaac Titterman, had been one of the few dukes of Mars to side with the Solar Government during the Secession Wars. In return for his loyalty, Isaac had been granted dominion over the moon in perpetuity. A member (or more) of the sprawling Titterman family had lived or worked there ever since.

Today, though, that work proved difficult. After getting up and having a quick bite to eat, Quinn usually sat with his computer to look at what was scheduled to come in and go out of the shop on any given day. But shortly after that morning's delivery, the inventory bots had gone out of service. Again.

Quinn stared around the room that his great-grandfather kept for him, trying to think of a solution. He barely saw the pennant for the Martian War Mongers VR Sector team or the poster proclaiming "Iash's Quotable Quotes" in stylized script. Instead, he wondered, not for the first time, if his great-grandfather was awake yet.

With no other solutions at hand, Quinn toggled the intercom.

At 107 years old, Abe Titterman felt he was entitled to a few creature comforts. Though humans lived much longer than at any other point in history, Abe had aged particularly well and resembled a spry seventy-year-old.

His morning routine began as it did on most days, regardless of whether any of his grandchildren or great-grandchildren were staying with him. Abe awoke in the penthouse apartment above the antique shop and prepared his usual breakfast of Arcturan egg whites and fresh-squeezed orange juice made from produce grown in the hydroponic orchards of the Red Planet. Sitting at his dining table, he spent the first half hour of each day eating and reading the news headlines from around the galaxy:

Labor strikes continue on Titan for the 33rd straight day, with union officials no closer to a resolution...

In a stunning turnaround, the Martian War Mongers beat the Venusian Brambles 178-172 in the Solar VR Sector Championships...

And—

Abe raised an eyebrow as his chest filled with mocking glee.

Nimbus Steele has been arrested again, this time for trying to smuggle Xidari artifacts out of a quarantined archeological zone. Based on an anonymous tip, the government raided Steele's antiques shop on Mars and found a number of other contraband items.

He'll be going away for a while this time, Abe thought with a satisfied smile.

Abe closed the headlines and brought his calendar up on the screen. Three appointments that day: a woman interested in expanding her collection of diamond stalactites from Quemos-7, an ice industrialist from Europa with a penchant for twentieth-century Earth coins, and an alien from Nalaxis who had given his name simply as Bob and wanted to find a series of heirloom erasers that his family had sold three generations prior.

His excitement quickly waning, Abe sighed, considered opening the news headlines again and then, with a hand on his creaking back, got up from the kitchen table.

"Another day, Grace..." Abe said to the framed portrait of his late wife that hung on one wall of the dining room.

Dropping his dishes in the washing machine, Abe grabbed his blazer and was about to head out the door when a voice sounded over the intercom.

"Pop-pop?"

Abe went over to the wall-mounted speaker. "Good morning, Quinn."

"Are you coming downstairs?" Quinn asked. "We're having a problem with the robots again."

Abe pressed the button to speak and let out a whine that was louder and longer than necessary.

"I know," Quinn went on. "Plus, your first appointment of the day is in fifteen minutes."

"Yes, Missus Finegraft. The Quemos stalactites."

"That's right," said Quinn. "I'll meet you in the shop."

Abe proceeded down the stairwell that connected the penthouse to the shop and came in through the doorway directly behind the front counter. He looked out onto a round room finished in warm brown wood, with shelves and display cases creating a flowing path throughout the store. A narrow staircase led to a balcony that served as the story's upper gallery and was filled with even more goods. Quinn stood waiting at the counter.

Abe craned his neck to catch the sightline to the front entrance. The transparent docking bubble adjacent to the front entrance was empty; beyond that, the view of Mars was even better than from the dining room, a rusty metal ball left out in the rain.

"She's not even here yet," Abe complained while resting his elbows on the counter and cradling his chin between his hands. "If I could just have a few minutes..."

"The philosopher Iash says that a gracious host is always punctual, even if his company is not," Quinn intoned.

The older man glared at his great-grandson, who was fond of quoting alien philosophers. At twelve years old, Quinn was far too smart for his own good, in Abe's opinion, and Abe kept meaning to talk to his granddaughter about that.

"Well," Abe retorted, "what does Iash have to say about old ladies from Saturn who have too much time and money on their hands?"

"Not much, I'm afraid," said Quinn, who had moved to straighten a display of stone-hewn weapons from some primitive planet or another.

Abe sighed again and consulted his watch. "What deliveries were due this morning?" he asked. "Anything good? Anything *exciting?*"

Without looking up, Quinn recited, "That overdue shipment from Neptune Station, the tapestries for Mister Fisher, and a consignment lot."

"We'll have to take a close look at those tapestries," Abe said, "make sure they're really made out of that underwater sea fern from Elchoir."

"Didn't you smell them in the stairwell?" Quinn asked.

"If that's the case, Mister Fisher *will* be pleased," Abe said. "But what about this consignment lot? Where did it come from?"

"The Halloran Estate," Quinn said.

"Reeeeally?" Abe said with more interest than he had given anything else that morning. "I didn't expect anyone to consign their heirlooms for another day, at least. Goodness, they didn't even wait until her bones were cold."

"Her bones were probably cold days ago, if we're getting technical," Quinn said.

"You know what I mean! Did you run an inventory yet?"

"No, because the robots are broken," Quinn said in exasperation.

"Let's see what we can do about that."

Abe booted up the computer embedded into the front counter, the excitement of discovery coursing through him for the first time in weeks. It was the thrill of the hunt that he loved, even after all these years. Getting called to examine an estate or appraise some long-stored-away treasure, even going to tag sales—these were the things that kept the monotony from becoming terminal in the years since Grace's passing.

Abe's eyes ran down the screen. "Let's see what we've got." He stared for a moment longer before exclaiming, "Ha! It was strictly a donation. We get to keep all the profit!"

"It's probably not worth anything then," said Quinn, who had finished with his straightening and now joined his great-grandfather at the front counter.

"Sometimes these fools don't know what they've got," Abe replied without lifting his eyes from the screen. "Or some favored niece thinks she's getting the grand piano and ends up with a collection of handmade Pyrem dolls. She assumes they're worthless and donates them in a fit of anger. And we reap the benefits. It's happened before."

Abe went silent as he tried to see if there was anything else to glean from the consignment ticket. But without the robots...

"Did you try turning them off and turning them on again, like you're always telling me to do?" Abe asked.

"Yes, Pop-pop," said Quinn with just a hint of exasperation. "That was the first thing I did."

"Well then, we'll have to go down there later today. Maybe after the Finegraft and Fisher sales, we can get that upgrade you keep talking about."

"It *would* make things easier." Quinn looked up at a sound from the direction of the landing pad. "Speak of the devil."

Abe followed his great-grandson's gaze. A black luxury yacht with severe boxy corners and a bluish skylight covering most of its top hull had passed through the airlock aperture and was in the process of landing.

Abe frowned. "Unless Missus Finegraft has finally invested in something the rest of us call taste, *that* is not her ship."

CHAPER TWO

Gabriella strode through the front door of Intergalactic Curios, her eyes expertly appraising the place as well as—if not better than—the four Nalaxan bodyguards behind her. The placement of the display cases made the shop feel stocked but not cluttered, using the space to its maximum efficiency while concealing how little room there was to maneuver. She was pleased to see one of the bodyguards—all of whom resembled rhinos stuffed into designer dress suits—split off and make his way toward the second-floor gallery while Gabriella and the other three continued toward the front counter.

The two people there were a study in contrasts. The older man was short with parted gray hair, a lined face whose maturity was mostly in the jowls, and a small gut that was typical—even expected—of men his age. The younger boy, not yet in his teens, was tall and wiry with slightly unkempt hair.

Gabriella and the three Nalaxans stopped in unison about a foot away from the counter. The young man nudged the older man slightly.

"How may I help you?" the latter said while wearing a salesman smile.

"Do you know who I am?" Gabriella asked.

"Someone I hope will be a valued customer for years to come," the old man replied.

The young man nudged his companion again, this time more aggressively, and said, "You're Gabriella Rossi."

Gabriella turned slightly to face the young man. "I knew you were smart just by looking at you." She turned back to the old man. "I presume you're Abraham Titterman, the owner of this place."

Abe bent slightly at the waist. "At your service."

"Good," Gabriella continued. "Now that we're acquainted, let me tell you what I want. This morning you likely received a consignment from the Halloran Estate. Is that correct?"

Abe shook his head. "I'm not at liberty to discuss store inventory with customers before I've had a chance to process it."

This time, the young man made no attempt to conceal the elbow that dug into the ribs of his companion. Abe grunted while the young man said sharply, "Stop it, Pop-pop!" Then to Gabriella: "Uh, yes, we got a small shipment from the Halloran Estate."

Gabriella nodded once. "What's your name, son?"

"Quinn. Quinn Titterman."

One of the old man's great-grandchildren, Gabriella remembered from the file she had read on the way over. Very smart, the notes had said, with prospects for academic scholarships to university several years ahead of schedule.

Aloud she said, "Quinn, I have a problem that I hope you and Abraham can help me with." Gabriella shifted her body and moved closer to the counter, separating slightly from her bodyguards. "A gentleman who is no longer in my employment accidentally donated to your shop a number of goods that I received from the late Minnie Halloran. My associates," she indicated the Nalaxans, "will show you the writ of inheritance from the Winkroot Law Firm. I am interested in one item only: a rectangular metal box about twelve inches in length. I will allow you to keep the rest of the donation to sell at profit."

"That shouldn't be a problem," said Quinn.

Now it was Abe's turn to look aghast. He glared at the younger man for a moment, then resumed his salesman smile and turned back to Gabriella. "Uh, legally speaking—"

Quinn grabbed the old man by the shoulders and steered him toward the door behind the counter. Gabriella heard Quinn sputter, "Just get what she wants!" before pushing Abe toward the door. Abe glowered at Quinn for a second, mumbled something, and disappeared through the doorway.

"He'll be just a minute," Quinn said. "I'll be happy to wait with you until he gets back."

Gabriella gave a hand signal to one of the bodyguards. Without a word passing between them, the black-suited Nalaxan lumbered around the counter to follow Abe through the doorway.

"You won't mind if my associate oversees the retrieval," Gabriella said. It was not a suggestion.

Carved from the bedrock of Phobos, the subterranean storeroom of Intergalactic Curios resided two stories underground and had once served as Duke Isaac Titterman's extensive wine cellar. The room had not held libations in two generations, and Abe had had the storeroom expanded and modernized when he had taken over the shop eight decades earlier. Industrial, low-emission lighting ran across the walls and ceiling, and security systems monitored everything from the temperature to the amount of cosmic radiation penetrating the moon's surface. Robots typically handled inventory receipt and requests from the front counter, though Abe and Quinn had found themselves going down to the storeroom more and more often since the start of Quinn's school break to correct mistakes that the aging robots were prone to make—that is, when they weren't broken down entirely.

Abe stepped up to the entrance door of the storeroom and submitted to both a palm and retina scan while Gabriella Rossi's bodyguard waited two steps behind him. With the security protocols clear, the door swung open and the lights came on to illuminate cages and safes, shelves and cabinets, tables and workbenches, all crammed with assorted goods not yet ready or suitable for display, or inventory that was simply not needed. The warren was an archeologist's dream, and the slightly musty smell of preserved goods filled the air.

Abe moved toward a six-by-six-foot hypersteel shipping container in the center of the room, then glanced over his shoulder to check on the bodyguard. The Nalaxan had not moved from the base of the stairs. Abe was about to tell him to come and help when he realized that the reason why the creature had not moved was to block Abe from escaping back up the stairs. Taking in the bodyguard's bulk framed in the doorway, his pinched ears and gray horn, the way the dress suit barely contained his muscular build, Abe turned back to the shipping container without a word.

The container, stamped with shipping brands from a dozen planets and pockmarked with micrometeor strikes and rust, sat on a square section of floor that could be raised and lowered from the moon's auxiliary docking station. This was where freight deliveries occurred and where Abe kept his own personal ship, *The Lady Grace*. Abe had had the system installed specifically for ease of inventory, and, indeed, this was where the shipment from Minnie Halloran's estate had ended up, along with the other goods that had been delivered that morning from the shipping transfer station planetside.

"Just, uh, just a moment," Abe said to the immobile bodyguard. "It's, uh, likely mixed in with the other goods."

Abe grabbed a plastide printout from the side of the container—the shipment's inventory—and scanned the list.

"There's several items here from the Halloran Estate," Abe said to the bodyguard. "Which one was it that your boss wanted?"

Abe didn't think the bodyguard would respond. But after about three beats, the Nalaxan said, "It'll be a rectangular metal box, twelve inches long."

Abe was so taken aback by the Nalaxan's high-pitched, nasally voice that he said, "I'm sorry?"

"I said, it'll be a rectangular metal box, twelve inches long."

Must be the horn, Abe thought. Aloud, he said, "That's not giving me a lot to go on."

The bodyguard said nothing else.

Abe sighed. With a resigned grunt, he unbolted the side of the container, which swung out and blocked his view of the Nalaxan.

An overhead lamp inside the container flickered on to shed a weak glow in the cramped space. Abe squinted and could make out crates and a few pieces of wooden furniture.

It won't be with the bigger items on the floor, Abe thought. Instead, he scanned the cargo netting on the inner wall of the container, his eyes moving past some kind of scepter, a few cloth jewelry boxes and—yes!—a nondescript metal box about the length of Abe's forearm. Abe fingered the box, was about to remove it from the cargo netting, then changed his mind and exited the shipping container.

"It's a mess in here," Abe said. "The freight hauler must not have put on the artificial gravity in his cargo bay. I'm gonna need some help. Call down my great-grandson, will ya?"

The bodyguard took a step forward. "I'll help you."

"No!" Abe replied. The bodyguard stopped abruptly and twitched his ears. Abe continued, "There's, uh, there's very delicate goods in here, and I don't want the likes of you blundering about wrecking anything."

Now the bodyguard lowered his horn slightly, and Abe could see that the creature's gray eyes were lidded in anger.

Abe cleared his throat. "That is, my great-grandson is much more accustomed to helping me. He's trained, you know."

The Nalaxan looked around the room at some of the un-moving robots, cylindrical machines about two feet tall with multiple arms and pneumatic tools jutting from their bodies.

"Have one of the robots help you," the bodyguard said tersely.

Abe let out a mirthless chuckle. "These things? They're worthless." He kicked the nearest one, eliciting a hollow metal clang. "Broken down half the time anyway, and I don't trust them any more than I trust you. Look, just ask Quinn to come down."

The bodyguard looked as if he was going to continue walk-ing toward the shipping container. Abe's heart hammered in his chest. Then the Nalaxan turned toward the stairs and yelled, "Send the kid down!"

Uncomfortable silence hung between Gabriella and Quinn as they waited at the front counter. Gabriella could see that the young man was unsettled and made no attempt at conversation, reveling in his discomfort. Just when he seemed on the verge of starting some awkward small talk, she turned half away from the counter and began scanning a set of stone-hewn weapons in a nearby glass cabinet.

"Those are from Itvero Prime," Quinn said. "The, uh, civili-zation there is extinct. Which is strange because the inhabitants of Itvero Beta developed into a space-faring culture."

"With weapons like these, I'm not particularly surprised," Gabriella said.

"The philosopher Iash says that it is our capacity to wage peace, not war, that determines the civility of a civilization—"

"Send the kid down!"

A shrill voice echoed up the stairwell, interrupting Quinn's next statement about the philosophy of Iash in regards to sentient development.

Quinn glanced at the exit door, and Gabriella said, "You better go help. I'm sure Iash would say, 'It's not wise to keep a Nalaxan waiting.'"

Footsteps sounded in the stairwell down to the storage vault. Abe inched out from behind the open door of the shipping container, hoping Quinn was coming alone. Within seconds, his great-grandson passed through the security door. The Nalaxan bodyguard turned to look at the new arrival.

With the alien's back to him, Abe leapt forward while swinging the heavy metal scepter he had found in the storage netting. The bludgeon connected with the Nalaxan's neck where the collar of his white shirt peeked above the black suit jacket. The rhino creature crumbled to the ground.

Abe and Quinn looked at each other in surprise. Abe recovered first, letting his arm relax and the head of the scepter rest on the ground. The impact had sent what felt like an earthquake up his shoulder.

"Well," Abe said, "that was easier than I thought."

Quinn's eyes went wide. "What are you *doing*?!"

"I'm protecting *my* personal property." Abe pointed to the Nalaxan with the scepter. "Is he dead?"

Quinn came fully into the storeroom and knelt by the Nalaxan.

"I think you hit the Nalaxan Nerve," the younger man said after a moment's examination.

"The *what*?" Abe asked.

Quinn stood. "It's something we learned about in xenobiology. Nalaxans evolved to be tough frontal-assault warriors. But there's a trade-off: a weak spot at the base of their neck called the Nalaxan Nerve. A blow there knocks 'em out cold."

"Good," Abe said. "Let's get the box and get out of here."

Quinn shook his head emphatically. "Let's just give her what she wants, Pop-pop! That's Gabriella 'Mama' Rossi upstairs. The *head* of the Martian Mafia. You don't just take things from her. As it is, I don't know how we're gonna explain this." Quinn waved at the unconscious Nalaxan.

"We'll be long gone before he comes around," Abe countered. "Besides, if she wants this box so badly, it must be valuable. I'm willing to take some risk for that."

"Some risk?" Quinn stepped toward his great-grandfather.

Abe held him off with the scepter, then darted inside the shipping container and grabbed the box in question from the cargo netting, gripping it close to his chest with his free hand. It was lighter than he thought it would be.

"We can hide out for a few days," Abe reasoned as he exited the container, "until this whole thing blows over."

"This isn't going to *blow over*," Quinn countered. "This is the Martian Mafia!"

Abe ignored him. "I'm going now," he said as he pushed a button that lowered the whole platform into the auxiliary docking bay.

"You can't fly the ship without me," Quinn said.

"Then I guess you'd better come along."

Quinn scowled and jumped onto the moving platform. In moments, the lift came to a halt in a decidedly less spectacular landing platform than the one outside of Intergalactic Curios' front entrance. Excavated from the bare rock with no adornments except those needed for utility—light strips, a few tool chests, and a bay door that was currently closed—the hangar was large enough for three small spacecraft to fit side by side. The only ship currently present was *The Lady Grace.*

Named for Quinn's great-grandmother—Abe's late wife— the ship was a graceful recreational cruiser with a pointed cockpit and a cylindrical body. Along with its nose landing gear, the ship rested on two Whyte Industries Limited Pulsar Class Faster-than-Light engines, which hung below the fuselage at the rear of the vessel.

Abe hurried to the side hatch and punched in the combination. As he and Quinn stepped inside, Abe rushed past the midship sleeping quarters and kitchen and headed straight for the cockpit.

"Can we please just go back upstairs?" pleaded Quinn, who followed hesitantly behind. "You don't even have your license, and I only have a learner's permit."

Abe shrugged. "Guess I'll start pushing buttons then." He flopped into one of the two pilot seats and began punching buttons and toggles at random. The side hatch closed, the engines roared to life within the confines of the hangar, and the coffeemaker in the kitchen began brewing a fresh pot.

"Stop!" Quinn cried, though Abe had already started the launch sequence quite by accident. In front of the cockpit's broad viewport, the bay door split open into the black vacuum of space.

Quinn fell into the second pilot seat and pulled on his restraining harness. He too started pressing buttons on the dash, checking indicators and verifying the clearance outside the port window. In his head, he ran through the preflight sequence he had learned and practiced in his flying class at home: *FLAGS,* he thought, *Fission reaction, Launch area, Anticollision lights, Gravity generator, Safety harness.*

"I'll fly around front so we can give the box to Mama Rossi and she can leave us alone," Quinn said.

Abe was about to object, but Quinn gunned the cruiser out of the hanger faster than was necessary, pressing Abe back forcefully into the comfortable confines of the seat. Banking a hard left, the cruiser began its quick orbit of the moon—only to be jolted to a stop by a powerful suspension field.

Abe and Quinn stared out of the forward viewport and directly into the prow of a small but heavily armed Solar Government special forces ship.

CHAPTER THREE

The airlock between the two ships snapped into place with a pressurized *hiss*. Quinn and Abe had barely had time to react before the suspension field had drawn *The Lady Grace* into docking position. Now, they waited for the ceiling hatch in the midship living quarters to open, all the while wondering if they were somehow being rescued from the Martian Mafia boss or being arrested themselves.

The airlock opened, a metal ladder descended, and a heavily accented voice called down, "You will ascend into my vessel slowly and one at a time. I know there are two of you aboard. You will bring the box with you."

Abe had been in the process of hiding the metal box inside the kitchen stove. Now he withdrew it with a frown that seemed to say, *No point now.* He straightened, closed the stove door, and followed Quinn up the ladder into the special forces ship.

Once inside, Quinn surveyed the interior of the vessel, observing the bulkheads covered with computer, surveillance, and analysis equipment. It was warmer than was comfortable, and a strange smell, like an exotic cooking spice, hung in the humid air.

Finally, his eyes came to rest on their host. The ship's operator was an alien, seven feet tall, thin with disproportionately long limbs that made him appear lithe and agile. He wore some kind of body armor over his gray skin, and piercing green eyes looked out from a head that was hairless and had two slits for nostrils.

"Greetings. We meet you in peace and goodwill," Quinn said politely, using the standard greeting for an undetermined species.

Abe scowled. "This certainly *looks* like a government ship, but I've been around long enough to know that if you're with the police, you're supposed to give us your name and rank."

The alien twitched its head to one side. "I am Agent Aerius," he said. "Registration SOL3468-23 with the Solar Government Special Forces." He produced a badge from somewhere on his person and held it briefly aloft.

"Thank you, Aerius," Quinn replied before his greatgrandfather could say anything insulting. "Why did you stop our ship?"

The alien moved his rangy body to one of the computers and tapped a key to bring the screen to life. The display was in some kind of alien language—probably the agent's native tongue. When Aerius read aloud, the translators Quinn had had implanted behind his ears since birth—like most people—conveyed the message in a language he could understand.

"Pursuant to Solar Code 4734.45, section thirty-two, you are required to aid me with a special operation of external security," said Aerius. "Failure to do so will result in your being charged with obstruction of justice and other penalties under Solar Law. If you are required to miss work as part of this operation, the Solar Government will reimburse you wages equal to your current rate of pay and—"

"Look," Abe interjected, "we were just about to make a delivery. Whatever 'operation' you're involved with has nothing to do with us."

"Unlikely," replied Aerius, turning back to them. "My commander has traced an important item from the estate of Minnie Halloran to this shop. With a vessel owned by known criminal Gabriella 'Mama' Rossi at your main docking port, it is reasonable to assume that you were fleeing with the object in question."

Abe puffed out his chest in an attempt at intimidation, even though he was nearly two feet shorter than the government agent. "And what object would that be?"

"The Key to the Universe," Aerius replied, his green eyes unblinking.

Abe deflated like the core of a collapsing star. Quinn stared at the alien agent, dumbfounded.

Quinn managed to speak first: "That's not possible."

"It's a myth," Abe added. "A fairy tale. Every dealer on both sides of the Asteroid Belt knows that."

"Then open the box and find out," Aerius challenged.

Abe had been holding the box in the crook of his right arm since he and Quinn had come aboard. Abe's arm twitched, but he did not release the box.

"How do you know that's what we have?" Quinn asked before his great-grandfather could recover. "How do you even know this is what you're looking for?"

Aerius continued to stare at them for a minute. Then he said, "According to my briefing, Solar Government Intelligence has long known that the Key to the Universe was under Minnie Halloran's protection, and we possessed a rough description of the box in which it was stored. Following Halloran's death, myself and other agents have been watching for signs of the box, monitoring communications from the Halloran Estate and trying to ascertain its new owner. Yesterday, we intercepted a coded transmission from a junior associate at the Winkroot Law Firm, and I was dispatched to follow our most promising lead.

"The Key must not be allowed to come into Gabriella Rossi's possession. I have been authorized to tell you this much so that you may understand the importance of my mission. If Gabriella Rossi has the Key, she will use it for acts of terror."

Quinn turned to his great-grandfather. "I agree, Pop-pop. If the Key's in there, we can't let her have it. It's much safer with Agent Aerius."

"Bah!" Abe said, clutching the box tighter to his body and backing slowing toward the airlock entrance. "You think the government wouldn't misuse such an object? For all the reading you do, Quinn, I'm surprised at your naivety. What would the government do with the Key that Mama Rossi wouldn't? Huh?"

Aerius rose to his full height within the confines of the ship, the alien's shadow spilling over Abe and Quinn.   "The Solar Government wants only to keep the Key safe," Aerius said with conviction. "Give it to me so that I may verify its identity and transfer it to the care of my commander."

Abe was almost to the airlock and Aerius was about to lunge when an explosion rocked the government craft and sent its three occupants sprawling. Abe fell bottom-first into the hatch and stuck there, like a clog in a drain, while Quinn and the alien both slammed into the equipment along the port bulkhead. Another explosion hit seconds later.

Aerius said something in his native language, an exclamation that sounded like a curse. Then the alien lumbered toward the front of the ship, his detainees temporarily forgotten. "The Rossi human attacks us!"

A third explosion hammered the special forces ship. Abe popped through the airlock hatch and fell back into *The Lady Grace*, crying out as his tailbone struck the floor of the ship. He remained sprawled on the floor as Quinn scrambled back into the cruiser, triggering the release that raised the ladder and closed the hatch.

"Don't move!" Quinn exclaimed as he made his way to-ward the cockpit. "Those shots are gonna trigger the emergency release!"

Sure enough, a shrill alarm sounded inside the ship as, with another hiss, *The Lady Grace* separated from the special forces vessel.

☆

In the cockpit of her luxury cruiser, Gabriella stood at the shoulder of the Nalaxan pilot and watched as the bulky rhino creature operated the controls in a U-shaped console with a grace that belied his size. Seated in a thick-backed chair with massive armrests, the Nalaxan swiveled between the controls and readouts that surrounded him, including a board with numerous switches, a small screen that showed the ship's status, and a large tactical display that overlaid most of the viewport. The display currently showed a detailed readout of the government special forces ship.

Illuminated by the emerald glow of the screens, Gabriella leaned slightly forward and pointed to a spot on the tactical grid, saying, "Another shot. Aim for the armor *above* the engine assembly. That's the weak point in those models."

The Nalaxan did as he was told, pressing a series of buttons with his wrinkled and studded hand to send another volley from the luxury cruiser's retractable LAS-er Cannon.

"Impact is good," the Nalaxan pilot said in his nasally voice. "Target correct, but the computer is reading no damage."

"That should have disabled it," Gabriella replied, standing bolt upright. "The ship's been modified. Keep firing at will. Be careful not to hit the Titterman cruiser."

The Nalaxan continued shooting, some of his volleys going wide in brilliant arcs of light as the government ship spun from the impacts it had already received. Moments later, it disengaged from *The Lady Grace* and the two vessels began to float in opposite directions.

"Emergency separation," Gabriella said. "Keep firing on the government vessel. I want it out of commission. Then we can deal with the Tittermans and figure out who has the Key."

"I'm getting us out of here," Quinn said from the cockpit of *The Lady Grace.* "This isn't a battleship, and we won't last long in a fight."

Abe, still sitting on the floor beneath the airlock hatch and nursing a sore bottom, said, "What, no platitudes about upholding the law and the philosophy of justice?"

Quinn didn't look back at his great-grandfather. "Something isn't right. We should go to the Martian Police before handing over that box."

"I'm not handing it over to anyone!" said Abe, springing up from the floor, his bruises temporarily forgotten. "You heard what that—that thing up there said. The Key to the Universe, Quinn! The greatest antiquity in all the galaxy, and it walked into *my* shop!"

"Hold on!" Quinn said by way of a response.

"Why? What are you doing now?"

"FTL drive ignition in three… two… one!"

Abe barely managed to grab onto the stove as *The Lady Grace* jolted in acceleration. He watched as the bulkheads and appliances rattled briefly with the transition to hyperspace. When the ship stabilized, he limped forward and strapped into the cockpit next to Quinn.

"Where are we going?" Abe asked. "And how did you even know how to do that?"

Quinn looked away sheepishly. "Well…"

"Well what?"

Quinn still wouldn't look at his great-grandfather. "That is, I've never actually *used* an FTL drive before."

Abe stared at the young man, slack jawed.

"I mean, I've read about it," Quinn went on hastily. "But you're technically not allowed to fly faster than light until you've had your license for a year. We didn't blow up though, so there's that."

"Great," Abe said sardonically.

"As for where we're going," Quinn consulted the instrument panel, "I decided to set a random course."

Abe stared out of the forward viewport, trying not to think about the pain in his backside or the fact that they could end up crashing into a star and instead focusing on the no-color brightness of hyperspace. He remembered the holo-serials of his youth and how the speed of light had always been portrayed with streaking colors, the great galactic heroes sharing drinks with attractive companions as their ships split the void and the zooming stars cast colorful tattoos over their faces and bodies. But reality was never like fiction. Abe had taken his first FTL trip when he was Quinn's age. He regarded the disappointment of seeing real hyperspace as the end of his childhood and the beginning of young adulthood.

Thinking about the holo-serials suddenly reminded Abe of a familiar storytelling trope in old adventure tales. The bottom fell out of his stomach. "What about tracking beacons?" he asked.

Quinn turned to look at his great-grandfather, and Abe was momentarily satisfied to see that he had thought of something Quinn had overlooked.

"Uh…"

"Well?" Abe pressed. "Any bright ideas in that big brain of yours?"

Quinn scanned the buttons, levers, and readouts on the instrument panel, apparently looking for something that wasn't there. "Well, it's *your* ship, Pop-pop," he finally said. "How would *you* find a tracking beacon?"

Abe considered this for a moment. This was the kind of problem that Grace would have known how to solve at once, a challenge that would have delighted her. Distractedly, he pulled up the display on his side of the dash and began navigating through the ship's various operations. He barely saw the text and diagrams until something clicked on a subconscious level and he whooped in triumph.

Quinn craned his neck to see what his great-grandfather had found.

"Hull diagnostic," Abe said, pointing to one of the menu options. "It'll scan for imperfections on the outside of the ship."

A worry crease appeared between Quinn's eyebrows. "Will that work?"

Abe shrugged. "Unless you can think of a better idea, it's worth a try."

Quinn said he couldn't, so Abe began the diagnostic. In seconds, the computer started beeping rapidly as a red dot appeared on the ship's schematic diagram. The dot was located right next to the top docking hatch.

Abe uttered an oath and said to Quinn, "Better pull us out of hyperspeed."

Quinn hit the appropriate sequence and grabbed the controls. The ship jolted again as it returned to normal space, the brightness transitioning immediately to black as if someone had thrown a giant blanket over the heavens.

"What are we gonna do?" Quinn asked.

Abe was navigating the operational menus again, working as quickly as his liver-spotted hands were able. "Service bots" was all the older man said in response.

After tapping the screen for a few more seconds, Abe had what he wanted. He sat back in his seat and said to Quinn, "Watch your screen, will you?"

Both displays showed a video feed from outside the ship. The first-person, fisheye view shambled as it moved along the graceful, seamless hull of the ship. In a moment, the camera operator had come within view of the top docking hatch while another creature angled into the hemispherical shot.

This second creature was a spidery service robot, its small body suspended on a number of spindly legs that attached magnetically to the hull. Resting in a sealed alcove on the outside the ship, the bots could perform a variety of functions between regularly scheduled maintenance (which, on *The Lady Grace*, was every three months or every three thousand light-years). The bot currently in view of the camera had a small welding laser attached to its body to repair minor damage made by micrometeors or other stellar debris. And though Abe and Quinn couldn't see it, the camera operator was a similar robot with a video feed attached to its body.

"I told the computer that the tracking beacon was a hull breach," Abe explained with delight at his own ingenuity.

Almost as soon as the words left his mouth, the camera panned down to give a better shot of the hull. There, next to the circular docking hatch, was a small round transmitter that had embedded itself into the ship's otherwise-flawless metal skin.

The service bot with the laser aimed its tool at the transmitter and fired. The transmitter glowed orange for a second, sparked, flared, and smoked for barely an instant before the oxygen-starved environment outside the ship stole even this away.

"Someone's watching out for us," Abe said, patting the wall of the cockpit. "Now hit it!"

As soon as the service bots were back inside their alcove, Quinn reactivated the FTL drive on another random course.

It was early evening, ship's time, when Quinn announced he was finally taking *The Lady Grace* out of hyperspeed.

"We'll get our bearings, then decide what to do next," he said, back stiff from piloting longer than he ever had before.

"And hope there's no one waiting for us on the other side," Abe replied as he took his seat in the cockpit with the box securely on his lap.

Their collective anxiety throughout the day had prevented them from focusing on much else, including the alleged Key.

Quinn had tended to his great-grandfather's injuries with the first-aid kit on board, using a macromolecular repair tool to mend the bruising from Abe's fall through the airlock. After that, Abe had paced the ship restlessly, sometimes playing with the kitchen appliances, while Quinn had spent the remainder of the day at the helm. Now they waited for the ship to transition out of hyperspace.

"Hold on," Quinn said.

Abe nodded as the ship jolted again and the outside heavens resolved themselves into a wall of darkness punctuated by countless stars.

"Computer's getting our coordinates now," Quinn continued. "We're in… quadrant seventy-two."

Abe sat up straighter in his chair. "That's an excellent choice! And you said the computer chose our destination at random?" He patted Quinn on the shoulder. "Well done!"

Quinn raised an eyebrow. "You know where we are?" he said with a chuckle. "We haven't even checked the charts yet."

"'The best food's in quadrant seventy-two,'" Abe recited. "Haven't you ever heard that jingle?"

Quinn stared at his great-grandfather.

"Anyway," Abe continued, "if memory serves—and mine's still as sharp as a Pyrem needle—we're rather close to the Adams Café." Abe patted his slightly protruding belly. "After the day we've had, I'm ready to relax a bit."

"With two ships on our tail?" Quinn exclaimed. "I don't think we have time to stop at a restaurant, Pop-pop."

"Ah, that's where you're wrong," Abe said. "Fastest service in the universe. And you'll see why when we get there. Besides, the prospect of a good meal has stoked my curiosity, and I don't intend to open this box on an empty stomach."

CHAPTER FOUR

Aerius ranged along the length of his ship, checking computer displays and assessing the damage to his vessel. He reached one elongated arm up to close a small valve near the ceiling, then moved to the computer that provided telemetry analysis. The Rossi human had thought to disable his ship with an attack that would have neutralized a standard special forces vessel; luckily, the special modifications to Aerius's ship had prevented her from doing anything more than superficial damage. After the disappearance of *The Lady Grace* into hyperspace, Aerius had taken the opportunity to escape as well.

Settling into a special chair adapted for his long body, Aerius switched on the computer and waited for a transmission from his tracking beacons. He had placed two on *The Lady Grace*—a trick he had learned during his days as a *chayat*. A fleeing ship almost always expected to find a tracking beacon on its hull; finding that beacon and destroying it created a sense of security so that a second beacon was usually overlooked. It didn't always work. Some captains were smarter than others; some had even used the trick themselves. But Aerius guessed that the humans Abe and Quinn Titterman would become less vigilant after disposing of the obvious tracking beacon near their docking hatch and completely bypass the one hidden near their engine well.

Aerius was still waiting for the transmission, and becoming increasingly worried that his gamble had failed, when a communications tone rang throughout the ship. Spinning the wheeled chair, Aerius moved to a different monitor and powered it to life. A human woman with fair skin and blond hair appeared on screen. One of her eyes was blue, the color of clear water, while the other was green behind a hologram that projected from a computer implanted on part of her right cheek and temple. As Aerius watched, information from the hologram spun in concentric circles that the woman's eye, with assistance from the C-shaped bio-computer, could probably detect and interpret.

"Greetings, Special Agent Aerius," the woman said.

"Greetings, Madeline," replied Aerius, recalling the name of the commander's personal lieutenant.

"Commander H on the line for you. Voice only, as usual."

The woman disappeared, replaced by the seal of the Solar Government. A green dot on the bottom right of the screen was the only indicator that someone was listening on the other end of the line.

"Greetings, commander," said Aerius.

"Greetings, special agent," said the voice with its usual military efficiency.

"I was going to check in momentarily, sir," said Aerius. "To be honest, I had hoped to deliver some good news alongside the bad."

"Bad news?"

"I intercepted the antique dealer as ordered, sir, but his apprehension was interrupted by Gabriella Rossi, the criminal known as Mama Rossi." Aerius paused, tilting his head slightly to one side. "Commander," he continued, "though I have studied the Rossi human's files extensively, I still fail to understand the meaning behind the honorific 'mama.'"

"It'll have to wait for another time," Commander H said impatiently. "What happened?"

"The Rossi human attacked us. The antique dealer escaped in a vessel designated *The Lady Grace*. I was in the process of tracking it when you called, sir."

"That woman has meddled in my affairs for too long. Are you confident you'll be able to track the Tittermans?"

"Yes, sir. That is, I hope so, sir."

"Good. Then I look forward to your next report, special agent."

The light on the bottom of the screen turned from green to red. Aerius switched off the monitor and returned to the computer he had been working at originally. Windows opened on the screen in quick succession: star charts, telemetry patterns, flight paths—all coming from quadrant seventy-two.

Success!

During his call with Commander H, the computer had intercepted a transmission from one of the still-active tracking beacons. His long fingers a blur at the controls, Aerius got to work on his pursuit analysis.

From her console on the bridge, Madeline closed the program she was using to record Commander H's latest communiqué with Agent Aerius. She had initially opposed the alien's commission—he was from one of the far outlying worlds, and she had personally witnessed the kind of problems that non-integrated species could pose during her formative years in the Solar Orphan-o-trophia on Venus—but the commander was convinced that Aerius's chayat skills would prove invaluable.

So far, she was less than impressed.

Aerius had botched the apprehension of an old man and failed to retrieve the artifact they sought. The agent apparently didn't even have any leads on his target.

Madeline scoffed. "And the commander will blame *me* if this all goes sideways," she said quietly to herself.

With a sigh, she brought up the data that had automatically been uploaded from Aerius's ship and began sifting through the information in the hopes of avoiding a future verbal lashing.

The Adams Café floated on the edge of a blue-and-purple nebula with waves of colored distortion washing over the base of the restaurant. The establishment itself wasn't much to look at—a lot of tacky chrome and a domed hover propulsor along the bottom—but the enclosed parking area was crammed with ships ranging from the cabs of long-distance space haulers to family sedans to entry-level luxury vessels.

"This place looks like a dump," Quinn complained as he maneuvered *The Lady Grace* into a parking spot next to a neon green coupe with jutting engine cones.

"Yes, but this place has something no other restaurant does," said Abe as he unbuckled his harness.

"And what's that?" Quinn asked, his head swerving to follow Abe through the ship.

"A time nexus, of course."

Quinn unbuckled his own harness and followed Abe out into the rather full parking area. As the two made their way to the restaurant lobby, Quinn was surprised to see no one milling about waiting for a table. Indeed, there were no other customers ahead of them as Abe and Quinn walked past a plaque describing the man for whom the restaurant was named and approached the hostess kiosk.

The hostess was a Dar'morian woman, beautiful, with purple hair arranged in a complicated array of braids. Somehow she had found—or had had manufactured—eyeliner in the exact shade as her locks, and the color accentuated her almond-shaped eyes in an alluring fashion. She looked up at her guests out of pupils the shape of hourglasses.

"Misters Abraham and Quinn Titterman," she said in a soothing voice that one could—and would—listen to all day. "We've been expecting you."

Quinn leaned into his great-grandfather. "How did they know we were coming?"

"A first-time visitor?" the Dar'morian exclaimed before Abe could answer. "How wonderful!"

The woman took Quinn's arm, pressed her body close to his, and led him ahead of Abe toward their table. The young man blushed, unable to do anything except be led along.

"The Adams Café," the woman explained above the restaurant's ambient noise, "is situated at the edge of a nebula that radiates a type of temporal particle that is unique in the whole universe. It allows the staff a brief glimpse into the future so as to provide the finest service possible."

"Which means your food is ready when you get here!" Abe interjected as his eyes followed a plate of steaming meat carried by an alien waiter. The charbroiled spices set his mouth to watering.

The Dar'morian leaned even closer to Quinn, her scent a mixture of blossoms that, somehow, made his face turn even redder. "We have reservations and customer orders several hours ahead of time, give or take a few minutes depending on the nebula's output."

"And who, I mean, uh, who is Adams?" Quinn managed to ask despite his shortness of breath.

"Oh, a great writer from more than a thousand years ago," the Dar'morian replied with a practiced amount of awe. "He wrote about a restaurant that traveled to the end of time every evening. Strangely prescient for a human who came from such a primitive era."

The hostess released Quinn's arm and waved the two guests toward a circular booth set into one wall of the restaurant. When both were seated, she said, "Your meal will be out momentarily."

When the Dar'morian had disappeared, Abe looked across the table at his great-grandson and smiled. Quinn was staring straight ahead with a glazed look in his eyes.

"Surely you've met a Dar'morian before?" Abe said, his voice ringing with amusement.

"I don't think there are any at my school," Quinn replied without breaking his gaze.

"There's a reason they make the best courtesans in the galaxy. And a reason why places like this use them as hostesses." Abe leaned in a bit as if sharing a secret. "They make the customers tip better."

Quinn shook his head to clear it. All around them were aliens of a dozen species—and several humans, as well—dining on foods and conversing in dialects as varied as the stars. The dim light between booths and tables lent a bit of privacy to the dining room, even if the sounds and smells floated among the patrons without boundary: gibberish that Abe's and Quinn's translators couldn't pick up; the sizzle of hot fryers served by multi-armed waiters; and cooking aromas that ranged from burning spice to nausea-inducing carrion.

Quinn's stomach rumbled audibly in their booth.

"I think you're hungrier than you let on," Abe said.

Quinn craned his neck around to look outside of their booth. "What do you think I ordered?"

"Well, what do you feel like?" Abe replied, resting one hand on the tabletop and another on the alleged Key box on the seat next to him.

"Feel like?" Quinn turned around again. "I haven't even seen a menu. I don't know what they serve here."

"That's part of the fun, isn't it?" Abe said. "Me? I've had a craving for their meatloaf for a good week. I'm fairly confident that's what I ordered."

"There's a place at home that serves hydroponic sprouts," Quinn mused. "Grown right on Mars, but surely they don't import—"

A waiter of some species unfamiliar to either Abe or Quinn arrived at the table carrying a plate of sliced meat patties and a platter of round green vegetables covered with a brownish-yellow sauce.

"Who gets the meatloaf?" the waiter asked in a voice that sounded like an air recirculator.

Nimbus Steele looked up from the bar at the Adams Café where he was nursing his third glass of Titan Stout. The beer's flavor had been "inspired" by the hard-working miner society of Saturn's moon, which meant it tasted like something brewed in an industrial toilet. But it was the only drink Nimbus could afford in any great number with the cash he had on hand; all of his other assets were still frozen.

He scanned the other patrons at the bar in the center of the restaurant, then glanced toward the entrance hoping to get another glimpse of the Dar'morian hostess.

The eyes on her… Nimbus thought as she led two patrons to one of the booths set along the perimeter of the dining area.

Nimbus did a double take, his gaze moving reluctantly from the hostess to one of the men she was seating.

Abe Titterman! Nimbus's mind screamed. *Of all the places in the galaxy, why is he* here?

Nimbus was on the verge of standing up when a waiter arrived with food for Abe and his young companion. Content to let the old man finish his meal, Nimbus flashed an inebriated smirk at the four-armed Rauskon sitting next to him, downed the last of his drink with a grimace, and ordered another.

"This is amazing," Quinn said as he forked the last bite of sprouts into his mouth. "A restaurant that knows what you want before you get there. How did I not know about this?"

"I keep telling you," Abe replied, resting one hand on his belly, "you're not as smart as you think you are."

Quinn ignored the comment and used his fork to scoop up a small, final bite of sauce, then set the utensil on the edge of his plate.

"This was delicious and all," the young man said, "but don't you think we should get the check and get moving?"

Abe waved a finger at his great-grandson. "Now that I'm fed and watered, I want to see what's inside this box." He swung his head from side to side. Satisfied that no one was paying any particular attention to them, Abe brought forth the box from the seat beside him.

"We should do that on the ship," Quinn protested.

"I'm comfortable here," Abe said obstinately. "Besides, when are we ever going to see these people again?"

Before Quinn could object further, Abe opened the hinged lid. The interior of the box was almost as plain as the outside: just a lining of some black velvet-like material. An object sat cradled within.

"Hmmm," Abe said. "It looks like an actual key. I thought maybe it would be a crystal or something exotic."

He spun the box around so Quinn could get a look.

Made of a burnished gold material, the object was about six inches long with a cylindrical shaft two-thirds of its length that attached into a four-sided handle. Two square-like teeth jutted up from the end of the shaft, and another halfway down. The handle was carved with intricate patterns and strange symbols. A ringed planet formed a kind of pommel at the end.

"It's really interesting," Quinn commented. His earlier caution forgotten, he lifted the key gingerly from the velvet and turned it over in his hand. "Too bad there's no way to tell if it's real."

"Well, what do we know about the Key?" Abe asked.

The two began trading facts that had become embedded in the collective consciousness of the galaxy since time immemorial.

"The Key can unlock great power," said Quinn, "but no one knows if this power is knowledge, a weapon, or something else."

"There are no physical descriptions of the Key, which is why people like Minnie Halloran have claimed to have had it in their collections for ages," said Abe.

"But there's a saying about the Key that 'You will know it if it opens the way.'"

"One legend says it was made by the faeries of Zebulon."

"Another says—"

Quinn stopped and turned the key over again to look at one of the symbols on the handle that was not like the others: a vertical slash with a kind of "X" at the bottom and smaller, perpendicular slashes at the top.

"Do you know what this is?!" Quinn said as he pointed to the symbol. "This is the Mark of Iash!"

"Hmph," Abe snorted. "That philosopher you're always going on about?"

Quinn balked but went on. "That 'philosopher' was one of the greatest thinkers in the galaxy, Pop-pop. I mean, his teachings are studied by people everywhere even though he's been dead for centuries."

Abe crossed his arms over his chest. "How could he possibly be connected to the Key?"

"I don't know," Quinn admitted. "There's never been any mention of the Key in the books I've read about him. Although…" The young man put a pensive finger to his lips.

"Well?" Abe said. "I'm not getting any younger."

Quinn lowered his finger and smirked. "Well, it's just that there's always been these legends about the tomb of Iash on Shyoph-2. They're usually paired with a lot of key and lock imagery. Symbolism. Archeologists and treasure hunters go there every so often, hoping to find something new. But they always come back empty-handed. For most people it's just a neat historical site. For others, it's a great mystery."

"We have to go there!" Abe said, returning the Key to its box. "We have what all those others have been lacking: the Key to the Universe. The Key will unlock whatever secret is buried in this Iash fellow's tomb and prove itself at the same time. 'You will know it if it opens the way.' That's what you said, right?"

Quinn leveled a glare at his great-grandfather. "We can't do that, Pop-pop. We've had our fun. Now we have to give this to the police."

Abe snorted. "I told you before that I have—"

A shadow fell over their booth. Both Quinn and Abe looked up to see a handsome man in a leather jacket standing over them. Lantern-jawed with auburn hair that was slightly out of place, the man smirked at them with a roguish grin. He smelled like some kind of grim intoxicant.

"Well, well," the man said, his words a bit slurred. "Abe Titterman. Fancy running into you here. Isn't that what they always say in the holo-serials?"

"Nimbus Steele." Abe spat the name as if it had been a bad-tasting bit of his dinner. "I thought you were in jail."

"On trumped-up charges!" Nimbus raged. "Even I'm not stupid enough to smuggle goods out of Xidari. Someone in the Solar Government set me up. Convenient timing, huh? Didn't want me to get a piece of all that bounty coming out of the Halloran Estate."

"That's a great story," Abe said in a way that indicated he wasn't interested whatsoever. "Isn't it time for you to be going?"

Nimbus blocked one side of the booth. "You still owe me from that unfair trade. And with my assets frozen, I think it's about time you paid up."

Abe started. "That thing with the spoons from Talos-4? That was seven years ago! Besides, *you* were the one who approached *me*. How was I supposed to know the Monet was fake? Even the authenticator said it was the best forgery he had ever seen."

Nimbus leaned forward, bringing his face to within inches of Abe's nose. Abe recoiled from the smell of beer on the man's breath.

"You wouldn't know a Monet from a meteorite," the handsome man said quietly.

"I've been in this business since before you were born," Abe growled, his face growing redder by the second.

"You're incompetent."

"You're a liar."

"An *imbecile.*"

"Would an imbecile have the Key to the Universe?"

The words were out of Abe's mouth before he could realize what he had said. Nimbus stiffened and took a step back as if struck, speechless for the first time. Abe shot a glance at Quinn that seemed to say *Oops!*

Nimbus finally mastered himself. "The Key—"

"Hey you!" Quinn waved to a four-armed alien at the bar in the center of the dining room. "This guy just told us that your mother belongs to *Greem Tor-Kana!*"

The alien bolted upright as if he had been shocked in the backside with a LAS-er disruptor. Winding up with his two right arms, the alien howled and struck Nimbus simultaneously in the gut and the chin.

Nimbus reeled, scattering the plates, utensils, and drink glasses on the table—a sound made all the louder by the sudden absence of conversation in the restaurant. Patrons turned in their seats to gawp at the melee. Quinn, meanwhile, scooted along the booth, grabbed his great-grandfather by the arm, and steered him away from the fight as the alien lifted Nimbus bodily from the floor.

"What did you say to him?" Abe asked as they approached the hostess stand at a rapid walk. The Dar'morian woman was staring at the fight with wide, beautiful eyes.

"He's Rauskon," Quinn replied. "They have a complex caste system on their planet. *Greem Tor-Kana* is the, uh, sewage cleaning class."

Abe threw a fifty-note solar bill on the hostess kiosk as he and Quinn passed.

"Keep the change," Abe said.

 "You gonna tell me about the spoons from Talos-4?" asked Quinn as they scrambled inside *The Lady Grace*.

Abe followed his great-grandson to the cockpit and settled into the passenger seat, the box with the Key resting on his lap. Looking out the viewport, he could see that no one had followed them out of the restaurant; they were too preoccupied with the fight.

"Oh, an honest mistake," Abe said as Quinn powered up the ship as quickly as possible. "I had what I thought was an original Monet in the store. Something with an aquatic plant."

"Water lilies?" Quinn asked as he went through the pre-flight mnemonic in his head and toggled the appropriate switches.

"Maybe," Abe said. "In any case, I was selling it on the floor and everything. Nimbus Steele, who was just starting out at the time and didn't have nearly the reputation he has now, came to me and offered a trade. He had a set of very rare Talos spoons that he couldn't move and wanted the painting for a quick sale. I traded him."

"But the painting was fake?" Quinn said.

The ship lifted out of the docking area and glided back into open space.

"Nimbus had it appraised for insurance purposes," Abe continued. "Of course, he couldn't use any old adjuster; he had to use the best expert of Mars. And it turned out the painting was a fake. Best forgery the authenticator had ever seen after nearly a century on the job. Can you imagine?"

Silence fell between the two as the ship drifted away from the Adams Café and its time-warping nebula. Quinn had not yet set a course, but there hung in the air an unspoken need to act with haste.

Finally, Abe said, "Listen, Quinn. I want to check out this tomb you mentioned. I want to see if this Key will open… something."

"We should go to the police," Quinn said with what sounded like less conviction than before.

"And what if this thing is *real*?" Abe said, the passion returning to his voice. "What will it unlock? Riches? Knowledge? The meaning of existence? Aren't you the least bit curious?" He nudged Quinn's shoulder. "Aren't you this philosopher's biggest fan?"

Quinn smiled at that.

"I'm one-hundred-and-seven years old," Abe went on. "I think it's about time I went on an adventure. And…" He paused. "And I'd like it to be with a member of my family."

Abe searched his great-grandson's eyes for a moment before Quinn turned away to look out of the forward viewport. Without looking back, he said, "When I was nine, you gave me my first holo-serial, even though my mother didn't want you to."

Abe shrugged, a crooked half smile playing across his lips. "I didn't want to bring it up, but now that you mention it…"

Quinn sighed, shook his head and flashed a grin of his own. "Okay, Pop-pop. We'll check out the tomb of Iash."

From a stealth position high above the Adams Café, Aerius watched from a monitor as his quarry blinked into hyperspace. He noted the coordinates of their jump and set his computers to track their destination. There hadn't been enough time for an apprehension. But in moments, the computer received a transmission from the still-hidden tracking beacon.

Aerius scanned the screen with unblinking eyes. Then he set a pursuit course.

CHAPTER FIVE

Gabriella Rossi stalked into the well-appointed office of her Martian compound, the mostly private center of her empire. She heaved a sigh, her large chest rising and falling tremendously, before setting down her purse.

It had been a long and ultimately fruitless day, and Gabriella was beginning to think that she was cursed in all things where the Key to the Universe was concerned: a seemingly gung-ho Solar agent interfering in her business, and Abe and Quinn Titterman disappearing, along with the Key. Not much else could have gone wrong.

She was considering her next move when the computer on her desk beeped twice, indicating an incoming video call. Gabriella composed her hair, face, and dress, sat in the office chair, and hit the answer button on the screen. Johnny DiBiaso's face—moss-green skin with a dark blue band across red eyes—filled the display.

"Johnny," Gabriella said by way of a greeting. "What can I do for you?"

"There's a call coming through the intranet from one of your agents," Johnny replied with a deferential nod.

"Put it though."

Johnny's face disappeared, replaced seconds later by that of a stunning (but weren't they all stunning?) Dar'morian woman.

"Agent zero-three-four, designation Sofia, reporting in, Mama," the woman said.

"Just a moment," Gabriella replied, taking in the Dar'morian's purple hair and matching eyeliner. On another screen, Gabriella brought up the agent's file, including her posting location and service record. Sofia had orange hair in her file photo, though she had gone without eye makeup on the day it was taken. Gabriella noted that the Dar'morian had been in her employ for approximately six months, all of them stationed at a restaurant called the Adams Café in quadrant seventy-two.

Gabriella turned her attention back to the caller and smiled. "It's a beautiful day for a picnic on Rilium-5."

"Unless the saw-tooth ants join you," Sofia replied with the countersign.

"Code in, please."

"Nine-three-zero-eight-three alpha."

"Thank you," Gabriella said, pleased that Sofia had passed the verbal code checks. "What do you have for me?"

"A positive ID on the humans you notified the network about this afternoon," the Dar'morian replied. "Abe and Quinn Titterman had dinner at the Adams Café just moments ago. Identification confirmed by a DNA sample on the bill Abe handed me. They left as a fight broke out at their table."

Gabriella's heartbeat quickened. "Do you have the fighters detained?" she asked, projecting an outward appearance of calm.

"Yes," Sofia replied. "They're under the impression that the police are on their way. I haven't called them yet, but the manager will keep them in the office as long as need be. He generally does what I want."

"I'll bet he does," Gabriella said with a smirk. "I see from your file that you've never called in before. You've earned your keep today, Sofia. I'm glad to have you with us."

"Thank you, Mama," the woman said, batting her eyes.

"We'll be there shortly."

Gabriella ended the call and placed another, this one to the compound's shuttle bay. One of the Nalaxan bodyguards answered.

"Prep the ship again," Gabriella said. "We're getting take-out."

"What do you know about this Mama Rossi person, anyway?" Abe asked from the midship living quarters of *The Lady Grace*, where he prepared for bed.

Quinn glanced away from the white glow of hyperspace outside the cockpit viewport and regarded his great-grandfather. "I suppose I know as much as what's in the news. She's been head of the mafia for about eight years now. Supposedly she's a real traditionalist and makes all of her employees take Italian names—I guess those were the people who ran organized crime on Earth all those years ago. No one even knew who she was before she became Gabriella 'Mama' Rossi.'"

Abe came back to the cockpit and took a seat next to his great-grandson.

"She looks rather matronly," Abe said. "Not what I would have expected for a criminal mastermind."

"'A *broq* hold the sweetest fruit,'" Quinn said. "That's Iash's way of saying that looks can be deceiving. If the stories are true, she's controlled, emotionless, and deadly."

"What do you think she wants with the Key?" Abe asked. "And for that matter, why would a smart woman like Minnie Halloran leave such an important object to her?"

"Minnie Halloran was rich. That doesn't mean she was smart," Quinn pointed out.

"Oh, she was smart," Abe said. "Had to be to run that terraforming business of hers. You don't become a multi-trillionaire by being dumb." He paused. "Your great-grandmother and I met her once you know."

Quinn, distracted by the instrument panel, said, "Who?"

"Minnie Halloran."

The younger man looked up, one eyebrow raised.

"It's true," Abe continued. "Minnie was quite the collector. Never had a chance to sell her anything—I probably could have retired on *that* commission alone—but we met her at an auction once. Exceedingly clever, if a bit eccentric. But the rich always are."

"And you don't know why she would have left the Key to Mama Rossi?" Quinn asked.

"I said I'd *met* her, Quinn. I didn't say I *knew* her." Abe stood and waggled one finger at his great-grandson. "You better get some sleep. After all, we're gonna visit the tomb of your idol tomorrow."

Gabriella and one of her Nalaxan bodyguards strode up to the hostess kiosk in the Adams Café where the beautiful Sofia was waiting for them.

"Greetings," Sofia said cheerfully. "I'll have your take-out orders ready to go once we finish our business. Tortellini Abruzzi with a Martian-style sauce for you and Nalaxan truffles with *rugout* paste for your associate."

"I'd heard about the exceptional service here," said Gabriella. "I'm glad I finally had a chance to visit."

Sofia waved past the kiosk to a door marked "Employees Only" in several different languages. "This way."

The office was typical of many food establishments, furnished with a computer, filing cabinets, and security monitors. The one exception was the thickest metal trap door that Gabriella had ever seen set right in the center of the office floor. Warning stickers of every kind—*High Radiation! Beware Temporal Displacement! Hardhat and anti-magneto footware required beyond this point!*—were plastered to the surface of the door, which looked heavy enough for six Nalaxans to lift.

"What is that?" squeaked the bodyguard, drawing his LAS-er Pistol from inside of his suit jacket and pointing it at the trap door.

Gabriella forced the Nalaxan to lower his gun arm and shot an apologetic glance at Sofia. The Dar'morian had tensed noticeably at the sight of the gun, her purple hair puffing out like the tail of an agitated housecat.

"I'm sorry," Gabriella said. "He's just being cautious."

Sofia relaxed a bit. "I understand. That's the door to the restaurant's core in the hover propulsor. Only certain species can handle the conditions down there, and then only for a short period of time. It's where our Seers go to get the orders for a given six-hour period." She pointed to another, unadorned door at the far end of the office. "That's the cleaning closet. They're in there."

The Nalaxan raised his pistol again—slowly this time—and opened the door to reveal what appeared to be a plain storage room, complete with the headache-inducing smell of disinfectant. A four-armed Rauskon and a human male sat on the floor inside, backs against a metal shelving unit that contained bottles of various cleaning supplies. The human had a black eye and some blood caked around the corner of his mouth. He didn't look up when the closet door opened. The Rauskon seemed unharmed but morose.

"You don't look like the police," the Rauskon said in a rumbly voice that came from deep within his chest.

Gabriella sidled up to her bodyguard, arms crossed over her chest. "Tell me what happened at the table where the fight started."

The Rauskon pointed at the human with his two right arms and said something that Gabriella's translator didn't pick up.

"*Slowly*," Gabriella said menacingly.

The Rauskon stared at her, growled, and took a deep breath. "He. Called. My. Mother. A. Sanitation worker!"

"And do you know him or the men at the table where the fight started?" Gabriella asked.

"I don't associate with *humans*," the Rauskon spat. "I come here because it's the only place for light-years around that can prepare a proper Rauskon *imaud*."

"Thank you," Sofia said automatically.

Gabriella looked from the Dar'morian to her bodyguard with an impassive look on her face. "He doesn't know anything," Gabriella said. "Let him go."

Sofia pointed over her shoulder toward the door that led from the office. "You're free to go."

The Rauskon stood, face brightening at the prospect of not having to deal with the authorities. He grunted at Gabriella, then leveled a lingering stare at the Nalaxan bodyguard as if to say that he would welcome a chance to tangle with the rhino-like creature. After an unspoken battle of wills that lasted only a few seconds—during which the Nalaxan's ears flattened against his skull—the Rauskon levered past his would-be persecutors and left the office.

Gabriella, Sofia, and the Nalaxan turned their attention back to the human, who was now looking completely away from them. Gabriella squinted.

"Look at me," she ordered.

Like a chastised child, the human did as he was told, turning his face toward Gabriella but avoiding eye contact.

"Humph," Gabriella grunted. "Nimbus Steele. I was told you had been taken care of for good."

"Assets frozen and half my inventory confiscated," Nimbus said, finally looking up. "I think the Solar Government has pretty well 'taken care' of me."

"And yet you show up in the same place as the man I'm seeking: Abe Titterman," said Gabriella.

"Oh yeah," Nimbus said with a sneer. "Abe and I go way back."

"What did you talk about?" Gabriella asked.

"Nothing of importance before his companion—"

"That's his great-grandson," Gabriella interjected.

"Fine," Nimbus said. "Before his great-grandson got that thing to jump me. It was a personal matter, if you must know. A debt he owed me."

Gabriella turned to the Nalaxan. "I'd suggest interrogating him, but I don't think it would be worth your time." Then she addressed Sofia in a sweeter tone, "Thank you for calling, dear, but it seems our trip out here was unnecessary. Except for the food, of course."

"Apologies, Mama," Sofia said. "I'll show you out."

Gabriella and the others turned to leave when Nimbus said, "I know where he's going."

Gabriella stopped but didn't turn around. "Your lame attempts to impress me really don't add to your charm, Nimbus."

"Something about the Key to the Universe," Nimbus teased.

Now Gabriella *did* turn around.

"I was standing next to their table for a while before they noticed me," Nimbus continued. "Heard all about it, especially where they plan to go next."

Gabriella rummaged in her purse and brought out her own LAS-er gun, holding it in a relaxed grip.

"And I suppose you want something for this information," Gabriella said. "Besides your life."

Nimbus shot a hesitant glance at the delicate weapon but went on. "I want my name cleared. I want my assets unfrozen. And I want my inventory back."

"That can be arranged," Gabriella said. "Provided I get what I want first."

"And I'll be coming with you to make sure you hold up your end of the bargain."

Gabriella considered this for a moment. She had already gotten into one firefight over this Key business. If something were to "happen" to Nimbus the next time things got tense, he would be out of her hair permanently. In the meantime, having him close could ensure that he didn't cause any more trouble for the time being.

"I suppose it'll have to do," she said with a false note of resignation.

The roguish grin finally crossed Nimbus's bruised face.

Gabriella returned the gun to her purse and said to the Nalaxan, "Grab our to-go bags and get the ship ready. Nimbus here will be giving you a pursuit course."

CHAPTER SIX

Shyoph-2 hung brown and dirty in the void outside the cockpit viewport of *The Lady Grace*. From orbit, the planet resembled a barren desert rock with a barely breathable atmosphere. Quinn stared out the window with a pensive look, index finger covering his lips as he considered their destination.

"Ready to land yet?" Abe asked. "You're the one who's been harping on about how little time we have."

Quinn tore his gaze away from the planet.

"I've always wanted to come here," he said. "Ever since I read *The Essential Teachings of Iash*. This is where he came from, Pop-pop. This is where he walked and lived."

Abe patted his great-grandson's shoulder. "And just think what it'll be like once we're actually *down* there."

Quinn flashed a wry smile, nodded, and set the ship's entry course.

"Much of the planet is barren," Quinn narrated as the ship descended and Abe strapped in next to him. "Huge deserts. The people live in oases where the *lapyk* springs from the ground."

"Lapyk?" Abe asked. The ship rocked slightly as they entered the atmosphere, the black of space transitioning to blue blended with brownish earth tones.

"It's a green gel," Quinn said while making minor adjustments to the instruments. "The Shyophians drink it—kind of what we would think of as water. But don't try it; humans can't tolerate lapyk."

"Thanks for the tip," Abe said.

"Sometimes the lapyk will fall from the sky," Quinn continued. "It'll even accumulate for a while. For offworlders to see a lapyk storm is rare. They only happen once every two or three years."

A beeping noise sounded from the control console. Quinn hit a button to silence the notification tone. "That's the tourist beacon near the tomb," he said. "We'll be there shortly."

Outside the viewport, Shyoph-2 had resolved itself into a flat wasteland of brown dirt punctuated by clusters of bizarre rock outcroppings. The nature-made monuments rose singly or in groups, rock spires with holes punched straight through their girth. Where the peaks of the oldest and tallest spires had crumbled, there lay ruins of giant boulders and other spires that had toppled under the tumult.

Occasionally, the ship passed settlements or shepherds in the desert with herds of scaly domestic animals. Moving en masse, the creatures resembled mobile rocks slowly making their way across one fraction of the planet's massive deserts.

"There." Quinn pointed through the viewport.

A settlement cradled in the foothills of a desert mountain range emerged from the sameness of the arid waste. People moved along the outskirts of the village and among the sparse vegetation of the oasis: trees with hard-looking bark that seemed more akin to the rocklike animals than to any vegetation that Abe or Quinn had ever seen.

Taking manual control of the ship, Quinn steered *The Lady Grace* several hundred feet away from the outskirts of the settlement, the vessel raising a small tornado of sand.

"Did you have to park so far away?" Abe complained as he tried to measure the distance from the ship to the oasis.

"We don't want to upset anyone by stirring up a dust storm," Quinn replied. "We'll just have to do a bit of walking."

Abe and Quinn grabbed sun goggles, backpacks (one of which held the Key), and two canteens from the ship's store.

Extending a collapsible hypersteel walking stick that he kept on board, Abe moved to the side hatch and opened it.

Dry, acrid air flooded into *The Lady Grace*, along with a wall of heat. Abe took a step back, coughing as he wielded the walking stick in front of him like a ward. "Gah! I'm too old for this!"

Quinn patted his great-grandfather on the shoulder. "You're the one who wanted an adventure. C'mon, let's get started."

The walk took some time as Abe and Quinn struggled to keep their footing over the uneven, shifting sand. Passing a shepherd, Abe noticed the Shyophian wore some kind of tear-shaped sandshoe that distributed his weight and allowed him to walk with an even gait. Abe pointed out the footwear to his great-grandson.

"It looks like they're made from the bark of those trees," Quinn observed.

"Maybe we can buy some in the village," Abe said. "I don't care how much they cost!"

Hot, sweaty, and tired after only fifteen minutes, the two arrived at the oasis in need of respite. Sitting with their backs against one of the trees, Abe and Quinn sipped measured gulps of water from their canteens while getting their first good look at the Shyophians.

Tall in a manner reminiscent of the government agent Aerius, the Shyophians were wrapped head to toe in rough, homespun strips of fabric about two inches thick. Where their bodies were exposed, often at the elbows, knees, and eyes, the Shyophians seemed to lack definition. The edges of their bodies appeared to waver like a heat mirage.

"They're a bit ethereal, aren't they?" Abe said quietly to Quinn.

"They've evolved to survive here," Quinn replied. "Their clothes help give them shape and identity, as much to each other as to outsiders like us."

After a few more moments of rest and another healthy draught from his canteen, Quinn rose and helped his great-grandfather to his feet.

They proceeded through the oasis, clothes sticking to their bodies as they wound between huts carved from the native rock and held together with baked clay. The smells and sounds of people living close together with one another and their animals filled the settlement as Shyophians young and old (the young ones were only as tall as Abe) went about their lives of cooking food, mending garments and houses, and herding the rocklike animals into pens.

"These are *unwor*," Quinn said as they passed a group of cubs wrestling under the watchful eye of a parent animal. "They retain lapyk in their hides, which they shed several times a year. A thick fiber grows on the inside that the Shyophians use to make clothes."

"You really do admire this Iash fellow," Abe said.

By way of response, Quinn pointed to a pool of bright green gel next to a cluster of trees. Wrinkles had formed on the pool's surface, and the splash of color seemed almost offensive in the otherwise bland environment.

"Lapyk," Quinn said.

Abe rubbed his chin. "How do you think some of this would look in one of those decanters from Ava Gamma? We could sell it in the shop. With the appropriate caution labels, of course."

Quinn eyed his great-grandfather with a look of reproach. "Don't even think about it. It's the lifeblood of these people."

Before his great-grandfather could get any other ideas, Quinn nodded past the pool toward a modern dynoplas structure that seemed as out of place as the green lapyk.

"That's where the tourist beacon must be transmitting from," Quinn said. "Let's check it out."

They moved around to the front of the structure, where a bored-looking human with hair down to his chin and sun blisters on his forehead and upper lip stood at an information window.

The man didn't perk up with the arrival of two fellow *Homo sapiens*.

"Here to see the tomb, I suppose?" the man said while examining something under his fingernails. "Don't recommend you stay long, or else your skin and cuticles will start to look like mine."

He held up one long-fingered hand, which to Abe and Quinn appeared meticulous compared to the rest of the man's grooming.

"You're part of the Galactic Tourism Bureau," Abe said while examining the weather-beaten and sun-bleached walls of the structure. From what he could see through the information window, it appeared the man lived in the building as well.

"You got it," the man replied. "Lucky me, helping travelers from under the light of the Solar Government experience the pleasure of cultural tourism." He spat the word "pleasure" as if he had inhaled a mouthful of sand.

"But lots of people like to visit the Tomb of Iash," Quinn said.

The man glared. "Don't patronize me. I used to run a five-star resort on Elchoir."

"Wait," Abe said. "You weren't involved with that incident with the toilets—?"

"That was two years ago!" the man barked. "A solar system—a *galaxy*—full of news, and people still remember that!"

"Well, your establishment *did* embarrass the wife of the Prime Prolocutor rather badly," Abe said.

The man rolled his eyes and sighed, barely containing his anger. "Just tell me what you want."

"The tomb," Quinn replied quickly.

The man pointed to a mountain pass at the edge of the village. The alley carved into the rock led somewhere they couldn't see from their current vantage point.

"Thank you," Quinn said, and led his great-grandfather away from the kiosk in the direction the man had indicated.

"I wonder how long they'll keep him stationed here," Quinn mused when he and Abe were out of earshot.

"Probably as long as it takes for the Prime Prolocutor's wife to grow back her caudal," Abe said. "Which is to say, at least another year."

CHAPTER SEVEN

The walls of the mountain pass loomed on either side of Abe and Quinn, and though the pass itself was in shadow, the heat of the desert refused to fall away. Feeling even more stifled within the confines of the rock, Abe shuffled as quickly as he could through the pass, sweating more than he had been in the open desert.

Quinn pointed up one side of the rock wall. "You see those caves?"

Abe could just barely make out a series of hollows in the rock that he had initially mistaken for deep shadows.

"Those are where Iash and his followers used to meditate," Quinn continued excitedly. "He probably wrote some of his epistles on bark paper *right here*."

"And I'm sure he reached some kind of transcendental state where the heat didn't bother him either," Abe said.

"Actually—"

"Shut it."

Blinking into the sunlight at the end of the pass, Abe found that he and Quinn had entered a box canyon surrounded by mountainous cliffs on all sides. Inside the canyon, more caves had been scooped out of the cliff walls, all of which stared down at an obelisk in the center of the canyon.

Rising about a hundred feet, the obelisk had been crafted with a level of workmanship unlike anything else they had seen so far. Hewn from mountain-sourced rock, the four-sided monument flared slightly from its base to a pyramid-like capstone, its surface completely smooth despite thousands of years of exposure to the elements.

With their goal in sight, they rushed forward with renewed energy. Abe reached out one hand to touch the speckles and whorls of color formed by minerals in the rock. Reds and browns and grays flecked the sides of the obelisk in nature-made patterns that were obviously random. But as Abe stared at the monument, it seemed, at the very edges of his consciousness, that the patterns were *not* random, that there was something *deliberate* about them, as if the rock itself paid homage to the great thinker entombed within.

"Have you ever seen anything like it," Quinn asked, nearly breathless.

Abe admitted that he was impressed as he circled the massive base of the obelisk, examining it from all angles.

"Look at how carefully it was carved," Quinn went on. "I know it's just rock, but it feels like something more."

"You feel it too?"

Quinn nodded.

Abe finished circling the tomb. "It's like an emotional… generator," he said, grasping for the right words to describe what he was feeling. "Can you imagine what this would look like in the shop under the right lighting? People would come from light-years around to see and feel *this*."

Quinn blanched. "You wouldn't dare!"

"You're right," Abe said with a regretful shrug. "Intergalactic regulations. And the transportation costs alone!"

Quinn rolled his eyes and went back to examining the obelisk. Abe removed his backpack and withdrew the box containing the Key. Setting his walking stick to rest against the wall of the obelisk, Abe held the box in front of him and began circling the tomb again.

"I don't see any kind of keyhole," Abe said.

"I didn't think we would," Quinn replied. "People have been studying the tomb for years. They've taken every kind of reading short of a physical sample, which the Shyophians would never allow. If there's something hidden here, no one has ever found it."

"Yeah, but they've never had the actual Key with them," Abe said. "If this is the real thing, I wonder how long it's been since these two were brought together."

"Who knows," Quinn said with a shrug. "Maybe not since Iash's own lifetime."

Abe continued circling, the box held before him the whole time. A vulture-like bird cried at the top of the canyon.

"I thought it'd be easier than this," Abe complained.

"Be patient," Quinn said. "The answer isn't going to just jump out at us."

"How about we go back to the ship and make something to eat?" Abe said.

"You're hungry already?!" Quinn exclaimed. "We just had breakfast!"

"Well, adrenaline hastens digestion, you know," Abe countered. "I say—"

Whatever Abe was going to say next was cut short as he tripped on a loose rock on the canyon floor. Propelled forward, he lost his grip on the box as he put out both hands to break his fall. The box with the Key skipped across the ground as Abe watched it from all fours. It skittered to a stop—then started edging toward the obelisk on its own.

"Look!" Abe cried.

Quinn had rounded one corner of the tomb to help his great-grandfather. Now he watched open-mouthed as the box with the Key moved slowly toward the obelisk as if placed on an invisible conveyor belt.

"It's being drawn to the tomb!" Quinn said.

He helped Abe to his feet, made sure his great-grandfather was unharmed, and bent to retrieve the box from the pebble-strewn ground. Holding it out, Quinn said, "Go on and open it, Pop-pop."

Abe finished brushing the dirt from his clothes and reached forward to open the hinged lid. The Key lay inside, as unassuming as before. He took it out.

"Concentrate," Quinn instructed. "Relax your hands and arms. Do you feel it being pulled anywhere?"

Abe held the Key out toward one wall of the obelisk, teeth forward.

"I think I feel something," Abe said. "It's very slight, like a weak magnet."

Abe fully extended his arm and let the muscles go as slack as possible. *Yes!* The attraction was there. He let himself move closer to the polished stone, the draw becoming stronger with every inch. Closer. Closer. The magnetism was distinct now, and Abe concentrated on nothing else. *Closer. Closer.*

With a slight *tap*, the Key touched the obelisk, the linking site undeniable. There was a rumble, the sound of giant rocks scraping together, and a door swung open in the side of the tomb.

"That's amazing," Abe said, pulling the Key away from the surface of the obelisk, conscious now of the pull between the two objects.

"That's impossible," Quinn said. He stared at his great-grandfather with conviction burning in his eyes. "This wasn't here a second ago. The *seams* for this weren't here a second ago. All those tests, all those researchers—they would have found this."

Abe barely heard. He was staring down the length of the Key, his whole body shaking with the energy of a compressed spring. "Do you know what this means?" he breathed. *"We have the Key!"*

Abe's exclamation echoed among the walls of the box canyon, the stone unable to contain the joviality in his voice as it leapt toward the sky. He slapped Quinn on the shoulder and turned the Key over in his hands, all while muttering things like, "Unfathomable" and "In all my years…"

"If you're done screaming at the rocks," Quinn said with a grin, "maybe you'd like to have a look inside?"

Abe motioned toward the door. "After you. I'll wait here and make sure you don't get stuck inside that little crawl space."

Quinn stepped inside the threshold and said, "I don't think that'll be a problem."

Abe looked past Quinn into a chamber far larger than the obelisk could possibly contain. The domed space was carved roughly from rock with veins of green lapyk running through the stone in strange, linear patterns. In the darkness of the chamber, the gel provided an iridescent green light, which illuminated a burial mound in the center of the room three times the height of a man and ringed with tall, carved stones.

Abe took a step back and examined the obelisk, then looked through the door to the massive chamber beyond, then back at the obelisk again. "I don't think this door, or whatever it is, leads straight into the obelisk."

Quinn nodded in agreement as he took a few steps farther into the domed room. "That would explain why the scans never showed anything like this *inside* the tomb." He craned his neck to take in the scene. "Could the Key have opened a door to somewhere else?"

Abe stepped inside to have his own look around. "'You will know it if it opens the way,'" he said, repeating the mantra that Quinn had uttered in the Adams Café.

"It's the only explanation I can think of," Quinn said. "I mean, I can't even explain how a door like this would work."

Abe laughed again, the sound echoing off the chamber walls. "Shall we have a look around?"

He watched as his great-grandson nodded, set down his pack, and began rolling a large rock just outside the obelisk toward the door. Quinn propped the stone against the portal inside the chamber's threshold.

Abe nodded in understanding. Now the door wouldn't swing closed and lock them inside. Together, they ventured farther into the chamber.

Compared to the heat in the desert canyon, the cavern was quite cool. Each footfall raised little clouds of dust, disturbing dirt that had not been trod in ages and adding to the dry smell inside the cave.

About fifty paces brought them to the circle of stones ringing the mound. Like the obelisk in the canyon, each four-foot-tall hunk of native rock had been carved with exquisite workmanship and had been placed equidistant from its fellows. Altogether, they seemed as flawless as the day they had been set in formation.

Abe circled one side of the mound while Quinn circled the other. They met on the far side of the burial mound, the bulk of which blocked their view of the crypt door.

"This looks like the entrance," Quinn said.

The final marker had been placed directly opposite the chamber door on the far side of the burial mound. It stood in front of a colossal stone block embedded in the base of the mound.

Abe stared dubiously at the stone block, which must have taken dozens of Shyophians to lift. "You're not thinking of going in there."

"I don't think we could move that even if we wanted to," Quinn said. "It could be that we need to use the Key again." He paused and knelt by the marker across from the stone block. "Hold on a minute."

Abe watched as his great-grandson brushed his hand across a portion of the marker's surface that seemed to have some kind of bumpy marking. Then Quinn bolted upright, eyes wide, as the chamber exploded in a burst of blinding light.

Abe cried out in alarm. He shielded his eyes and reached out with his free hand to grasp for Quinn. Moving his arm incrementally away from his face, Abe caught a vision of galaxies and scientific formulae and religious axioms projected within the vastness of the cave, an enormous theater for… for…

"A computer?" Abe gasped, wonderstruck. Then remembering that Quinn was in danger, Abe began grasping even more wildly until he grabbed Quinn's shirt.

"Quinn!" Abe shouted. "Quinn!"

There was no audible response; just a flare as the projection reached some kind of climax. Whole systems of data whirled and flashed by in a kaleidoscopic display faster than the human eye could process. With a final burst of light, the whole scene disappeared.

Quinn dropped to his knees, taking Abe with him. Blinking away the flashes of light in his eyes, Abe felt for his great-grandson, laying both hands on Quinn's shoulders.

"Quinn!" Abe repeated over and over.

Quinn just stared. His pupils were nearly as big as his irises, and a dazed look had settled over his face.

"Pop-pop?" Quinn said, reaching out blindly with one hand. "Pop-pop, I'm all right. But everything's blurry, distorted."

Abe scrambled forward to hug his great-grandson.

"I'm all right," Quinn repeated with a sigh of relief. "I'm all right."

Abe pulled away with a reproachful look on his face. "Don't ever do that again… whatever *that* was!"

Quinn smiled, though it was clear his eyes were unable to focus. "Is that worry I hear in the voice of my fearless, impetuous great-grandfather?"

Abe grunted and pointed his finger for emphasis before realizing that Quinn couldn't see the gesture. "Say what you want about me," he said, "but I take care of my family."

"By making sure they evade arrest and get chased by mobsters?" Quinn asked.

Abe stammered in response, but Quinn simply laughed. "I'm kidding, Pop-pop."

Abe lowered his finger and smirked. He removed the canteen from his pack, unscrewed the top and handed it to Quinn. When they had both taken a long drink of water, Abe said, "Let's rest for a minute, then get out of here and get you to a doctor."

"I think my eyes are just dilated," Quinn said. "But I'd like to head back to the ship."

"What was that? What did you see?"

"It was…" Quinn inhaled deeply. "It was amazing!" The excitement rose in his voice again. "Pop-pop, it was a transmission! A transmission left here by Iash! I—" he was nearly breathless "—I can't make it all out yet, but I think *he* found the Key. He's been waiting for someone to return here with it, waiting to share his knowledge. And Pop-pop, somewhere in all that data is the location—a map with directions on how to use the Key."

"Well then," Abe said. "What are we waiting for? Let's get back to the ship and get you checked out. Then we can work out what you saw."

He helped Quinn to his feet and put one arm around the young man's shoulders to lead him. Together with Abe's walking stick, they made their way back around the burial mound.

"How are your eyes?" Abe asked.

"Getting better already," Quinn said. "I can see the shape of the mound and some of the stones in the shadows. But it's harder to see where it's brighter." He paused. "It was like Iash needed my eyes fully open to absorb everything."

"You can tell me all about it back on the ship. Just think about it—air conditioning, food, showers. We'll have you sorted out in no time!"

They started toward the obelisk exit, the green lapyk casting their faces in a ghastly light. Rounding the final curve of the mound, they were almost too distracted by what had happened to see that someone was waiting for them.

CHAPTER EIGHT

E ven without the use of his eyes, Quinn could feel his great-grandfather stiffen in alarm. The instinctual part of his brain warned of danger ahead.

"What's wrong, Pop-pop?" Quinn asked.

The entrance to the crypt and the desert beyond was too bright for him to look upon, a blur of light seen through eyes teary from the strain.

"Is someone there?" Quinn pressed.

Before Abe could respond, a figure moved from the brightest part of the light and came another step into the crypt. It held something in one outstretched arm.

"I am sorry that things worked out this way, but I must take you into custody," a voice said.

"Who is that?" Quinn said.

Abe cleared his throat. "It seems Agent Aerius has finally caught up with us."

"Indeed," said the alien.

"You saw everything?" Abe asked.

"Since you entered this structure? Yes," Aerius said. "You have the Key as well, I presume?"

"We have it," Abe replied. "But I'm ready and willing to sue the Solar Government over my right to possess it. It came to my shop, and you spooks don't have any claim to it."

"That is for Commander H to decide," said the alien. "Come outside, please."

Abe, still supporting Quinn, did as he was told. The young man grunted in pain as they reentered the canyon; the desert sun shone as unrelentingly as before.

"Too bright," Quinn muttered.

Abe turned to Aerius and said, "His eyes! He needs the goggles in his pack."

Aerius steadied his weapon with an aim on Abe's head. "Put the pack on the ground," the alien said, "and remove the goggles *slowly*."

With deliberate movements, Abe left Quinn to stand on his own, then slid the pack from his great-grandson's shoulder. Opening the top, he retrieved Quinn's sun goggles with pains-taking slowness. Abe handed the goggles to Quinn and straightened as the younger man adjusted them on his face.

"My ship is just outside the settlement," Aerius said when his captives were ready again. "You will lead the way there. Understand that my weapon will be aimed at you at all times and that I will not underestimate you again."

"You make me sound like a criminal mastermind," Abe said with a smile.

"I think you should take this more seriously," Quinn replied, all the excitement of the past hour gone from his voice.

"Listen to your great-grandson, Mister Titterman," Aerius said. "Let's go."

They made their way out of the box canyon and back through the mountain pass, Abe and Quinn sweating freely again despite the advancing day and their respite in the coolness of the cavern.

"Does it ever cool down in this frying pan?" Abe complained as they returned to the village outskirts, feet unsteady on the shifting sand.

Aerius, who appeared not to be sweating at all despite wearing his full body armor, replied, "My survey of this planet indicates that the high temperatures persist past sunset during the warm weather months. I rather like it."

"You mean there are *cool weather* months?" Abe asked, raising one hand over his eyes to block out the punishing sunlight.

"Fourteen months out of this planet's sixteen-month rotation are considered warm-weather months," Aerius replied drily.

"How convenient," Abe said. He turned toward Quinn. "You all right?"

"Better with the goggles," Quinn said, though he still moved unsteadily.

As before, the Shyophians didn't notice them, and if the natives found it odd that two offworlders were being marched through their village at gunpoint, none of them made any move to interfere. Within moments, Aerius, Abe, and Quinn passed the kiosk structure, where the man from the Galactic Tourism Bureau gawped from his window. He shouted to Aerius, "Right where I said they would be, huh? You'll make sure to mention me in your report, right? Put in a good word with the Tourism Bureau?"

"Your assistance will be noted," Aerius said without looking at the man.

Abe shot a scowl back at the tourism agent, who retreated into his shelter and slammed the dynoplas cover over the information window.

The special forces ship was parked just outside the settlement, much closer than Quinn had dared to land *The Lady Grace*. Menacing, red-tipped wings toward the rear of the vessel made the ship look like a giant bird of prey ready to leap off the desert floor, while a nose-mounted LAS-er cannon seemed ready to turn on them at any moment. Aerius produced a remote control from his person and used it to open the side hatch.

"After you," the alien said.

Abe and Quinn started for the hatch just as the sound of weapons fire filled the air. Abe turned in time to see a pulse strike hit the center of Aerius's chest, the shear-thickening material of his body armor rushing forward to coalesce at the impact site. While the material stopped the pulse from getting through, it didn't prevent Aerius from being propelled backward. The alien fell with a grunt, sending up a spray of sand.

"There!" Abe shouted. He pointed to a group of huts on the outskirts of the settlement, where four Nalaxans were rushing from their hiding spots with LAS-er weapons drawn. Waiting behind them with her own pistol aimed at the special forces ship was Mama Rossi.

Then everything seemed to happen in fast forward. Abe dragged Quinn to the ground and watched as the Nalaxans continued firing to keep Aerius pinned down. Laser bolts, barely visible in the blinding desert sunlight, streaked across the open space, sending up miniature volcanoes of sand whenever they struck the ground. The smell of burnt ozone filled the air.

One of the bodyguards broke from the main group and raced toward Abe and Quinn. Watching as the rhino creature barreled toward them, feet making small craters in the desert floor, Abe pulled Quinn toward the landing gear of the special forces ship, sure they would never be able to outrun the Nalaxan.

Aerius, however, was not about to lose his prize. The alien coiled his rangy body and sprang up from the ground, limbs moving with a liquid speed to bob and weave among the oncoming weapons fire. Raising his own gun, the government agent whipped off a shot that hit one of the Nalaxans in the head, then ducked, crouched, and sprang at another of the bodyguards, taking him down with some kind of leg-propelled tackle almost too fast for the eye to see.

"My goodness," Abe said. In spite of the pursuit, he had stopped to watch the government agent in action.

Suddenly, a hulking shadow fell over Abe and Quinn. Abe shouted as yet another Nalaxan leaned down and laid both burly hands on Abe's shoulders.

Quinn pounded on the trunk-like legs of the bodyguard as the Nalaxan lifted Abe into a restrictive bear hug. Kicking Quinn so that he struck the landing gear of the special forces ship, the Nalaxan turned and ran back toward Mama Rossi.

If Aerius was aware that Abe had been taken, there was nothing the alien agent could do about it. Shots continued to issue from the group of huts, effective cover fire from Mama Rossi, the one remaining bodyguard, and another figure at the edge of the settlement who seemed incapable of using his weapon properly. It was only when the Nalaxan carrying Abe got closer that Abe could see that it was Nimbus Steele.

"You!" Abe seethed.

Nimbus ignored the comment and continued fiddling with his pistol without success.

"Let's go!" Mama Rossi said. She grabbed Nimbus by the arm and angled him toward her luxury cruiser, which was parked a few yards back at the edge of the oasis. Abe and the Nalaxan took up the rear.

Aerius seemed to realize he would not be able to retrieve the elder Titterman. Instead, he fired off several random shots, then ran in a bullet-like crouch toward where Quinn kneeled helplessly in the sand. With one wiry arm, Aerius scooped Quinn into his momentum and propelled them both toward the open hatch of the special forces ship. Abe watched as the hatch of the government vessel closed with an airtight *hiss*.

Realizing they now had the upper hand, the Nalaxans fired a few shots at Aerius's ship—to no avail. In seconds, the vessel's engines powered to life with a roar, the landing gear retracted, and the ship began hovering a few feet off the ground. It sped away from the settlement as it gained altitude.

Abe slumped within the arms of his captor, his body limp with defeat. Mama Rossi, Nimbus Steele, and the other Nalaxan lowered their LAS-er weapons as the ship disappeared into a sky that had grown increasingly gray with clouds.

Abe felt something hit his cheek and roll onto the arm of his Nalaxan detainer. It was bright green. The Nalaxan put on a burst of speed toward the cruiser. It took a moment for Abe to realize what was happening: lapyk was falling from the sky, coating everything in an outrageous emerald gel.

CHAPTER NINE

With the young human subdued in the rear of the vessel, Aerius steered the ship away from the battleground and into the sky. He had arrived at Shyoph-2 only minutes after *The Lady Grace*, but a quick communiqué from Commander H had convinced Aerius to observe his targets before apprehending them. The wait had paid off. Aerius had seen the elder Titterman use the Key to open a door in the canyon obelisk. Surely Commander H would find that useful.

Aerius punched in the coordinates of their agreed-upon rendezvous and sat back as the ship made a hyperspeed jump. Emerging back into regular space with a small jolt about an hour later, the government agent signaled his arrival over an encrypted frequency and waited for a return message from Commander H's battle carrier.

Aerius didn't have to wait long. The instruments on one console of the ship's sophisticated instruments beeped to indicate that another, larger vessel had entered the vicinity. Aerius brought up the new arrival on his viewfinder display.

The ship was a battle carrier but of no configuration that Aerius had ever seen before. Long and lean with a pointed prow, quad ion engines, and side- and top-mounted LAS-er canons, the vessel was bred for combat and likely supported by a large and experienced crew. Aerius was considering a retreat when his computer received a signal from Commander H.

Cautiously, Aerius answered.

"Commander?" the agent said hesitantly.

The commander's voice came through the speech-only transmitter. "Agent Aerius, how nice that you've arrived. Report."

"Your ship... startled me, sir," the government agent replied.

"Everything will be explained once you're aboard. Do you have the Key, Aerius?" Commander H insisted.

"I do not, sir. But I do have the younger Titterman in custody, and I believe he has valuable information. Something about a transmission related to the Key."

Commander H sighed, the disappointment obvious when he spoke. "Very well. Prepare to be brought aboard. It's time we met in person."

Aerius felt another jolt as a suspension field locked onto his ship. As the field guided the vessel safely toward the docking bay of the battle carrier, Aerius unfolded his body from the cockpit chair and moved down the row of surveillance instruments toward the back of the ship.

Quinn had been placed against a rear bulkhead, a large power cell digging into his back. He still wore the sun goggles over his dilated eyes, and his hands had been bound with dynoplas ties.

"We are being brought aboard my commanding officer's battle carrier," Aerius said to Quinn, bending down to address the young man. "You will likely be asked a series of questions. I recommend you answer them truthfully."

"I want to call my family," Quinn replied stiffly.

"I am sure Commander H will fulfill your request once we are aboard." The alien agent turned and opened a storage locker built into the one part of the bulkhead that wasn't covered in computing equipment. He withdrew a fitted special forces jacket that displayed his rank and slipped it over his body armor. Taking a tube from somewhere within the depths of the locker, the alien squeezed a glob of lotion onto one long-fingered hand, which he proceeded to rub over his bare pate.

"It is important to look one's best when meeting with one's superior officer," Aerius said when he noticed Quinn staring at him through the goggles.

There was a beep from the instrument panel at the front of the ship. Aerius finished his grooming and strode the length of the vessel in just a few steps to check the display.

Looking up from the screen and back at his captive, the alien announced, "We have docked."

When he had first been asked to contract his services with Commander H, Aerius had read all the regulations related to his new employer, the Solar Navy. Thus, he knew something was wrong as soon as the hatch to his vessel opened inside the cavernous docking bay. For one thing, none of the battle carrier personnel wore any kind of standard-issue uniform, which broke at least thirteen different directives of the Navy dress code. For another, the weapons trained on Aerius and his captive as they stood in the hatch were highly modified and not the regulation LAS-er pistols provided to every enlisted man, woman, and creature.

"Stay where you are," said a burly Rauskon, who looked as if he had just stepped out of the mines of Titan. He held long-barreled weapons in two of his four hands.

"Where is Commander H?" Aerius asked, taking a stronger grip on Quinn's arm.

A woman stepped out from behind the Rauskon. Petite, blond, and with a green hologram over her left eye, Aerius recognized her as Madeline, the lieutenant who often contacted Aerius on behalf of Commander H.

"I've been instructed to bring you to the commander now," Madeline said in a polite, placating tone. "These men are here for your safety and safety of the prisoner."

"I demand a comm call," Quinn announced to no one in particular.

"Quiet," Aerius said to the young man. To Madeline, "Why are you not in uniform? What is the configuration and origin point of this vessel?"

"Commander H will explain everything," Madeline replied as the hologram cycled through its patterns in a mesmerizing fashion. She gestured toward a door behind the Rauskon and the rest of the security detail. "If you'll come this way."

Aerius made to take a step forward, but Quinn was reluctant to move.

"Something's not right," Quinn said softly to Aerius. "Even I can see it."

"We do not have much of a choice," the agent replied.

They stepped down from the special forces ship and into the midst of the gun muzzles pointed in their direction. With a word from Madeline, the Rauskon and the others lowered their weapons slightly, then stepped out of the way so she could escort Aerius and Quinn through the ship.

The interior of the battle carrier was a showcase of technological sophistication and finish to rival anything built at the shipyards of Vortas. Gone were the exposed pipes and conduits, the unadorned industrial functionality of a military vessel, replaced instead with bright corridors outfitted in neutral composite materials. Narrow strips of lighting embedded in the walls formed continuous lines that raced down the hallways, intercepted occasionally by glossy touch terminals, which Aerius assumed could access any number of shipboard functions.

"What is the origin of this vessel?" Aerius asked again as they passed into the transit core of the ship, a huge cylindrical space that spanned every deck with lifts and curving walkways along the outside wall.

Compared to the previous corridors, the transit hub was a buzz of activity as crewmembers—none in uniform—went about their assignments. A constant hum of white noise filled the air: the low mechanical buzz of the lifts as they moved between decks and indistinct conversation as personnel from a dozen species moved from one section of the ship to another.

Leading the group to one of the lift platforms, Madeline said to Aerius, "Commander H had this ship specially commissioned. She's a twelve-deck heavy cruiser with a crew of two hundred fifty. All the latest in armaments, communications, and FTL technology."

The glass-sided lift arrived and whisked them past the lower and central levels of the transit core to the top deck. Stepping off the elevator, Madeline led them down one final corridor to a set of double sliding doors. The word "Bridge" was stenciled on the hypersteel portal in three languages.

"After you," Madeline said with a gesture.

The doors slid to either side. Aerius and Quinn were immediately greeted by a magnificent view of the heavens, courtesy of floor-to-ceiling viewports at the far end of the roughly triangular bridge space. Crew members sat at various stations, controlling ship functions by swiping their hands and fingers over projected displays and the same glossy screens that Aerius and Quinn had passed in the lower corridors. In the center of the bridge was a square navigation table with interactive star charts currently on display. A man with a computer visor over his eyes used a stylus to plot the ship's course, bypassing planets and nebulae with a pulsing red mark. The bridge hummed with discourse as the various stations conversed with one another in controlled tones, reporting everything from radiation readings to engine performance.

"This way," Madeline said, waving toward a door at the rear of the bridge.

The commander's study, Aerius thought as he steeled himself for his first in-person interview with Commander H.

The door opened to reveal elegantly furnished quarters with wooden furniture that was quite a contrast from the composite workstations on the bridge. There were shelves with what Aerius knew the humans called *books*, though he had never actually seen one in person, and everything in the room spoke of comfort, not of military utilitarianism: the tapestry-like area rug on the deck; the wide desk, littered with trinkets, that on a normal ship would seat three; and the gilt-framed paintings on the wall. Commander H stood at a round viewport, his back to the door.

"Agent Aerius and his captive, Quinn Titterman, sir," Madeline announced as they stepped into the room.

"Thank you, Madeline," Commander H said without turning. "You're dismissed."

Madeline nodded and left the room, closing the door behind her. Commander H waited a moment for dramatic effect, then turned from the viewport to confront Aerius and Quinn.

Aerius was not one to scare easily, but he almost visibly started at the commander's appearance before reining in his emotions.

The commander, Aerius guessed, was bispecies, half human and half... something else. His muted red skin tone contrasted nicely with black eyes set in a strong, square face with a small ridge between the eyebrows. Middle aged and tall, Commander H had a bearing that spoke of military service.

None of this was out of the ordinary. What was unusual was that Commander H seemed to be missing part of his head.

From his right temple to a point near the back of the skull, the flesh had been replaced with a quarter sphere of polished metal. Where his ear should have been, there was a panel with a micromedia drive and several empty ports.

"Commander," Aerius acknowledged, trying not to break eye contact.

"Agent Aerius," said the commander as he sat at the desk, "how nice to finally meet you in person."

"Sir, if I may: Why is your crew not in uniform?" Aerius asked.

"I'll get to that in a moment." Commander H turned his attention to Quinn. "And who is this?"

Quinn looked pointedly toward one corner of the ceiling.

"Answer him," Aerius hissed.

"I have rights," Quinn said. "I don't have to say anything."

Aerius turned to Commander H and tried to approximate a smile, which made his nostril slits flare. "This is Quinn Titterman, great-grandson of Abe Titterman of Intergalactic Curios."

"Interesting," said the commander. He placed his palms flat on the desk. "To save us all some time, I'll get right to the point—where is the Key to the Universe?"

"I don't have it," Quinn said brusquely. "And I won't say anything else until I can call my parents. This is a Solar Navy vessel and—"

Commander H interrupted Quinn with a harsh laugh. "This *isn't* a Solar Navy vessel. Whatever gave you that idea?"

Aerius shot an unblinking glare at the commander. "Sir, as a special agent of the Solar Government, I would like to request information regarding the parameters of this operation. I will repeat my previous question: Why is your crew not in uniform? What is going on here?"

Commander H returned the stare evenly. "You aren't," he said by way of a reply.

"Sir?" Aerius asked.

Commander H stood and began pacing behind his desk. "You aren't a special agent of the Solar Government. This isn't a Solar Navy vessel. And I work for neither the government nor the military."

"Sir, I do not understand," Aerius said, the anger in his voice making his accent more pronounced. "Your representative hired me on contract for the Solar Government."

"I wanted the best," the commander said, "and I was told that you were one of the best, up until that case with the Cherhovan prince. Since I couldn't risk you turning me down, I stretched the truth and claimed to be enlisted with the Solar Navy. A deception, I admit, but a necessary one. I *needed* your skills."

Quinn looked hard at the commander while Aerius struggled to process the information he had been given. "Who are you?" the young man asked.

"My name is Peter Halloran," the commander said. "You're aboard the Solar Free Ship *Melee*, my personal battle carrier. And my mission, as Agent Aerius so finely put it, is to reclaim the Key to the Universe, which my mother—" he spat the word "—gave to Gabriella Rossi instead of me."

Aerius was at a loss for words, as if his embedded translator had failed to operate.

But Quinn exclaimed, "You're Minnie Halloran's *son?*"

Peter Halloran sighed, closed his eyes, and rubbed the ridge between his eyebrows. "Where is the Key?" he asked again, voice filled with frustration. "That's all I need to know."

"I told you, I don't have it," Quinn said. "Now let us leave."

"*Where is it?*" Peter shouted.

Quinn stammered. "I, I—"

"Do not tell him anything," Aerius cut in. "Under Solar Law F-37, section B, you are entitled to have a lawyer present."

Peter slammed his fist on the desk, making the trinkets rattle. "This isn't a Solar Navy ship! Get that through your idiotic alien skull! I could make you both disappear right now, and no one would be any the wiser!"

Aerius ignored the insult. "Do not say anything further," he advised Quinn.

The commander's eyes narrowed. He seemed on the verge of spouting more vitriol but instead pressed a button on the computer embedded in the desk. The door to the room slid open, and the four-armed Rauskon framed the entrance with weapons drawn.

"Take them to the brig," Peter ordered. "We'll begin the interrogation soon."

Quinn shouted in protest, drawing looks from the bridge crew as he and Aerius were led from Peter Halloran's study and back toward the elevator. Aerius, though, remained silent all the way down to their holding cells.

CHAPTER TEN

Thinking back on the past six months, Aerius could piece together how he had been tricked by Peter Halloran. There was an old human saying about things being too good to be true, and the offer made by Peter—by Commander H—had certainly been that.

"Are you all right?" Quinn asked from their conjoined cells.

Aerius looked up, unblinking, at his fellow captive. Like the rest of the ship, Peter had spared no expense on the brig. Brightly lit in a glaring fashion, the prison was comprised of six narrow cells with laser "bars" that crackled with megawatts worth of electrical energy. Just standing near the three-sided barriers was painful to Aerius's electroreceptors. Touching one of the bars, he imagined, would be excruciating, if not outright deadly.

"I owe you an apology," Aerius said.

The human looked taken aback.

"I believed I was working in the best interests of your government," Aerius continued. "It seems I was deceived."

Quinn regained his composure. He stared at Aerius with probing brown eyes, his sight now fully restored. The sun goggles lay discarded on the floor of his cell.

"If you're not a special agent, then who are you?" Quinn asked.

Aerius folded his long limbs into a sitting position, leaning against the one un-electrified wall of his cell. "I am—or was—a chayat. Do you know what that is?"

Quinn shook his head.

Aerius thought for a moment. "The best way I can explain that you will understand is that I found people for money," he finally said.

"A tracker?" Quinn clarified. "A bounty hunter?"

"Yes. And no. The chayats on my home world are famous, though few of my people are selected to train for the privilege. We are taken as striplings to learn the *Hinlid*, our code of conduct. When we can recite it, when we can *live* it, then we learn the secrets of finding from our elders."

"How did you come to work for Peter Halloran?" Quinn asked. As he said this, he appeared to notice something on the floor near the front of his cell and began crawling toward it.

"Do you know this human?" Aerius said, trying not to wince at Quinn's proximity to the electrical field.

Quinn shrugged. "Everyone who grows up on Mars knows the Halloran family."

Both were silent as Quinn scratched at the bulkhead inches from the lasers.

"What are you doing?" Aerius finally said when his anxiety had reached a fever pitch.

Quinn looked up. "There's a panel here. I want to see what's underneath." He paused for a moment as he worked one fingernail into the seam. Then he said, "You can keep going if you want. I'd like to hear about how you met Peter Halloran."

Aerius exhaled, trying to collect his thoughts. "It was not long ago. Maybe half a cycle. I usually do not take work in your solar system since it is far from my home world and rarely profitable. But on my last job I was tracking a Cherhovan prince who had come to one of the moons of Saturn to 'seek his fortune.' The young man disappeared. No one knew where he was. I was in the middle of my search when Commander H sent me a communiqué. The Solar Government, he said, needed experienced individuals and wanted to recruit me for its special forces because I was a chayat of some renown. Shortly after, I learned that the prince had died in the mines of Titan. He had lost all of his money on games of chance. His father was not pleased. He said my search had taken too long and blamed me for his son's death. Then he began to spread falsehoods about my reputation. So, I took work with the commander. He gave me a new ship. He even gave me a uniform with my rank."

Aerius fingered the military jacket that he had on over his liquid armor. Then he looked up to find that Quinn had succeeded in prying the panel loose from the floor.

"What did you find?" Aerius asked.

"I'm not sure," Quinn said without looking up. "It looks like these may be conduits that feed power to the cell walls. I read a book on electrical wiring once. Iash says, 'A well-rounded individual is never prevented from rolling forward.'"

There was a pause as Quinn fumbled around inside the hole. Aerius didn't know who Iash was, so instead he said, "Tell me more about Peter Halloran."

"What do you want to know? The Hallorans are like the royalty of Mars."

"They are your rulers? Your kings?"

Quinn shook his head and spoke more plainly. "Sorry," he said. "They're not our rulers. But they're so rich that people think of them as celebrities. Does that make sense?"

"No, I do not understand."

Quinn took a deep breath. "Okay, uh, let's see. The Hallorans are a very rich and powerful family because of their terraforming company."

"Okay."

"Minnie Halloran—that's Peter's mother—ran the company until she retired about a year ago. She died last week."

Aerius didn't understand all of the cultural references that his translator picked up, but he got the general idea.

"Minnie was married—uh, mated—for a while to a diplomat from Delta Proxima. They had a son named Peter."

"The brow ridge," Aerius clarified. "He is half human, half Delta Proximan."

"Yes," Quinn said. "Pop-pop told me that the media on Mars covered the pregnancy like a planet-wide election. It was—*Ow!*"

Quinn's hand shot out of the hole as if he had been bitten by a burrowing *umkala*. The young man shook the appendage rigorously, forcing his fingers to clack together.

"Are you all right?" Aerius asked, pressing as close as he dared to the bars.

"Well, that's definitely a power conduit," Quinn said. "I wonder if I can bypass the flow. That may cut power to the cell walls."

Aerius nodded and shifted into a more comfortable position.

"Anyway," Quinn went on, "Peter was a bit of a troublemaker in his youth, always going to parties, getting kicked out of school. He dated supermodels, drove fast ships—the usual."

"The usual?" Aerius asked.

"Uh, it's a little hard to explain," Quinn conceded.

"And is such behavior normal for human striplings?" Aerius asked.

"No, only those with lots of money."

Aerius tilted his head but didn't have much time to puzzle through Quinn's riddle of words.

"Peter went into the Solar Navy," the young man continued. "I think his family hoped it would teach him discipline. And from what Pop-pop told me, Peter did pretty well. He served on the front lines during the Europa Crisis, and of course the news made a big deal about it. But then there was an accident on his ship—Peter got hit in the head by a falling piece of bulkhead. I guess it was pretty bad because he was in a coma for days and the doctors didn't know if he would live. I'm sure the tabloids had a field day with that one too."

"But he *did* live?"

"Yeah," Quinn replied, "he came out of it. After that, he became kind of a recluse. Every now and then, some reporter
would try to track him down for a story, but Peter would always
turn them down. Some said he had been... *altered* by the accident. But he had his family's money, so he could spend his time
doing whatever he liked—which apparently included buying a
custom battleship, hiring a crew of mercenaries, and reliving his
glory days in the Solar Navy."

Aerius's chayat mind processed this new information, making connections between the various elements of Quinn's story.
But there was an important element that was still missing.

"What about the Key to the Universe?" Aerius asked.

Quinn chuckled. "I bet Pop-pop wishes he had just given it
to Mama Rossi now." Then, still focused on the panel in the
floor, he added, "I wish I had an electrical resonator rod."

"What is this word 'pop'?" Aerius said, placing too much of
a pause between the syllables.

"It's what I call my great-grandfather. It *is* normal for human children... er, striplings to give their parents and
grandparents terms of endearment."

Aerius nodded again.

"The Key," Quinn went on. "No one knew if it was even real, much less how the Halloran family got it. But we—you, me,
and Pop-pop, anyway—know that Minnie Halloran left it to
Mama Rossi in her will, instead of Peter."

"Why would she do that?"

Quinn blew out his breath. "Who knows. But it looks like
Peter really wants it back."

"By this I am not surprised," Aerius said.

Quinn stopped working inside the bulkhead. "You aren't?"

"Most planets in the known galaxy have legends about the
Key to the Universe, some going back a thousand years to the
Golden Age of Missionaries. My own people call it *Briak Mor*.
The stories say that the Key will lead to much influence."

Quinn sat up straighter, the panel and the electrical current momentarily forgotten. "What else do the stories say?"

Aerius thought for a moment. "On my world, the tales are told to striplings. They say that a wise elder or elders crafted the Key and that the finder will unlock a new age of peace and prosperity for the galaxy."

"Do your people study Iash as well?" Quinn asked.

There was that word again. Aerius thought that maybe his translator had malfunctioned. "I do not know what 'iash' is."

Quinn frowned and nodded, turning his attention back to the panel. "It doesn't matter. But based on what we've seen, I don't think Peter Halloran is interested in peace and prosperity for the galaxy."

"In this, human, we are in full agreement."

For a moment, the silence was punctuated only by the constant electrical hum of the bars and the sound of Quinn scraping around inside the floor panel. Then the young man said, "I think I got it!"

Aerius watched as Quinn triggered something inside the bulkhead. There was a burst of light as the laser bars *intensified*. Aerius shrank back, his electroreceptors stinging in discomfort. He caught sight of Quinn scrambling back as well, the hair on his arms standing straight up with all the electricity in the air.

"Ugh!" Quinn groaned as he used one arm to shield his face.

"What happened?" Aerius shouted.

"Now it's my turn to apologize," Quinn replied. "I think I just made things worse."

Aerius squinted at the new flow of power running through the bars. *This is going to be a long day.*

CHAPTER ELEVEN

After cleaning up the ship from the lapyk storm, which involved the Nalaxan bodyguards scraping the pernicious gel from every nook and cranny of the hull and engine wells, it took Gabriella's party nearly two days to arrive back on Mars, during which time Abe Titterman complained endlessly. The old man whined mostly about his abducted great-grandson, and when he wanted a break from that, he grumbled about the food, his accommodations, the Nalaxans' odor, Nimbus Steele, and the fact that Gabriella had left his ship, *The Lady Grace*, back on Shyoph.

By the time they got back to Gabriella's compound, she was about ready to shoot him and be done with it. She had the Key now, certainly, but Abe kept saying something about a "map"— a map that was apparently in the possession of his great-grandson. In the interest of gathering everything associated with the Key, Gabriella would need to find out more about this map. Which meant that, sooner or later, she would have to rescue Quinn Titterman from that accursed alien agent.

Abe stalked down one of the sublevel corridors of Mama Rossi's military-grade compound, escorted by the Nalaxan bodyguard who had accompanied Abe from his "prison room"

to the lavatory. The facility was very industrial, the passages crafted from hypersteel-reinforced concrete, and Abe got the impression that the whole structure could probably survive a bombing from orbit.

"Don't you ever bathe?" Abe wheedled the stoic bodyguard.

The guard did not reply. In fact, Abe noticed that all of the Nalaxans who had been assigned to guard him no longer responded to any of his barbs. Abe smiled to himself in satisfaction. *At least I don't have to listen to their nasally voices any more.*

The door to Abe's room was ajar as they rounded one corner of the guest wing. As far as "prisons" went, Mama Rossi's compound was anything but cruel. Abe was essentially under house arrest in a well-furnished room with a bed, desk, and entertainment platform that had access to the Solar Network and holo entertainment (though no outside communications). One of the Nalaxan bodyguards stayed outside the room at all times, bringing Abe his meals and accompanying him to the restroom around the corner.

Abe pushed open the door, which he didn't remember leaving open, and was greeted by the sight of Nimbus Steele rifling through the drawers in the room's desk.

"What are you doing?" said Abe and the Nalaxan at the same time.

Nimbus looked up, an expression of surprise and fear passing over his features for just a second. Then he mastered himself, flashed an oily smile, and said, "Just looking for the Key. I wanted to get a good look at it. I feel confident that Mama Rossi will give me part of its value as compensation for the money you owe me."

"You charlatan!" Abe shouted. "Out!"

"You're not supposed to be here," the Nalaxan added more reasonably. The bodyguard crossed his meaty arms, his voice and body language at odds with each other. "Where is your escort?"

"The last I saw," Nimbus said, "he was in the middle of a sneezing fit. You get plenty of mold spores in the corners of these underground complexes."

"Get back to your room," the Nalaxan ordered, eyes narrowed.

"Very well," Nimbus said. To Abe he added, "We'll talk more about this later."

Nimbus exited the room. Abe followed and shouted down the hall, "You're a thief, Nimbus Steele! A no-good thief!"

Nimbus simply waved over his shoulder.

Abe returned to his room. The Nalaxan was looking over the debris that Nimbus had scattered in a circle around the desk.

"Well, what are you still doing here?" Abe asked irritably.

The bodyguard looked up at his charge.

"Unless your orders are to sit on me, I suggest you get back to the hallway and leave me alone!"

The Nalaxan didn't argue but simply strode from the room and closed the door behind him.

Abe sat wearily in the desk chair, pulse pounding in his ears. His chest felt heavy.

Got to relax, he thought. *Can't get worked up like that anymore.*

He grunted.

Ugh, I sound just like Grace!

When he had calmed down a bit, Abe stood, walked over to the bed and reached up to a grate that was set halfway up the wall. The square vent, held by a screw in each corner, was part of the compound's environmental system, and Abe worked at turning the fasteners gingerly between his thumb and forefinger. When he had detached the grate from the wall, he placed it on the bed and reached inside the recess to draw out the box containing the Key to the Universe.

Mama Rossi had allowed him to hold onto it after he had thrown such a fit on the way back to Mars that she had to threaten to subdue him with sedative drugs for the sake of his own health. In the end, she begrudgingly assured Abe that he could temporarily keep the Key in his own room in her compound, after which Abe was completely silent for the rest of the trip.

After opening the box to make sure the Key was safe, Abe replaced it in the ventilation shaft and began reattaching the grille.

It was then that the communications tone on the entertainment console sounded in the otherwise-silent room. Abe jumped, dropping the screw he was holding.

"Oh jeez," Abe groaned as the screw clattered out of sight. He finished with the remaining three screws and walked over to the console. "What?" he said irritably as he touched the screen.

Mama Rossi appeared on the console. "Did I catch you at a bad time, Mister Titterman?"

Abe grunted. "Time is something we've been wasting since we left Shyoph. We should be out there finding the scoundrel who kidnapped Quinn."

"We can discuss that," Mama Rossi replied. "In fact, we have a lot to talk about. Why don't you come to my office? One of my bodyguards will escort you."

"More talk, less action," Abe muttered.

"Come to my office," Mama Rossi repeated.

Abe nodded resignedly and cut the communications link. The Nalaxan must have been alerted as well because he was waiting expectantly when Abe exited the room.

Nimbus Steele watched the Nalaxan's immense backside lumber down the hall, accompanied by the less steady steps of Abe Titterman. Nimbus shuddered.

I hope I never get that old, he thought.

Shaking his head to clear it, Nimbus proceeded to tiptoe down the hall to the entrance to Abe's prison room. The door, of course, was locked, but that had never stopped Nimbus in the past. He rolled up his sleeve and pressed a number of nodules that had been implanted on the underside of his wrist. These were the best kind of lock picks one could possess—the kind that couldn't be confiscated.

Nimbus splayed his fingers and held them in front of the door's security panel. The equipment in his hand began scanning the lock's encryption code, the electronics searching for the combination that would release the bolt. In about twenty seconds, the door clicked open.

Getting slow, Nimbus thought. *I'll have to get back to Nyoploris for an update soon.*

Nimbus pressed the nodules on his wrist again and pulled down his sleeve. Looking down the corridor in both directions, he bolted inside Abe's room and shut the door behind him.

Abe's quarters were much the same as Nimbus's own accommodations. *Sure beats the prisons on the Moon*, he thought with a shudder.

Before taking another step inside, Nimbus scanned the room expertly. The sheets on the bed were turned down and the desk he had been rummaging through was a mess, but nothing else seemed disturbed. The room was so ordinary and without embellishment that hiding *anything* would be difficult.

Nimbus thought back to his own room and considered the places where *he* might hide something as valuable as the Key to the Universe—that is, assuming Mama Rossi hadn't already confiscated the relic upon their arrival, despite Abe's bellyaching.

Nimbus took a step forward to begin a more thorough investigation when he trod on a piece of debris. He lifted his foot and saw a small screw. He looked from the screw to the environmental grille on the wall next to the bed.

"No…" Nimbus said aloud.

He laughed. *You* are *getting old, whether you like it or not.*

Mama Rossi's office was elegant but not ostentatious, a mix of utility and class meant for actual work and to impress the occasional visitor. The focus of the room was a desk with built-in computer surrounded by several studded leather wingchairs. Lamps stood to either side, and Abe recognized them as having originated from Delta Proxima.

"Nice," Abe said, pointing to the lamps as he took a seat in one of the chairs, feet flexing on the ornamental rug underfoot.

"I knew you'd appreciate them," Mama Rossi said from behind her desk. "They're from the workshops of the Eighteenth Dynasty."

"Very rare to find them intact, lampshades and all," Abe said.

"They were a gift from the governor of Brahe."

Abe grunted. "I'm sure you did him some *tremendous* favor. Made the public works union sign a new contract, maybe? Or smeared some political rival?"

Mama Rossi pursed her lips. "Nothing of the sort, actually. I merely loaned him the services of my personal lawyer at Winkroot."

Abe leaned forward. "But you didn't bring me here to talk shop."

"Shop, yes," Mama Rossi said. "But about my lamps, no. Tell me, Mister Titterman, have you ever played VR Sector before?"

Abe folded him arms over his chest. "Call me Abe. And about the only sport I take in at my age is low-gravity golf."

"Then you're going to love it," Mama Rossi said. "I, for one, always think better when my hands are occupied. Follow me."

She stood and gestured toward another door to the left of the desk. Abe followed her through and found himself in a small lounge with several bookshelf cabinets and two well-worn but comfortable-looking chairs separated by a round end table.

"Have a seat," Mama Rossi said, indicating the chairs while she went over to one of the bookcases and removed something from the cabinet. When she returned, she was holding two virtual reality headsets. "Go ahead and put this on."

Abe looked skeptically at the headset, which resembled a helmet crossed with overlarge sunglasses.

"Go ahead," Mama Rossi urged.

She took a seat in the other chair and slipped the set over her hair bun, lowering the visual display onto her face. Abe did the same, glowering at the tinted lenses that made it all but impossible to see.

"Hold on," he heard her say.

There was a flash of white, and Abe gasped. In seconds, he found himself in a kind of arena with a twenty-sided spheroid in the center. He looked down at himself and saw a mirrored buckler strapped to his right arm and a kind of laser weapon encasing his left. Catching a glimpse of himself in the reflective shield, Abe noticed his virtual reality avatar was a young man, handsome and athletic.

"What do you think?" came a voice from behind Abe.

Abe spun and saw that a fit, attractive young woman in a sports top and leggings had entered the arena. She had Mama Rossi's voice.

"Wishful thinking, huh?" the young woman went on. "Me and an old goat, transformed into a princess and a prince. Just like in the old fairytales."

Abe flexed his arms and examined his well-toned biceps. Then he looked down at a flat chest clad in a form-fitting tank top. "This is amazing," Abe breathed, momentarily forgetting everything else. "I'd heard about the latest VR sims, but I never dreamed…"

"Come on," Mama Rossi said. "I'll show you how to play."

She led him over to the spheroid and pressed a button on her gun arm. Abe watched as different sides of the sphere cycled through various colors—red, blue, green—that lasted about two seconds each.

"Each of the sphere's twenty sides is called a sector," Mama Rossi explained. "A green sector will get you one point. A blue sector will get you three. A red sector will take away one. The goal is to score as many points as possible while preventing your opponent from doing the same. Normally there's four blockers with bucklers called mirrormen and one scorer with a gun called a rusher. But since we're playing one-on-one, we serve double duty. Give it a try."

Abe looked down at his gun arm. He lifted it and shot at a portion of the sphere that was illuminated green. A tone sounded in the arena, and a floating scoreboard that had previously escaped his notice registered one point. Abe shot again, this time at a blue sector. The tone sounded a second time, and the scoreboard registered three more points. Abe lifted his arm to shoot a third time, but the young woman stepped in his way and blocked the laser bolt with her shield. The shot went wild, disappearing into the no-space that surrounded the virtual court.

"See?" Mama Rossi said. "Easy."

"If you say so," Abe replied.

"I'll set the clock for a five-minute period," the young woman said while pressing a series of buttons on her gun arm. "Go stand over there to start."

Abe looked over his shoulder and saw an octagon of light on the arena floor. He walked toward it and stood in the center. A second octagon appeared about twenty feet away, occupied by Mama Rossi's avatar.

"So," she began, "tell me about your findings on Shyoph."

"Just a cultural visit with my great-grandson," Abe replied.

A buzzer sounded in the arena. Mama Rossi's avatar left the octagon at a run, gun arm raised and aimed at the twenty-sided spheroid. Abe took a second to realize that the round had started, then walked out of the octagon at a leisurely pace.

The young woman looked over her shoulder. "What's wrong?"

"I haven't run in fifty years," Abe replied, lifting his own gun arm before realizing that he was too far away to make any kind of reasonable shot.

"You're not restricted by your physical body here," the woman said with a touch of condescension. *"Run!"*

She shot a laser bolt at Abe's avatar. By reflex alone, Abe crouched and lifted his mirrored buckler, deflecting the shot at a 90-degree angle. Before he could stand, the athletic young woman was running again toward the spheroid, shooting at green and blue sectors with abandon.

Abe got to his feet and gave pursuit, his stride lengthening from a jog to a run. A thrill of exhilaration pulsed through his body as he exercised muscles that were no longer stiff, cramped, or painful. He lifted his gun arm and got off two shots at a green sector before Mama Rossi realized that her opponent was back in the game. She deflected Abe's third shot.

"Better," the young woman said. "Now, what did you find on Shyoph?"

Abe dodged around the woman and got off two shots at the spheroid, one of which hit a blue sector.

"I told you," Abe said. "A cultural visit. We went to the tomb of Iash. Quinn's a big fan."

Mama Rossi shot at Abe again. The laser bolt hit his shoulder and sent a shock of electric pain running down his arm. Abe shouted and raised his buckler in defense.

"Don't lie to me!" the young woman said. Her face was covered in a sheen of sweat, and a few flyaways had come loose from her ponytail.

"I'm not lying," Abe said from behind his shield. "Quinn's a huge fan of that Iash fellow. Always quoting him, usually at the most inappropriate times."

"Fine," said Mama Rossi. She turned and ran to the opposite side of the spheroid, then shouted, "I was beginning to doubt that Minnie Halloran had the genuine article anyway."

Abe gave chase, shooting at blue and green sectors whenever they appeared. "Oh, the Key is genuine," he said with professional pride.

"You *did* find something on Shyoph then?" Mama Rossi said. She shot at Abe again as he rounded the corner of the spheroid.

Abe dodged, narrowly, and returned fire before ducking back to safety. "I don't see that it's any of your business. Besides, without Quinn none of this is worth a wooden Galavan spot-coin." He gritted his teeth. "We should be out there *looking for him.*"

Mama Rossi had taken cover behind the other side of the spheroid, the game momentarily forgotten. She said, "Tell me what I want to know, and we can make that happen."

"Oh, and I suppose I have your word on that," Abe replied.

"Of course."

Abe bobbed his head from left to right, looking for an opening with which to strike. "If any harm comes to him while we're arguing like this…"

"The sooner you tell me," came Mama Rossi's voice, "the sooner we can begin."

Abe sighed. "Fine. It was a transmission."

"A transmission of what?"

"I don't know!" Abe said angrily.

Leaping from the other side of the cube, he leveled a shot that hit the young woman square in the chest. Mama Rossi's avatar gasped and skidded backward on the arena floor.

"That's what I've been trying to tell you for two days," Abe continued. "It's all inside Quinn's head, including the location of where to use the Key. Which is just another reason why we have to rescue him from that—that government agent."

Abe turned and shot the spheroid at will.

"That creature from N-31 Alpha is *not* a government agent," Mama Rossi said as her avatar got to its feet.

Abe turned, ready to play defense again, and aimed his gun arm at the young woman. "And how would you know that?"

"Because *I'm* a government agent."

Abe's shot went wide, missing its intended target. The buzzer sounded in the arena again, and a robotic voice said, "Period end. Score: Abe Titterman, 54. Gabriella Rossi, 82."

CHAPTER TWELVE

Quinn walks through an alley of rocks, feet shifting on a floor of desert sand, pebbles, and scree. The place carries with it a sense of déjà vu, but when Quinn tries to grasp where he is and when he has been there, the memories flee like grains of sand pouring through an outstretched hand. He keeps walking, hoping that his journey will evoke more recollections.

There is a clearing ahead, a place where the rocks draw away and the sand runs down a gentle slope. Quinn stands at the edge of the ridge, looking down. There is a crater below, and the land is black and charred where the object struck.

Footsteps behind him—!

Quinn wasn't sure how much time had passed, but his dream ended as loud footfalls entered the brig. Both he and Aerius looked up to find the human woman Madeline, the Rauskon, and Peter Halloran enter the confinement area. Madeline wore blue surgical gloves.

"What's going on?" Quinn asked with a mounting sense of dread.

Peter noticed the open access panel inside the cell and the increase in power running through the laser bars. He chuckled and crossed his arms. "I see you found the power regulator. Unfortunately, the one *inside* the cell only increases the juice."

He reached for a control panel near the door of the brig and pressed a button that returned the laser bars to their original intensity.

"There. Now we won't risk my own people as well." He turned to Madeline. "Open it."

Madeline deactivated the bars in Quinn's cell. With a quick sidestep, the Rauskon shifted to obstruct the entrance, all four arms spread out.

"Hold him," Peter ordered.

Out of instinct, Quinn looked left and right before his brain registered that there was nowhere to go. He was cornered.

"Whatever you're doing…" Quinn began.

The Rauskon advanced silently and used two of his arms to pin Quinn against the back wall. Quinn shouted, but the Rauskon used his other two arms to hold the young man's chest and prevent him from struggling. Madeline, meanwhile, edged into the cell with what looked like a medical injector in one hand. Quinn, heart racing, began to plead, "Please, don't—"

"Keep him still," Madeline said, "or else I won't be able to get a good implantation."

The Rauskon clamped down harder but still didn't have enough hands to cover the cries of fear that came from Quinn's mouth.

"Cease what you are doing!" Aerius shouted from his own cell.

Peter, Madeline, and the Rauskon all ignored him. Madeline placed the injector on Quinn's neck and depressed the firing mechanism. There was a brief flare of pain, then Quinn seemed to experience the next few moments as a passenger inside his own body: the Rauskon releasing him, his body falling against the back wall and sliding down to the floor, Madeline and the Rauskon leaving the cell, Peter reactivating the security bars.

110 · PATRICK SCALISI

Peter held out one hand and said to Madeline, "The control."

She placed a small remote in the commander's hand and left the brig with the Rauskon in tow.

"I will ask you one more time," Peter said to Quinn. "Where is the Key to the Universe?"

Quinn, his entire body shaking, grunted, "Stuff it."

Peter nodded and turned away from the cells for a moment. "Have you ever been to the techno world Nyoploris?" He didn't wait for a response. Turning back to Quinn's cell, Peter continued, "Wonderful place. You can get practically anything there. This device, for instance, when implanted in the neck and activated with this remote will stimulate the nociceptors—the pain receptors—in a person's body."

Peter turned a knob on the remote. Quinn cried out and lurched to the floor as a sensation that resembled touching a hot surface raced over every inch of his skin.

"Not very pleasant, is it?" Peter asked as he switched the control off. "Of course, I haven't tried it myself."

The pain disappeared as quickly as it had arrived. Quinn gasped, "Felt like my whole body was on fire…"

"The real beauty of this device is that I can interrogate without the mess of bodily fluids or fancy torture devices," Peter said. "The Nyoploris scientists have really put all of that into a complete package—this."

Peter turned the knob again, eliciting another tortured cry of pain from his captive. Somewhere far away, Quinn heard Aerius pleading, "Cease, please."

Peter ignored him. "Where is the Key?" the commander persisted.

Quinn would not answer. Another twist of the knob. Screams and a thud as the pain sent the young man convulsing against the back wall of his cell.

"I know who has the Key!" Aerius shouted.

The pain stopped. Quinn managed to lift his head and see that Peter's fingers were still poised over the control knob. But for the first time, the commander was focused on his other prisoner.

"*You* know where it is?" Peter asked Aerius.

"Yes," the chayat said. "The human Gabriella Rossi took it when I intercepted Abraham and Quinn Titterman on Shyoph-2. Now please leave him alone."

Peter looked back at Quinn. "Your fellow prisoner has earned you a respite. I'll be back later to talk about this 'transmission' that Agent Aerius mentioned, and I'll wager he knows less about that than he does about the location of the Key."

Quinn flinched as Peter returned the remote to his pocket. The commander saw this and flashed a feral smile before leaving, the brig doors sliding shut with a hiss of finality.

Abe removed his VR headset to discover that he had indeed broken a sweat while playing in the virtual arena. Perspiration covered his forehead, whether from simply wearing the helmet or from mental exertion he did not know, but he imagined that his hair was in quite a disarray. He put the headset on the table and watched as Mama Rossi removed her own gear and patted the hair around her bun.

"I'm not sure I heard you right in there," said Abe. "For a second I thought you said that you were a government agent."

Mama Rossi held a finger to her lips, reached under the lip of the table and pressed an unseen button here.

"Privacy field," she said. "Around this room and the office. You can't be too careful, even when you're feared and respected by most of your subordinates."

"So?" Abe pressed.

"You heard me right," Mama Rossi continued. "I'm an agent of the Solar Government."

Abe rose from his chair, perhaps a little too quickly. In just ten minutes, he had gotten used to being young again. Now his body creaked in protest, and he realized how people could become VR addicts, living their whole lives in an alternate reality.

Pacing for a moment to work the ache out of his lower back, Abe turned to Mama Rossi and shook his head. "I must be losing more of my faculties than I thought. How can you possibly be a Solar Government agent?"

Mama Rossi sat back and crossed her arms over her prodigious chest. "When the last don died in a turf war with the Martian Yakuza, the government saw a rare opportunity to implant one of its own as the head of the Martian Mafia. I can't go into classified details, but it's enough to say that if I hadn't taken the don's place, someone else would have. And the authorities would much rather have someone on their payroll in charge than some random heavy."

"But the killings? The crime?"

She shrugged. "I never said anything about not getting my hands dirty once and a while. And the government does give me a certain amount of carte blanche. But in the eight years since I took over, street crime has decreased forty percent, and we've actually legitimized many of our dealings. If my methods play their course, the Mafia will be out of illegal business trades by the time I retire. And they'll still be profitable."

She paused, as if considering what else to divulge. "I was ordered some time ago to cultivate a relationship with Minnie Halloran, knowing it would one day allow the government at least a small opportunity to get the Key to the Universe. Something that powerful shouldn't be in civilian hands. That's how I know Aerius isn't a government agent. I would have been informed if there was someone else working this case."

Abe glanced around the lounge, barely taking in the book-shelves and their contents as his mind worked through what he had just been told. He inhaled deeply.

"Aerius," he said, making the name into a kind of sigh. Af-ter a moment, he continued, "When I was just getting started in the antique business, I had the opportunity to buy an important cultural artifact from Earth, sight unseen, for a *very* reasonable price. My father, who taught me everything I know, warned me against such deals, but I rationalized it by telling myself that I would still be able to turn a profit, even if the condition was in-flated. There were red flags—the seller had 'lost' some of the paperwork; he needed a 'quick' sale to pay off some family debts—but I ignored them. In the end, I made the purchase."

"And let me guess—the thing was a wreck when you actu-ally got it?"

Abe met eyes with the mafiosa. "No, it was perfect. Too perfect, in fact. It was a replica. And by the time I had jumped through all the hoops to get the proper authentication papers again, the seller was long gone with my money."

"I'm guessing this little story has a point."

"It does," Abe said. "I accept few things without proof. And your story is still lacking in that department."

Without a word, Mama Rossi grabbed a fat, leather-bound book from a nearby shelf and opened it to the center. The book was hollow, the pages cut out to accommodate an object about the size of her palm. She withdrew the object and closed the book with a definitive *thud*.

"What is that?" Abe asked.

"See for yourself."

Mama Rossi handed him a metal badge emblazoned with the seal of the Solar Government. Abe quickly handed it back.

"Aerius had one of these too," he said dismissively.

"But did his do this?"

Mama Rossi held out her right thumb and made a display of lifting up the fingernail, which was synthetic and operated on a hinge. From underneath, she withdrew a small bio-chip, which she inserted into a slot on top of the badge. Immediately, the lines on the badge started glowing blue, and a blank space at the bottom of the Solar Government seal illuminated with a name and a Solar Registration code.

"It's keyed to my DNA," Mama Rossi said. "Every *real* agent of the Solar Government has one. They're made through a proprietary system known to only two people in the galaxy. And they're impossible to counterfeit. This is the best proof I can offer."

"So your real name is—"

"I'm not that person anymore," Mama Rossi cut in. "And the only reason I'm showing you this is to prove we both have a vested interest in finding your great-grandson. I need your willing cooperation, Abe."

Abe thought about it for a minute, weighing the risk of trusting the mafiosa against finding Quinn. Finally, he said, "Okay. But if Aerius isn't employed by the government, who does he work for?"

"That I don't have such a ready answer for," Mama Rossi replied. She removed the bio-chip and returned both it and the badge to their respective places. Then she walked to the door that led back to her office.

"I've been using my connections to try and find out," she continued, "but no one's turned up anything so far. A network across the galaxy and you'd think someone would know *something*."

Abe followed the mafiosa back to her desk. Mama Rossi was about to sit when a distinct rumble shook the room, sending trails of dust falling from the ceiling.

"What the—?" Mama Rossi slapped a button on her computer. "Report!"

"Mama!" Abe recognized the nasally voice of one of the Nalaxans on the other end of the line. "There's been an explosion in the docking bay!"

Mama Rossi's voice went from matronly to acid-tipped. "What?!"

"It looks like Nimbus Steele stole one of the shuttles," the Nalaxan said between coughing fits. "He set off some kind of bomb near the cruiser. Gianni is dead."

Mama Rossi pounded the desk, but Abe wasn't around to see her burst of anger. At the mention of Nimbus Steele, Abe had flown from the office at what could best be described as a jogging shuffle, retracing his steps back to his prison room. He arrived to find the ventilation grate set aside on the bed and the wall recess empty. He groaned.

Mama Rossi arrived a few seconds later, her small LAS-er weapon held in one hand. "What's wrong now?" she asked sharply.

Abe pointed to the empty ventilation duct. "He took the Key."

CHAPTER THIRTEEN

Gabriella felt like the world was crashing around her, both literally and figuratively. Her compound bombed. The Key and Nimbus Steele gone. Quinn Titterman—who had some larger role to play in all of this—kidnapped and lost somewhere in the galaxy. Gabriella thought back to her meeting with Nimbus in the Adams Café and wondered at all of the problems she might have solved by killing him then. But hindsight was always 20-20, and Nimbus was now another obstacle before the Key could be found and made safe again.

Gabriella lowered her pistol arm, loosening her grip so that the weapon almost fell to the floor.

"Damn" was all she managed to say.

The sound of heavy footfalls came from the end of the corridor. One of the Nalaxans, his black suit and white shirt singed around the sleeves and smelling like cooked fabric, lumbered down the hallway.

"What's the latest?" Gabriella demanded when the bodyguard reached them.

"The fire damaged your cruiser and the only other shuttle," the Nalaxan wheezed. "Steele somehow disabled the anti-theft protocols on the ship he took. We're not sure how. Mario is working on tracking the shuttle, but—"

"But without the anti-theft system, it's useless," Gabriella finished. She stared at the winded bodyguard. "Did you run all the way up here?"

"Yes, Mama," the Nalaxan replied. "The fire threatened one of the fuel cells. Mario took internal communications offline. We're working on fixing it now, but he wanted me to let you know that there's a call for you on the outside line."

"Whoever it is can wait," Gabriella said.

The Nalaxan shook his horned head. "The man said it was important. He said he has Quinn Titterman."

At the sound of Quinn's name, Abe turned from the plundered room, which he had been examining with his own sense of hopelessness and despair.

"What did you say?" Abe asked the Nalaxan. Then he turned to Mama Rossi, "What did he say?"

"There's someone on the outside communications line who says they have your great-grandson," replied Mama Rossi coolly. The rare outburst Abe had seen in the office was long gone, the mafiosa's voice returned to its calm, calculating tone.

Abe, though, couldn't hide his own impatience. "Was it that *creature*? That fake government agent?" he exclaimed. "Well, let's go talk to him! What are we waiting for?"

Mama Rossi pointed a finger at Abe's chest. "You're to stay quiet, you hear me?"

Abe waved off the command. "Fine, fine. Let's just go talk to whoever has Quinn."

They returned to the mafiosa's office while the Nalaxan went off to continue with repairs and fire suppression. Mama Rossi sat at her desk while Abe watched from over her right shoulder. There was a brief delay while the communications line was routed to the computer. Then a man—not Agent Aerius—appeared on screen in what appeared to be a room aboard a starship.

"Miss Rossi, how nice to see you again," the man said.

Abe saw the woman's shoulders tense almost imperceptibly and guessed correctly that she wasn't used to being caught off guard.

"To whom am I speaking?" Mama Rossi asked, the inquiry businesslike and lined with iron.

"I'm hurt you don't remember me," the man said, feigning a frown. "I always thought of myself as rather unique."

Now that the man mentioned it, Abe noticed that the caller wasn't quite human, or at least wasn't *fully* human. What Abe had mistaken for deeply tanned or perhaps even burnt skin was actually a muted red. And the man's eyes were unnaturally black, not to mention the small ridge between his eyebrows. Then again, who could keep up with the latest trends in plastic surgery and augmentation? This guy had plenty of it—half his head was missing!

"Look, I'm afraid I'm very busy at the moment—" Mama Rossi began.

"Too busy for Minnie Halloran's son?"

Abe watched as Mama Rossi tilted her head to one side, as if hoping to dislodge a memory.

"Peter?" she asked in a tone that was much less terse. "But—"

"Peter Halloran?" Abe leaned closer to the screen. "From the tabloids?"

Mama Rossi pushed Abe out of the way. "I told you to keep quiet."

"And who's this?" the man who claimed to be Peter Halloran exclaimed. "Don't tell me you up and got married? Not to this old fart!"

"Allow me to introduce Abe Titterman. And, no, we're not married," Mama Rossi said firmly.

"Titterman?" Peter said. "What a coincidence. I have a Quinn Titterman in my brig right now."

Abe sputtered a curse as Mama Rossi said, "Is that a fact?"

"It is," Peter countered. "Citizen's arrest, as it were. But I might be willing to negotiate for his release. Tell me: What is he worth to you?"

Mama Rossi shrugged. "To me? Nothing."

A sound that wasn't even close to intelligible escaped from Abe's lips as Mama Rossi used one large arm to hold him back.

Peter laughed. "I think Abe has something to say on the matter."

"You've got that right!" Abe burst out. "You and that alien scum can give me back my great-grandson!"

Mama Rossi sent an elbow into Abe's gut. The unexpected blow knocked the wind from his body, forcing him to double over in pain. The conversation between Peter and the mafiosa was blotted out for a moment as Abe coughed and struggled to breathe. He desperately needed to know what was being said, to know Quinn's fate, and forced gulps of air into his lungs.

"—does better than you and that he'll give me what I want in return for his great-grandson," Peter was saying.

"What do you want?" Abe wheezed.

Mama Rossi looked like she wanted to hit him again. Instead, she moved over so Abe could slide into range of the computer's built-in camera.

"I want the Key," Peter said, addressing himself to Abe directly. Then, turning slightly to face Mama Rossi, he added, "It's rightfully mine, Miss Rossi. You know that."

"If I recall, and I do have a signed copy from the Winkroot Law Firm, your mother left it to me in her will," the mafiosa said as if explaining a difficult concept to a child.

"It's mine!" Peter replied, now definitely sounding like a querulous infant. "It's been in my family for generations! And I want it back!"

"I'm afraid that's not possible," Mama Rossi said.

Peter seemed to master himself, his anger reduced one again to smoldering ashes instead of a bonfire. In a steady voice, he said, "Then this man's great-grandson will die. You have an hour to decide."

With that, the screen went dark.

CHAPTER FOURTEEN

Gabriella leaned heavily on the desktop, elbows jutting. She sighed.

"What are we gonna do?" Abe asked from over her shoulder.

"We don't exactly have a lot of options. And thanks in no small part to you, we don't even have the Key to bargain with."

"Well you were the one stupid enough to employ a rogue like Nimbus Steele," Abe retorted.

"He wasn't my—" Gabriella grunted and slammed her desk.

"You're really going to ruin that nice E'mourdian desk."

"It's a replica," she said icily.

Abe clicked his tongue. "I should have known from the rounded corners. The real ones have little flowery carvings."

Gabriella stared for a moment, then fought down a chuckle, embarrassed that she could be amused at a time like this. Her mind spun, weighing every possible course of action. Aloud she said, "I should just leave your great-grandson with that spoiled brat."

Abe's eyes widened in a look of furious terror. "You wouldn't dare! You heard what he said—he'll kill Quinn!"

"And you heard what I said—he means nothing to me."

She watched as, somehow, an even greater range of emotions crossed the old man's face. When he was able to speak again he said, "But Quinn has the map!"

Gabriella grimaced. "The map, the 'transmission.' What's all this about? I want an answer. Now. No lies. No exaggeration."

Abe crossed his arms. "It's a map of where to use the Key," he said, as if the answer should have been obvious. "Why else do you think we went to Shyoph?"

"Well, if Quinn had the map when he was captured, Peter Halloran most certainly has it now," Gabriella said.

"The map wasn't an object." Abe tapped his forehead. "It was up here, transmitted into Quinn's brain by Iash himself."

At that, Gabriella nearly started laughing again. "What, by some kind of dead philosopher?"

"Don't ask me," Abe said with a sigh. "Quinn's the expert."

Gabriella patted her hair bun. "I guess I don't have much choice then. I need to get the Key. And leaving this map out there is just as dangerous as giving Peter the Key itself. You've caused me a lot of trouble, Abe Titterman, and it'll be a wonder if I don't kill you before this is over. Come on."

She led the way out of the office, not looking back to see if Abe followed. He was, because seconds later he asked, "Where are we going?" as they made their way through the warren-like corridors of the compound.

Gabriella didn't answer. She wound her way through the hallways without pause, leading them down a metal stairway further underground. On the landing, they encountered another Nalaxan.

"Mario," Gabriella said, "how's the power situation?"

"I've rerouted as many systems as I can through the other fuel cells, but there's still a few things offline," the Nalaxan replied. "Internal communications are up and running."

Gabriella stood on the bottom stair so she could look the alien bodyguard in the eye. "What do we know about the call that just came in?"

"Originated from Mars orbit," Mario replied efficiently. "Transponder designates the ship as SFS *Melee*."

"Well, he's certainly not being coy," Gabriella said. "We may be able to use that to our advantage." She pointed one finger at the Nalaxan's chest. "Get me all the data on that ship, including schematics. I want them on the computer in suboffice three in ten minutes."

She didn't wait for a reply and continued down the stairs.

At the base of the stairs they came to yet another corridor with rows of uniform glass-fronted offices on either side. The offices looked unoccupied, plain and lonely, places where boring people did boring work. Each was painted taupe and furnished with a computer desk, chair and filing cabinet. Mama Rossi turned into one of the offices, seemingly at random, and went over to the filing cabinet.

"Now where is it?" she muttered, pulling up one file after another. "Ah."

There was a beep from somewhere overhead. The far side of the office shimmered and changed from taupe brick to solid concrete. Where a corkboard had been hanging on the wall there was now a metal door.

"Hologram," the mafiosa explained. She pointed to the filing cabinet. "Fake folder triggers it on and off. Switch on that desk terminal, will you? Then follow me."

Abe did as he was told and turned in time to see her complete the end of another security protocol that unlocked the metal door.

Inside was an arsenal. LAS-er weapons lined the walls, from guns and rifles to full-on assault weapons. There were dispensers full of grenades, each one labeled with notes like "Concussion," "Smoke," "Plasma" and "Iso-Fragmentary," as well as empty bandoliers and holsters. Weapon batteries were kept on shelf-like charging stations, organized by caliber and gun type.

"They don't all use the same battery?" Abe asked, stooping down to examine the shelves and the blinking lights that indicated charge levels.

"I think LAS-er Systems invents a new battery for each gun they put out," Mama Rossi replied. "A single-source LAS-er battery—wouldn't that be something!"

"If you're thinking of storming the *Melee* yourself..." Abe began. "Well, I can't say I don't admire the idea. But I think your chances are about as good as... as becoming that virtual reality lady."

"Well, I won't be alone," Mama Rossi said cheerfully. "You'll be coming too."

Abe scoffed.

Mama Rossi ignored him and continued, "Do you remember what the Key box looked like?"

Abe thought for a moment, squinting his eyes. "I guess. Rather nondescript, if I recall."

"Enough to have a matter printer reproduce it?"

"I don't see why not."

Mama Rossi turned to a wide, mostly empty shelf at the far end of the armory on which sat a clear cylinder held in a set of brackets and a spindle with six metal bracelets. She lifted the cylinder gingerly out of its bracket, trailing a complicated array of wires.

"If that's some kind of bomb—" Abe said.

"It is."

"Well, I don't see what that's going to accomplish," Abe said impatiently. "Except to kill us all in the process!"

"It's not *that* kind of bomb," Mama Rossi said. "This is the only prototype of its kind to emerge from a secret government lab on Nyoploris before it was raided by Drav insurgents. Took me a long time and a lot of money to get it. My supervisors don't even know I have it."

"More of your carte blanche, I take it?" Abe crossed his arms. "What does it do?"

Mama Rossi looked at him with a peculiar smirk on her face. "This bomb will stop all organic molecular movement in a fifty-foot radius for approximately one hour."

"Wonderful," Abe said. "Instead of getting blown up, we'll be frozen. Great plan."

"That's what these are for." Mama Rossi removed two of the bracelets from the spindle. "These create a barrier field of opposing particles that negate any effects from the device. You and I won't be affected."

Abe smiled a half grin, his attitude improving. "And what's your plan?"

She led him out into the office again and returned to the running computer. With a short sequence of keys and gestures, Mama Rossi brought up a screen topped with the heading FLOYD'S REGISTER OF STARSHIPS. A brief search yielded information about the *Melee*.

"This is what I had Mario prepare," she said without looking up from the screen. "Ah, here we are."

Registry information about the *Melee* was replaced with a 3-D schematic blueprint of the ship. It was massive, with quad ion engines and a hull bristling with LAS-er canons.

"We don't stand a chance," Abe groaned, his spirits dropping again.

"In armed combat? No. But we'll be inside, like a virus," Mama Rossi replied with grim determination. She pointed to a spot on the schematic, far forward in the ship's pointed prow. "Peter's a navy man," she went on. "That's what his mother told me. He almost certainly keeps a study or ops room on the bridge, here. That's where he'll meet with us. Setting off the bomb there should disable the entire bridge crew. Then we have an hour to find your great-grandson."

Mama Rossi panned through the schematic again, looking for something else. As Abe watched, she passed through the ship's central transit core, the shuttle bay, weapons terminals, and the engine room.

"I think this is it," she said finally.

The brig was located far aft, practically in the belly of the ship on its bottom deck. It was as far as possible from the bridge.

"It'll take us an hour just to get there," Abe muttered. "Not much room for error."

As he said this, a separate tone sounded on the computer display. Mama Rossi touched one corner of the screen, and the two listened as Mario's squeaky voice came through the speakers.

"The commander of the *Melee* is on the line again," the Nalaxan said. "He says your time is up."

Mama Rossi looked at Abe Titterman.

"Ready or not," she said.

CHAPTER FIFTEEN

Peter Halloran stopped polishing his metal skull as the door tone sounded. Today's headache was particularly bad, an enduring symptom of the injury that had ended his military career. The motion of polishing sometimes helped, but not often. Arranging his features into a stoic expression, he said, "Come in."

Madeline stepped into the room and stood at attention. Reaching up to her right cheek, she disabled the hologram that covered her right eye from the face-implanted computer. Both of her eyes now blue, she stared at the wall over Peter's shoulder and waited.

"What do you have for me?" Peter asked.

"Mama Rossi's ship will rendezvous with us in approximately thirty minutes," Madeline said.

Peter clasped his hands on the desktop. "Excellent. I want you and Lieutenant V'lari to meet them with an armed escort. Rossi's a wily one, so be sure to watch her every move. Make sure they're checked, Madeline, then bring them to me."

"Yes, commander," Madeline said.

When she did not immediately turn to leave, Peter said, "Was there something else?"

"Yes, commander," Madeline repeated. "I was hoping to broach the topic of my, uh, contract again, sir."

"Another time," Peter said dismissively, turning back to a plastide printout on his desk.

"Surely—" Madeline persisted.

"Surely what?" Peter cut her off. "There is no 'early release.' Besides," he added, "what would you do with your freedom?"

Madeline did not hesitate. "I was hoping for a command assignment," she said boldly.

Peter laughed derisively. "We'll see if you still feel that way in another ten years. That is, if I decide that someone whose contract I bought from an orphan-o-trophia has a place in my command structure."

As the words left his mouth, Peter could see that he had demolished what was left of Madeline's resolve. "I believe it's nearly time for you to meet our guests," he said. "You're dismissed."

Without a word, Madeline reached up to reactivate her facial computer and stalked from the room.

One of Gabriella's shuttles, repaired enough for its short trip into orbit, glided from the atmosphere of Mars as gracefully as a black swan, the heavens turning to full darkness as the engines sped the vessel toward its meeting with the SFS *Melee*. The shuttle was on autopilot based on coordinates given by Peter Halloran; he had forbidden Gabriella from taking any of the Nalaxans along. As a result, she sat in the thick-backed chair of the main pilot console, watching the ship's onboard functions do their work and feeling altogether useless. Abe sat at one of the unused auxiliary consoles holding the replica Key to the Universe box that the matter printer in Gabriella's compound had created based on Abe's description. Inside was the bomb, and both Gabriella and Abe wore metal bracelets from the armory.

Suddenly, the *Melee* drifted into sight directly in front of the cockpit's main viewport. The battle cruiser was even more massive than the schematic had led Gabriella to believe, a predator bred for combat and little else. Was this how Peter Halloran had spent his family fortune? Was this what he had been doing in the years since his accident in the Solar Navy? He certainly had the means to buy a ship of that size and equip it with a crew of mercenaries.

A communications alert sounded from the console. Gabriella leaned forward slightly to answer the call.

"Miss Rossi," came Peter's voice. "We have you in view now. Power down. We'll bring you in."

Peter's tone broached no argument, so Gabriella acknowledged the command and powered down all shipboard functions. To Abe she said, "Here we go."

There was a slight jostling as the *Melee* caught hold of them with its suspension field. Gabriella and Abe watched as they were drawn toward the maw of the battle cruiser.

Moments later, the shuttle bay swallowed them. Gabriella stood as they passed through the force field that prevented everything in the bay from being sucked into the void. Looking back at Abe, she noticed that he had gone pale, his skin the color of a deepwater Elchoir eel.

"Think of this as a game of VR Sector," Gabriella said, trying to sound reassuring. "Look at how quickly you picked that up."

"Except I'm ninety years older in the real world," Abe replied irritably. "And we won't be shooting at stable targets. And I don't have a mirrored buckler. In fact, it's nothing like VR Sector."

Gabriella shrugged. "I was just trying to make you feel better." There was another jolt as the artificial gravity of the *Melee* took hold and Gabriella's ship landed. "Get ready."

Clanks and bangs and hisses accompanied the shuttle as it settled onto the floor of the bay. Landing gear clamped down into secure holsters, and automatic fueling and environmental hoses snaked to their respective ports. Abe stood now as well, and Gabriella was surprised, based at least on his complexion, that his legs were able to support the rest of his body.

They moved to disembark. The hatch slid open to reveal the muzzles of at least a dozen drawn weapons. A four-armed Rauskon and a human woman with a computer grafted onto part of her face stood in the center of the security detail.

"Come slowly down into the bay," the Rauskon barked. "Hands where we can see them."

Gabriella raised her hands over her head and came slowly down the gangway. Next to her, Abe held the Key box far out in front of his chest, as if handling a load of nuclear waste.

"Commander Halloran welcomes you aboard the Solar Free Ship *Melee*," the human woman said. "I'm Madeline, his personal lieutenant."

"Is this how he treats all of his guests?" Gabriella said.

"Search them," the Rauskon said in response.

"It gets even better," Gabriella commented.

A creature of some species she couldn't identify came forward. Its body was clad in what looked like a suit of bulbous metal armor. Semitransparent tentacles emerged from the leg and arm holes, veins pulsing with purple and black fluids. Its head resembled a jellyfish from the oceans of Earth: featureless, with streamers of tissue hanging down at intervals.

The tentacles ran down the sides of Gabriella's body, checking for hidden weapons or devices. The mafiosa struggled to maintain an outward appearance of calm, though she shuddered in revulsion at the violation of her skin and personal space. She got the impression that the tentacles worked on a much more sensitive level of touch than anything humans could ever hope to experience, that they could feel every individual strand of fabric in Gabriella's dress, every ridge, crease, and pore of the skin beneath. She fought down an overpowering instinct to break contact, to fling the snakelike appendages away with a shove and a well-aimed blast from a weapon she did not possess.

After a moment that seemed like hours, the creature stepped back, turned to Madeline and uttered a series of noises that sounded like a child blowing spit bubbles. Madeline nodded and said to the Rauskon, "She's clean."

The tentacle creature took a step toward Abe.

Abe lifted the fake Key box over his head.

"Get that thing away from me," he said, indicating the tentacle creature.

Madeline shook her head. "I'm afraid that's not possible. You have two options: You can be searched, or the guards can kill you." As she said this, the Rauskon and his associates raised their guns again.

Abe looked helplessly to Mama Rossi, who shrugged as if to say, *Don't look at me*. Then Abe thought about Quinn, imprisoned somewhere on the *Melee* just because Abe had wanted to learn more about the Key, to have an "adventure." Quinn had wanted to bring the Key to the authorities from the start. Now, who knew what he had suffered because of Abe's impetuous selfishness.

Still holding the box over his head, Abe nodded his assent to Madeline. As if by unspoken command, the tentacle creature closed the gap between itself and Abe, its sensory appendages reaching out to begin their inspection.

Unlike Mama Rossi, who had a reputation to maintain, Abe had no qualms about letting his displeasure be known. He squirmed and shuddered as the alien ran its tentacles over his body, feeling the same invasion that the mafiosa had experienced moments ago.

"Oh, oh, is this *really* necessary?" Abe complained. "Ugh! I demand a shower facility before we're presented to your commander. Oh!" Abe let out a startled laugh. "That tickles, you brute! Finish up already!"

The tentacle creature stepped back and uttered its moist communication noise again.

"He's clean," Madeline interpreted. "Now, the box."

Abe froze in the process of lowering his arms again, sudden fear turning his insides to ice.

"No!" he shouted. "Absolutely not! We've suffered your probing, but what's in here is for Halloran's eyes only."

"You expect me to let you see the commander without looking inside that case?" the Rauskon growled.

"It's the Key to the Universe, nothing more," Abe said, the irony of his understatement lost on the assembled crowed.

"Or a bomb," said Madeline. "Or a gas emitter. Or any number of other threats to our commander. Your choice is the same as before: open it or die."

"I refuse," Abe said, trying to keep the desperation out of his voice.

The Rauskon sighed. "Someone grab him."

Hands gripped Abe from either side, holding his arms fast so that the Key box could be taken without difficulty. A human man dressed in a military uniform that looked as if it had been cobbled together from every branch of the armed forces handed the box to the Rauskon and took a cautious step backward.

Without ceremony, the Rauskon opened the box, simultaneously stopping all molecular movement in the shuttle bay— and every hope that Abe had of successfully rescuing his great-grandson.

CHAPTER SIXTEEN

There was no flash or explosion, no detonation of any kind that Gabriella could detect. One moment, the crowd watched uneasily as the Rauskon opened the fake Key box; the next, silence. Nothing. No movement. No breathing.

Gabriella took a tentative step forward. The man with the cobbled-together military uniform was next to her, so she waved one hand in front of his face. He made no response.

"Can they see us? Hear us?" Abe asked.

"I don't know," Gabriella said as she moved toward the Rauskon. Peering inside the box, she saw that a series of red lights blinked down the length of the clear cylinder. Looking back up at Abe, she continued, "I was never told."

Abe found his emotions again. "Well, this is going well!" he raged. "We're done for! Finished! You and me had better just kill ourselves now because we've got no chance of saving Quinn and getting out of here alive."

Gabriella pried a LAS-er rifle from the hands of one of the guards. "On the contrary," she said. "We have sixty"—she glanced down at her wristwatch—"*fifty-eight* minutes to find your great-grandson and get out of here." Then she laughed.

Abe shot her a look of such loathing that Gabriella couldn't help but laugh even harder.

"What's so funny?" Abe said as he too grabbed a weapon from one of the inert guards.

Getting control of herself, Gabriella said, "We're even closer to the brig than if we had detonated the bomb on the bridge. I don't know why I didn't think of that sooner. C'mon!"

She led the way out of the shuttle bay and down an elegantly designed corridor toward the aft of the ship, recalling the way based on her examination of the ship schematic.

"Quiet!" Gabriella hissed as they came to a bend. From somewhere ahead came the sound of footfalls and quiet conversation. "Relax. Don't hold your gun so tight. Act like you belong here."

Abe frowned and hoisted the LAS-er rifle over his shoulder. In another minute, two people rounded the bend: a human man and a Dar'morian male. They stopped their discussion long enough to nod at Gabriella and Abe, then continued down the corridor without another glance.

Abe raised an eyebrow. "That was easy," he said when the human and the Dar'morian were out of earshot.

"Two hundred fifty people on this boat and no uniforms," Gabriella replied. "You think they all know each other?"

Abe shrugged, and they continued on their way, passing through endless ship corridors as the bomb timer ticked away. Gabriella couldn't help but admire the mix of sophistication and military utility that comprised the ship, something that was influenced by, and yet strictly at odds with, the ornate trappings preferred by Peter's mother. Here was a midship auxiliary control station with flowing chairs and consoles that could accommodate a dozen different species configurations; there was a crew lounge with a winding bar topped by Dravian volcanic marble polished to deepest black. Peter Halloran's taste had not been stripped down by years of military discipline.

Though they had no problems with any further crew encounters, Gabriella suspected they would meet resistance at the brig. She was right. A Nalaxan and a Rauskon guarded the entrance.

Falling back out of sight, Gabriella huddled together with Abe to discuss their plan.

"Just two of 'em," Gabriella said. "But heavy hitters. The Nalaxan looks as big as any of my security guards. If I recall, there's a junction that runs parallel to this corridor. If I sneak around, we can come at the brig from both ends."

"How much time do we have?" Abe asked.

Gabriella consulted her wristwatch. "Thirty-three minutes."

"Not long enough," Abe said.

Before Gabriella could react, Abe stood, readied his weapon and rushed down the corridor in a kind of bow-legged jog.

"Wait!" she cried belatedly.

But he was already mostly at the brig, firing his LAS-er rifle randomly at the two guards. Gabriella arrived in time to see one of the wild bolts hit the Rauskon in the chest. The four-armed guard slumped back against the wall of the corridor and oozed to the floor, unmoving. The Nalaxan had a little more time to react—but not much. One of the bolts hit him squarely on the horn, which isn't particularly damaging to Nalaxans, but made the alien feel as if he was going to sneeze. Gabriella aimed her rifle at an angled piece of hypersteel that curved down from the ceiling and fired three shots in rapid succession. One bounced perfectly and hit the back of the Nalaxan's neck—the Nalaxan Nerve. The guard joined his companion on the ground.

Abe lowered his weapon, and Gabriella noticed that the old man was breathing heavily.

"Just like VR Sector after all," he said between breaths.

Quinn looked up as the door to the brig opened again, girding himself for whatever humiliation he would have to suffer next. He and Aerius had not been visited in—how long? Six hours? Twelve? It was impossible to tell. After the last interrogation session, they had each been given a plate of protein gruel and left alone. The passage of time was marked only by how long Quinn had to wait between "interviews" with Peter Halloran and his device.

But it was not Peter who entered the brig, nor was it one of the Rauskon guards or Madeline. Instead, it was the last two people that Quinn and Aerius expected to see in each other's company: Abe Titterman and Gabriella Rossi.

Quinn jumped to his feet, the phantom pain that seemed to linger between sessions temporarily forgotten. "Pop-pop?!"

Abe moved to the bars while Mama Rossi cut the power to Quinn's cell using the same panel that Peter had manipulated earlier. At once, Abe and Quinn embraced each other while the mafiosa kept watch on the door.

"Are you all right?" Abe asked, holding his great-grandson at length to examine his face and body.

"I am now," Quinn replied. "But what's Mama Rossi doing here? Are you working together?"

"For now," said Abe. "It's a long story."

Quinn nodded. "It's like Iash said—"

"Forget Iash," Mama Rossi cut in. "We've got less than thirty minutes, and there's no way your great-grandfather's frontal assault will go unnoticed for long. The full reunion will have to wait."

"Let's go," Abe said, indicating that Quinn should walk sandwiched between him and Mama Rossi.

Quinn, however, went straight to the brig's control panel. "We have to free Aerius."

"Are you crazy?" Abe exclaimed. "He's the reason you're here!"

"He's *not* a government agent," Mama Rossi added emphatically.

"He was duped," Quinn replied. "The commander of this ship is Peter Halloran, Pop-pop. *The* Peter Halloran."

"We know," Abe said. "He's trying to get the Key back."

"You didn't give it to him, did you?" Quinn exclaimed.

"Of course not!" Mama Rossi said. "But we don't have it either. Your great-grandfather can explain later. In the meantime, free that troublemaker if it'll make you happy and let's *get out of here*."

Quinn reached over to deactivate the cell. The vertical bars disappeared as smoothly as one turning off a light switch. Aerius took a deep breath.

"Come with us," Quinn said, holding out one hand. "We could use your help."

Aerius wriggled his long arms out of the military jacket and flung it back inside the cell. Clad now in just his liquid armor, he said, "Let's go."

Peter Halloran looked up from his notes and rubbed his eyes. After Madeline's departure, he had continued pouring over the information he had gleaned from Quinn Titterman, though the big picture of the so-called map in the boy's head was still incomplete. Peter gathered that Quinn had been the recipient of some kind of hyper-transmission, but the young man's human mind was still working through all the data. It was like trying to solve billions of calculations per second with an obsolete computer; the computer might get there *eventually*, but the calculations could take hours, days, or even years. And there was no more inferior computer these days than the human mind.

Still, Peter was confident that future interrogations would yield even more data. With the Key in his possession and Abe Titterman and Mama Rossi in captivity as well, Peter could take all the time he needed to find the ultimate end-use point for the Key.

Spinning away from his desk, Peter stood and gazed out of the study's small viewport. Mars floating below. His mother. Titterman. Rossi.

They should be here by now, Peter thought.

He turned again and slapped a button on his desk computer.

"Madeline!" he barked. "What's the status with Titterman and Rossi?"

There was no response. Peter hit the button again, knowing it should transmit directly to Madeline's wearable computer.

"Madeline! Acknowledge!"

When the call went unanswered a second time, Peter hit a series of commands on the computer that triggered a ship-wide alert. Toggling on the *Melee*'s internal communications channel, he said, "Attention all hands. This is not a drill. Fugitives Abraham Titterman and Gabriella Rossi may be loose aboard this ship. A year's bonus to the man or woman or thing that brings them to me first! *Alive!*"

Peter shut down the communications link and opened one of the desk drawers. Inside he found his LAS-er Eagle Sight pistol and holster, which he strapped to his waist. Checking the charge on the weapon, he rushed from the ready room and into the ensuing chaos aboard his ship.

Abe, Mama Rossi, and their party of prison escapees were rushing down a corridor near the shuttle bay when Peter Halloran's announcement blared over the ship's internal communications system. All four stopped in their tracks.

"A year's bonus to the man or woman or thing that brings them to me first! *Alive!*" Peter finished.

Within seconds, there were voices and the sound of running feet coming from all around them. A pair of human crewmembers appeared out of nowhere, speeding down the corridor with weapons ready. Mama Rossi fired at once, hitting both men in the chest and sending them flying against the wall. They were quickly replaced by a Drav and a Rauskon, who returned fire before Mama Rossi could get off any more shots. Abe fired his own weapon, the blast going wide to hit a piece of bulkhead three feet above the Drav's helmeted head.

"Your weapon," Aerius said to Abe, holding out one gray hand that, Abe noticed, had six digits including two opposable thumbs.

Abe handed it over and watched with a certain amount of awe as the alien aimed with expertise and confidence, firing off two rounds timed perfectly between the shots of their adversaries. The first blast hit the Rauskon on his upper right arm, causing him to howl in pain and drop his weapon. The second hit the Drav in the forehead, leaving a black score mark on the hammered metal. The Rauskon retreated down the corridor as he watched his companion topple forward.

"We'll never get back to the shuttle bay!" Abe shouted.

"We don't need to," Mama Rossi replied, whipping off a few shots of cover fire to keep the Rauskon pinned down. "There's an escape pod station this way. Let's—"

The Dar'morian they had passed earlier appeared at the opposite end of the corridor, surprising the group with a rear assault. There was a burst of light, a scream, and the smell of burning flesh and fabric as Mama Rossi was flung back against the bulkhead. Abe rushed to her side, waving away the smoke that wafted from her dress. When he saw that the fabric was still on fire, he slapped the mafiosa on the shoulder, hard. She cried out again, but the flames had been extinguished, leaving a gaping hole of charred clothing with blistered and bleeding skin beneath.

Meanwhile, Aerius had disabled the Dar'morian and was trying to edge the whole group back down the hallway.

"We can't stay here!" he cried. "Where are the escape pods?"

Mama Rossi pointed with her good arm. "Back to the t-junction," she said with a groan. "Right, if I remember from the schematic. The opposite turn from the brig."

Abe tried to lift the large woman to her feet but wasn't up to the task. With a painful *pop* that sent ripples of discomfort along his whole lower back, Abe slumped to the floor next to the mafiosa.

"Looks like we're done for," Abe said resignedly. "I knew this would happen."

Then Quinn was there, helping Abe back to his feet before crouching again to support Mama Rossi under her good arm.

"Can you walk?" Quinn asked.

Mama Rossi gritted her teeth. "I can if it means getting out of here. Let's go, old man."

The three of them shambled down the corridor while Aerius held point. The alien's senses, they learned, were incredibly honed. As soon as he detected a threat, he fired unerringly toward the source. Barely any of Peter's crew had a chance to fire shots against him, and the few that did either missed or hit Aerius's liquid armor.

"Yes," Mama Rossi said when they reached a t-shaped intersection. "To the right."

Soon they were passing signs on the walls that said "Muster Station F →" eventually coming to a door with a yellow-and-black emergency stripe running down the center. Aerius stepped back, gun at the ready, and indicated that Abe should open the door. But before anyone else could move, Mama Rossi's wristwatch went off.

"Everyone in the shuttle bay will be able to move again," she said. "We're out of time."

"You certainly are."

The door to the muster station had opened without Abe's help, and Peter Halloran stood framed in the doorway.

CHAPTER SEVENTEEN

A erius and Mama Rossi raised their weapons as one. Peter Halloran did the same, pointing the muzzle of his LAS-er Eagle Sight directly at Quinn's heart.

"Drop it," Peter said, "or none of us learn the Key's secrets."

"Do it!" Abe shouted, his pulse racing as he looked for a way to move between Quinn and the gun.

"Ah, ah," Peter admonished. "Stay right where you are."

Abe froze. He watched Aerius and Mama Rossi lower their weapons to the floor.

With his free hand, Peter pressed a finger to his right ear. "Madeline? Can you hear me now?" A pause. "Come to Muster Station F right away. Bring V'lari with you."

Peter lowered his hand again and turned his full attention back to Abe and company. "We'll all just sit tight until they get here."

"You are heinous," Aerius said as Abe watched the alien come forward.

"No, I just get what I want," Peter replied. "It's the privilege of my having money and power."

"*You* are the criminal, not these people," Aerius went on.

"And you were just a dirty little chayat from a dirty little world when I found you," Peter countered.

"I will give you one chance to let these people leave," Aerius said.

Peter turned his weapon fully to target the alien tracker. "I doubt even your fancy clothing would stop a shot at this range."

"This is your final warning," Aerius said.

Peter did not lower the weapon, and two things seemed to happen at once.

With the same speed that Abe and Quinn had seen on Shy-oph-2, Aerius flicked his right arm as if waving to a friend in the distance. At the same time, a spike that appeared to be made of bone sprouted from the center of Peter Halloran's chest.

Peter gasped, his mind apparently taking a moment to catch up with the damage that had been done to his body. He slumped against the doorframe of the muster station, his gun arm lowering before dropping the Eagle Sight from numb fingers. No words escaped his lips, just a kind of unintelligible gurgle as his body continued its way lifelessly to the floor.

"How did—?" Abe began.

Aerius cut him off. "No time."

As he said this, Madeline and V'lari the Rauskon rounded the corner in time to take in the scene at the muster station: Halloran on the floor with a spike through his heart and the prisoners on the verge of escape. V'lari raised his weapons half-heartedly.

"Your commander's dead," Mama Rossi said to Madeline and V'lari. "I suggest you find a new captain and get out of here before the actual authorities arrive."

Madeline and V'lari looked at each other. Aerius led the others into the muster station unopposed.

They were nearly all aboard the bulbous escape raft when Aerius finally collapsed. Quinn settled the wounded Mama Rossi onto the circular bench that ran along the wall of the raft's only compartment, then returned to help Aerius cover the last few yards to his own seat on the bench next to Abe.

"Thank you," Aerius muttered as Abe and Quinn secured the restraint harness around the alien's tall frame.

"What now?" Abe said.

Quinn reached overhead to press a button on the raft's curving bulkhead. A circular console rose from the floor in the center of the compartment, accessible to everyone on the bench.

"Nobody touch the controls," Quinn said as he took a seat and fastened his own harness.

With a simple series of commands, learned during the required emergency section of his driving course, Quinn dimmed the lights inside the raft and activated a countdown that appeared on every console screen.

3... 2... 1... 0.

A pneumatic hiss sounded from all around them as cables detached from the raft and docking levers within the *Melee* released their mechanical hold on the escape pod. The entire ship rattled as it sped toward its egress. Then Mars appeared in a small viewport that no one had noticed because it had been facing the inside of the battle cruiser.

"We're clear," Quinn announced. "Where to?"

"Head for my compound," Mama Rossi said. "We'll be safe there from any kind of aerial bombardment if the crew of the *Melee* decides they didn't like us killing their commander." She gave Quinn the coordinates and added, "A ship full of mercenaries, though—I don't think they'll care who's in charge as long as they get paid in the end."

After that, there was silence for a moment as the pod sped gently toward its destination. Abe looked over at Aerius, who was sucking in great gulps of breath with his strange eyes closed.

"Are you all right?"

Aerius opened his eyes and stared unblinking at the old man.

"I suppose I owe you some thanks for watching over Quinn in there," Abe went on. "Even though you got us into this mess in the first place."

"Pop-pop!" Quinn exclaimed.

"Well, it's true!" Abe said.

"No," Aerius said suddenly, causing the others to look at him. "Your pop pop—" again, too much pause between the syllables "—is right. I have brought shame to the chayat code."

"What did you do to Peter Halloran?" Abe asked.

"Yes, I'd like to know that as well," Mama Rossi chimed in.

In response, Aerius flipped over his right arm. Abe noticed that the underside of the alien's wrist was bruised purple and black. Not only that, but the skin was floppy and deflated, as if it had been stretched over something that was no longer there.

"When we are in extreme duress," Aerius said, "my people can form a calcite bone on either arm that can be used as a projectile. Firing one requires a tremendous amount of energy; firing both is often fatal."

"That's amazing," Quinn said. "The hunted becomes the hunter. It's like Iash said: 'Choose your battles wisely, because even the smallest rat is deadly in large numbers.'" He seemed on the verge of saying something else but stopped with mouth half open. "Iash didn't say that," he said incredulously. "At least, I've never heard that saying before."

"Just as I thought," Abe said. "You've been making these things up all along."

"No," said Quinn. "It just… came to me. That's how it's been since Shyoph. Every now and then I'll get these flashes. I'll learn a little bit more about the map in the projection. And I've been having dreams."

"Your brain is still processing the information," said Aerius, who had closed his eyes again. "It will take time for you to piece it all together."

"And then we'll know where to use the Key!" Quinn exclaimed.

"If we still had it," said Mama Rossi.

The rest of reentry was spent swapping tales of all that had happened since Abe and Quinn had been separated. Quinn was understandably dismayed at the loss of the Key, though little could be done from the cockpit of the escape raft. Abe was furious at how his great-grandson had been treated by Peter Halloran and was even gladder that Aerius had dispatched the renegade commander. Soon, though, the landing rockets fired and the pod floated to a halt on an outdoor landing pad adjacent to Mama Rossi's compound.

There was little time for talk once they landed. The mafiosa was whisked away to be checked by the private doctor she kept on staff. She told Quinn that she would make arrangements with the medic to have the torture implant removed as well. They were all given better accommodations in the compound and free reign within the facility, provided they didn't interfere with the Nalaxans and their repair work from Nimbus Steele's bomb. Aerius immediately disappeared to rest. Abe and Quinn returned to their room to do the same.

While waiting for Quinn's turn with the medic, Abe tried to cheer his great-grandson by turning on the room's entertainment console and reading the news headlines they had missed over the preceding days.

"'After a lockout lasting more than a month, union negotiators have finally hammered out a new three-year contract for the miners on Titan,'" Abe read. "That's certainly good news. Let's see. 'Pucker Gambol of the Martian War Mongers VR Sector will not be able to start next season because of an injury.'"

Quinn groaned.

"Right," Abe said. "Not so good. Um, oh, it says here that the infamous hacker shotel_0 breached a highly secure server operated by the Bank of Jupiter." Abe's reading slowed. "'Account numbers for roughly 1.3 billion customers have been compromised.' You know, let's just skip the news for now."

Abe closed the news browser and checked instead to see what film options were available. He was pleasantly surprised to find several selections from his favorite holo-serial, *Starchasers*. Still waiting to be summoned by the medic, Abe picked an episode for them both to watch and sat down to wait.

CHAPTER EIGHTEEN

It was early evening when Mama Rossi called all of her guests together for a meeting in her private study. As they arrived, they saw that she was sporting an arm sling to support her wounded shoulder. Otherwise, her hair bun was pulled tight atop her head, and she seemed to have regained the stern bearing that marked her as the head of the Martian Mafia.

Once they were all inside, Mama Rossi activated the privacy field and took a seat behind her desk.

"As Abe already knows," she began, "I'm an agent of the Solar Government."

Quinn placed a hand on his great-grandfather's arm. "Is this true?"

"Yes, I've seen proof," Abe replied. He couldn't help but notice that Mama Rossi looked rather pleased with herself.

"I was embedded in the Martian Mafia to reduce crime and dull the organization's power by quietly moving it toward legitimate business dealings," the mafiosa continued. "Some years ago, an opportunity presented itself for me to get close to Minnie Halloran, whom the government knew had the Key to the Universe. Through a series of favors that I won't go into now, Minnie became so indebted to me that when I requested she leave the Key to me in her will, there was nothing she could do to refuse. I think everyone in this room agrees that getting the Key back is of paramount importance. Am I wrong?"

Everyone was silent.

"Good," Mama Rossi continued. "We know Nimbus Steele has the Key. Mario has been trying to track his ship since he left the compound, but we haven't been able to come up with any leads yet."

As she said this, Aerius stepped forward. "If I may," the alien said.

The mafiosa nodded.

"The loss of the Key is my fault—" Aerius began.

"I think we all share part of the blame," Mama Rossi cut in, shooting a purposeful look at Abe.

Aerius shook his head. "Every instinct of my training disagrees. I am a chayat, and my disgrace in this matter demands that I undertake *laqhon*, a period of... penance to right the wrongs I have created."

"That's not necessary," said Quinn. "We forgive you. Iash teaches that forgiveness is more precious than gold—"

"And just as hard to come by," finished Mama Rossi. "Even I've heard that one."

"Do not be offended," Aerius said, "but your forgiveness is not enough. I must set in motion events to correct my digressions."

"What are you saying?" Quinn asked.

"I am a chayat," Aerius repeated. "I will track this Nimbus Steele, and I will find him. And then we shall all recover Briak Mor together."

The following morning, everyone was up early to send Aerius off. The discussion the night before had lasted a bit longer as everyone offered the chayat help on his laqhon. Quinn said he would accompany the alien, even if it meant missing school; Mama Rossi recommended that the tracker take her last ship. Aerius demurred every suggestion.

"Laqhon should not be easy," he explained. "It is struggle, suffering, pain. And, ultimately, redemption."

In the end, he would take only a bit of food before announcing that he would walk to the nearest spaceport to find passage. He did not elaborate on where he was going or how he would start his search for the Key.

After saying goodbye to everyone else, Aerius approached Quinn and looked down at the significantly shorter human.

"I enjoyed our talks," said Aerius.

Quinn brightened a bit. "So did I. It was the best part of an otherwise horrible situation."

"Agreed," Aerius said. "You are learning more about the transmission every day. Be vigilant. Take note of what your mind reveals. By the time I return, I believe you will know significantly more than you do now."

Quinn nodded solemnly.

Without another word, Aerius shouldered his pack of provisions and began marching in the direction of the rising sun. His journey had begun.

INTERLUDE

T he dream is always the same, but more is revealed each
time as his brain—his computer—processes more of the
raw data.

Quinn walks through an alley of rocks, feet shifting on a
floor of desert sand, pebbles and scree. The place carries with it
a sense of déjà vu, but when Quinn tries to grasp where he is
and when he has been there, the memories flee like grains of
sand pouring through an outstretched hand. He keeps walking,
hoping that his journey will evoke more recollections.

There is a clearing ahead, a place where the rocks draw
away and the sand runs down a gentle slope. Quinn stands at
the edge of the ridge, looking down. There is a crater below, and
the land is black and charred where the object struck.

Quinn begins the trek downward, feet sliding on the uncertain desert floor. He puts his arms out to keep his balance and
notices that they are not his arms. Instead, they are the arms of
a Shyophian, clad in rough strips of fabric about two inches
thick.

Like every time before, realization comes, though he knows
not from where. He is Iash. He is in the great philosopher's
memory, bequeathed to Quinn by the hyper-transmission at the
Shyophian's tomb.

He is almost at the bottom of the slope.

The object at the base of the crater is a ship, and it has
struck with such force that it has uncovered a small under-

ground pool of lapyk. Welling up from beneath the desert, the puddle of green gel surrounds the ship. By contrast, the walls of the crater are burnt black. Could anything survive such an impact?

Iash-Quinn edges around the ship in a full circle. It is of alien origin. He finds the cockpit and learns that the pilot, of a species he does not recognize, is dead.

Carefully, so as not to cut himself on the metal or any bits of broken stone, Iash-Quinn bends down to remove the body for a proper burial. He notices that the pilot is holding something: a burnished cylinder with a four-sided handle and a carved, ringed planet at one end.

Quinn-half wants to scream that he knows what this is: Iash-half has just found the Key to the Universe.

PART TWO

CHAPTER NINETEEN

Aerius hung in the void in a used spacesuit, his supply of oxygen down to ten percent. All around him, the rocks of the Koren Asteroid Belt spun and collided, an ancient ballet that would go on until the end of time. Aerius ignored the chaos around him, as well as the alert on his suit, and focused instead on the scanner held in the outer thumbs of his gloved hands. He wouldn't give up now, not after all it had taken him to get here.

He had spent a week at Copernicus Spaceport on Mars, scrounging for food and begging, before finding a ship that would give him passage in exchange for labor. The old freighter was hauling spent FTL casings to the smelt camps of Drav, and that was close enough for Aerius to get to Koren.

Once aboard, the chayat took as many shifts as possible, and his crewmates were often grateful for a little extra bunk time. The passage to Drav took six weeks by the freighter's flagging ion drive, and Aerius earned enough in overtime to purchase a twenty-year-old spacesuit from among the ship stores when he disembarked at the volcanic rock that was the Drav home world.

From there, he had hitched a ride with missionaries of *Ad-unt Elnor*, the infamous religious group whose name translates roughly to "People of Rock." Sworn to stop the wanton spread of technology, the missionaries were headed to Nyoploris to proselytize. They agreed to drop Aerius at the Koren Asteroid Belt, provided he pray with them twice a day.

Aerius had never spent much time with religious groups outside of his own, so he agreed to immerse himself in the Ad-unt Elnor culture for three days. The time was peaceful and introspective, though Aerius grew eager to leave the missionary ship, which was seemingly held together with spit and faith. Plus, the missionaries didn't take kindly to the spacesuit Aerius donned once they reached the drop point.

The alarm in the suit increased in volume, bringing Aerius back to the present. He looked down at the readout on his wrist: oxygen level at five percent. These were the coordinates, but the asteroid belt's dynamism meant that nothing stayed in one place for long.

Three percent.

Aerius tried to take small, shallow breaths, fighting against the panic rising in his gut. Maybe his ultimate penance, his laqhon, was to die out here, alone. If that was what the gods wanted—

A final alert sounded, then cut off abruptly. The suit's air supply was exhausted. In seconds, the atmosphere inside the helmet became stale. The air circulators would continue working until the carbon dioxide levels reached critical. Then the disorientation and the hallucinations would begin. It was not a good way to die.

Aerius toggled the switch on the suit's propulsion pack and turned in a small orbit toward the densest part of the asteroid belt. The space rocks spun and collided, sending debris in explosive patterns to strike other rocks again and again and again. Getting between one of the larger collisions would vaporize Aerius immediately. It was better than suffocating

Determined that his final act be a meaningful one, Aerius urged the propulsion pack forward. Now the air inside his helmet tasted acrid. In retrospect, the air circulators had probably failed around the same time that the oxygen ran out, if they even worked at capacity to begin with. The weight on his chest grew; soon it would feel like trying to breathe under water. A new alert sounded from somewhere nearby.

"Be quiet!" Aerius said.

Then he looked down at the scanner—it had found the signal!

Aerius moved his head left to right within the confines of his bulbous helmet. At nine o'clock, he spotted a massive asteroid, a rock the size of a dwarf moon that defied anything that came into contact with it. Aerius altered course; maybe the gods weren't done with him yet.

The signal on the scanner grew stronger, but as Aerius watched, the readout doubled, as did the arm that held the device. The chayat shook his head and blinked rapidly. *No, no!* He was so close.

Aerius closed his eyes and concentrated momentarily on the signal alert to guide him. Its beep was a life pulse. When he opened his eyes again, a blurry halo surrounded everything, but at least he could see only one giant asteroid looming in front of him.

Unlike a moon or planet, the rock was oblong, pockmarked with countless craters and crevices. Smaller asteroids flew everywhere, some crashing on the surface, others spiraling back into the darkness.

The scanner beeped frantically now; it had located the cave where Aerius had hidden his native ship nearly a year ago, before taking the commission from Commander H—the treacherous Peter Halloran. But which cave, which crater, held his vessel? He had time to explore one, maybe, before he was fully incapacitated. Time to trust the scanner to do its work.

With the propulsion pack at maximum, Aerius flew into the maw of a substantial cave, dodging several smaller asteroids. As he entered the darkness, the blurred halo of his vision disappeared—as did everything else. His eyes were unwilling to adjust; he flew on in blindness.

Remembering the headlamp on his helmet, Aerius switched on the light in time to dimly see his ship before colliding with the hull.

Something dug into Aerius's back. Without opening his eyes, he reached around and brought the offending object in front of his face. Squinting, he saw that it was a hyper-ratchet. He also noticed that his helmet was off and that he was lying on his back.

He was inside his ship's air lock.

Somehow, he had managed to get inside and activate the atmospheric equalizers before losing consciousness. His oxygen-deprived brain remembered nothing after the collision.

Aerius sat up slowly. The air was on, but the ship's heaters were running at minimum. His skin rippled as it tried to suck ambient heat from the air.

Standing now, Aerius moved to an auxiliary control panel and started the ship's warm-up sequence. Power hummed through the conduits as the vessel came out of hibernation, screens and light strips powering on gradually in sequence. The atmospheric system ramped up, sending even more fresh air into the ship and, for the first time, a breath of heat. Aerius retrieved his helmet and exited the air lock.

Everything was as he had left it. Coming out of the rear of the ship, there was a brief corridor with doors on either side that led to living spaces and a small galley. The other end of the hall opened onto the bridge, which included a small cockpit with two seats, a raised console that took up the nose area to accommodate Aerius's size, and a large, unbroken viewport that looked out into the darkness of the cave's interior. Parts of the console were already lit with pre-launch diagnostics.

Aerius dropped the spacesuit helmet into one of the seats and sat in the other. With a short sequence of buttons, more of the console came to life. In a moment, the vessel's fusion power plant would warm up and the engines would come online.

The chayat glanced at a string of beads tied to an unused portion of the console. The charm had been made by his first wife, Brit'mor, who had died some thirty years past in childbirth. It had kept Aerius alive, so far.

A rumble sounded from deep in the bowels of the ship: the power core was ready. Aerius brushed his hand over the beaded charm before grabbing the ship's control stick. It was time to get out of this cave and get to work.

CHAPTER TWENTY

With a soundless blast of light, *The Lady Grace* emerged from hyperspace a hundred thousand miles away from Nyoploris, the so-called "Techno World." As seen from the ship's cockpit, the planet resembled a chrome orb surrounded by a kind of cloudy membrane.

"What *is* that?" Abe asked from the seat beside Quinn, pointing out the forward viewport at the diaphanous haze.

"Satellites," Quinn replied. "The planet's orbit is choked with 'em. It's only safe to approach with telemetry from one of the guidance towers."

As if on cue, an alert sounded from the ship's communications system. Quinn, fully licensed now and familiar with all the ship's operations, pressed a button on the dash to receive the call.

"This is Nyoploris Tower three-seven-nine," a voice said. "Identify yourself and your destination."

"This is *The Lady Grace*, Solar registration F8BCPW5, requesting permission to land at—" Quinn consulted a small sheet of plastide "—coordinates sixty-four point oh-eight."

There was a brief pause as the tower verified Quinn's credentials. After a moment, the voice said, "Passage confirmed. Sending telemetry data now. Please set your vessel to autopilot."

Quinn did so and cut the communications link. Seconds later, *The Lady Grace* began its approach to Nyoploris on a path guided by the tower and the ship's autopilot system.

It wasn't long before they were in among the satellites, banking, diving, climbing on a path through the congestion that only a computer could calculate. Abe and Quinn winced as a boxy weather probe came within inches of the ship's viewport.

"That tower better know what it's doing!" Abe said. "We just had this thing fixed!"

After their return to Mars, it had taken nearly two months to arrange the return of *The Lady Grace* from Shyoph-2. The green lapyk of that world had done a number on the ship's finish and its engines. It had taken several more weeks to process the insurance claim and have the ship towed to a repair shop on one of the moons of Vortas, where it had to undergo a complete propulsion overhaul. Shipping *The Lady Grace* back to Phobos hadn't been cheap either.

In all that time, they had heard almost nothing from Aerius, except for occasional brief missives that he was tracking down various leads. Weeks stretched into months until a year had passed since they had all parted ways at Mama Rossi's Martian compound. Silence.

And then...

The message had been characteristically short, just two sentences: "Found Nimbus Steele. Meet me at coordinates 64.08 on Nyoploris."

After another zigzag through two communications satellites and a holo-broadcast array, *The Lady Grace* finally emerged from the morass, and Abe and Quinn got their first good look at the planet. Even from 30,000 feet, it was easy to tell that most of the continents were covered with megacities, their arms branching into the planet's few oceans with giant docking quays and interplanetary spaceports. As the ship zoomed through the clouds and toward a large continent on the planet's northeastern hemisphere, the cities resolved themselves into blocks of mile-high buildings, spires, complexes, and satellite dishes of every possible configuration. Air traffic clogged the lanes between buildings on several vertical levels, each one more congested than the last.

"All this technology and they still can't figure out how to solve traffic jams," said Abe.

Quinn replied, "As Iash said, 'Invention is an imperfect process.'" Then, "Look!"

Abe and Quinn could see that they were descending toward a rooftop park whose green color seemed slightly off-putting. The structure on which the park rested was huge, more than three miles long, and the rooftop was configured with a parking area for multiple vessels.

"It's weird to see a park in a place like this," said Quinn.

"And leave it to Aerius to set this as the meeting place," Abe replied.

The Lady Grace landed, its engines powering down, and Abe and Quinn disembarked into the mostly empty parking area. Looking around at the lack of tourists, they made for the park entrance and a sign that read "AAG Memorial Tree Museum." And under it: "Open daily, admission 30 credits."

"Thirty credits!" Abe exclaimed. "No wonder this place is empty. Why couldn't Aerius meet us in the parking lot?"

Quinn shrugged and said, "C'mon, Pop-pop."

They paid their admission at the ticket kiosk, which was run by a young woman from the Galactic Tourism Bureau, and proceeded into the park.

Abe expected the smoggy air of Nyoploris to diminish once they were on the cobblestone path between the trees, but the odor was not replaced with the earthy smell of soil and growth. He saw why almost immediately—as well as the reason for the disquieting shade of green they had seen from the air. All of the trees were holograms, projected representations of plants from around the galaxy. Apart from the spattering of tourists, there were no other living things in the whole park.

"Museum, indeed," Abe scoffed. "You couldn't find a real tree on this planet if it fell on you."

As if in response, the hologram next to them flickered, sending a wave of static up the length of its "trunk" and into the canopy of "branches." The sign next to the hologram identified the tree as "*Ulmus procera* (English Elm)—Earth" and gave a brief description of the species. Abe continued grumbling.

"Thirty credits," he muttered. "Robbery! And where's that blasted Aerius? These are the coordinates he gave. Why isn't he here yet?"

Indeed, the chayat was nowhere to be seen. A few other people mulled about the park, strolling along the path that wound among the exhibits or staring at the holograms as if each tree was a work of art instead of a cheap projection of light.

"Maybe he's farther in," Quinn suggested.

They began walking, passing hybrid trees from settlements throughout the solar system, as well as flora and fauna from other alien worlds. Here was a blooming leopard orchid from Dar'mor, spotted petals the size of LAS-er rifles dripping with blazes of cerulean; there was a Malodorous Stink Fern from Arctura, spear-like fronds heavy with spores. But whereas a park like this on Mars would be filled with smells and pollen and insects, the holographic museum maintained the sooty, acrid atmosphere of Nyoploris caused by overdevelopment and industry.

Abe and Quinn had just reached the center of the park when a voice from behind them said, "Pssst!" They spun around to find an imp-like creature floating in the air near a representation of the Shyophian Giant Cactus. Two flapping wings supported the alien's rotund little body, which seemed composed entirely of a ball-like head atop a ball-like stomach. A computer apparatus covered the imp's left eye, with a wire feeding around its bald head and straight inside one pointed ear.

"Greetings, we meet you in peace and goodwill," Quinn said.

164 · PATRICK SCALISI

The imp nodded. "Greet*iiiings*," it said in a voice whose pitch went up toward the end of the syllable. "Am I to pres*uuu-ume* that you are Abe and Qu*iiiin* Tittterm*aaaan*?"

"Who's asking?" Abe replied.

The imp fluttered twice in the air, as if it was used to answering this question. "I work for Salech-Com Couri*iiiier* Services. Your description was given to m*eeee* by a Mister Aer*iiiius*."

"Yes, that's us," Quinn replied. "But where's Aerius? Have you seen him?"

The creature removed a small device from a pouch on its belt and presented it to Quinn. The device had a square screen and a depression at the bottom where, presumably, one would press a finger or other digit.

"If you'll put your f*iiii*nger here for a DNA sample, I can deliver my message," the courier explained.

Quinn looked at his great-grandfather hesitantly, then shrugged and placed his finger on the depression. Quinn yelped when a pinprick struck his thumb. He wrenched his hand back and stuck his finger in his mouth to stem the dribble of blood.

The courier, meanwhile, withdrew a disposable sanitary wipe from another pouch on his belt, swabbed the device and tossed the crumpled wipe into a nearby trash bin. He consulted the information on the screen.

"Ident*iiiity* confirmed," the imp said. "Your friend Aer*iiiius* sends his greet*iiiings* and regrets that he cannot meet you in person. He has been arrested and is being held at the 37th Precinct."

CHAPTER TWENTY-ONE

One visit to the 37th Precinct was usually enough to scare wrongdoers into reforming their lives. As Abe and Quinn entered, they saw that the massive "Floor of Judgment" was overflowing with a crush of bureaucracy as offenders waited in mile-long lines for their turn with the Arbiters. Body odor from a hundred species filled the precinct, congealing into a stench that Abe and Quinn recoiled from immediately. How the stoic police officers, who stood guard throughout the floor in their helmets and riot gear, were not affected was truly a mystery.

"Ugh!" Abe groaned through the fabric of his shirt, which he had brought up to cover his nose. "If Aerius was stupid enough to get caught doing something illegal, I don't see how it's any of our business. I'm leaving."

"Stop being so grouchy," Quinn said, though he too had brought his hands up to cover his face. "There's an information grid right there."

Near the precinct entrance and separated from the Arbiter queues by a reinforced hypersteel fence was a wall-size screen with the word INFORMATION written on the top in several of the universal standard languages. Quinn walked over and touched one corner of the wall to begin his query, regrettably having to move one hand from his face in order to do so.

"Did Aerius ever mention a family name to you?" Quinn asked. When Abe shook his head, the young man continued, "I'll just type in 'Aerius' and hope for the best."

Quinn used the keypad to enter Aerius's name. Various windows that were floating behind and around the screen suddenly flew to the far edges of the display while a results window descended from the top. Thankfully, there was only one name on the resultant list of offenders: Aerius rel Drevet rel Lyrdem. Quinn touched the screen to bring up a dossier that included Aerius's mug shot, in which he looked as inexpressive as ever, and a list of crimes. Among them was operating a class-four vessel without a license and transporting unregistered waste.

"The jails here are too crowded," Quinn explained as he navigated the screens. "They only lock up the worst offenders. We just have to pay Aerius's fine, and they'll let him out in a few minutes." A few more taps on the wall. "There, I took it out of the store's account."

Abe sputtered in alarm. "What?!"

Quinn turned to his great-grandfather. "Think of it as an investment in the Key."

"I've 'invested' quite a bit in the Key already," Abe complained as he crossed his arms over his chest.

As they waited for Aerius's release, Abe and Quinn watched the lines on the Floor of Judgment move slowly, inexorably toward the Arbiters. The accused offenders had no choice but to wait for their turn with one of the handful of supercomputers that would decide their fate.

In the queue closest to the fence, a Nalaxan with a broken-off horn and a scar running down the left side of his gravelly face walked up to the Arbiter, a convex screen behind a protective force field. The screen shone white for a moment before the image of a fellow Nalaxan, this one adorned in a judge's mantle with tribal colors on the shoulder, appeared on the curved display.

"The computers must simulate an Arbiter from the offender's race," Quinn said as they watched.

The Arbiter Nalaxan cleared his throat and addressed the accused in the nasally voice that marked his species, "Do you have an Advocate?"

"No," the offender whined.

On screen, the Arbiter waved his right hand. The police officer on guard came forward holding a sturdy device with handles on either side. The officer placed the device in the offender's shackled hands.

"You have been given an Advocate," the Arbiter continued. "I will now compute the evidence."

The Arbiter on screen closed his eyes and paused for a moment. When he reopened them, he said, "Clarification inquiry: Were you armed before or after your confrontation began with one Wylett Anders?"

A voice issued from the Advocate box. "Objection. Under section three-twenty-seven-A of the Nyoploris Charter, my client is permitted to abstain from answering any questions that may incriminate him."

"Objection noted," the Arbiter said. "Do you wish to answer the question?"

"I wasn't armed before the fight began," the accused said. "The beam was on the side of the road. I used it in self-defense."

"Thank you," the Arbiter replied. "I will now uplink with the Advocate to deliver a sentence."

The Arbiter closed his eyes and paused again, this time for a longer period. A series of lights flashed on top of the Advocate box as the two computers shared information. Finally, the Arbiter resumed his sentencing.

"In light of the evidence presented by yourself and the police report, charges have been lowered from first degree assault to first degree breach of peace. A fine of three thousand credits is to be paid within thirty days in lieu of detention. This misdemeanor charge will appear on your record for one standard cycle. Go now, and keep the peace."

The Nalaxan offender grunted and handed the Advocate box back to the police officer, who also removed the rhino creature's shackles. No sooner had the Nalaxan stepped away than did the next accused criminal step up to the Arbiter screen.

Abe and Quinn would have watched more of the proceedings if not interrupted by a shift change for some of the detention officers. The peacekeepers, many of humanoid species with enhanced muscles and other augmentations from the Nyoploris doctors, streamed from a door near the detainment area. Some carried duffle bags full of equipment, riot helmets hanging from bag straps, and all were dressed in civilian clothes. The two Tittermans watched the parade, trying to catch snatches of conversation.

"Did you hear about the latest pirate raid in Sector 13?"

"How many is that in the last six months?"

"*Phht*, I lost count."

"You guys mean the pirates? They'll never come near Nyoploris."

"I wouldn't be so sure."

"If I were you, I'd be more worried about Shotel Zero destabilizing the carnivorous space worm market. He promised to compromise the Berlero Soil Farm's environmental systems in his latest video."

"We ever get that hacker in here, I doubt he'd make it halfway to the Arbiters…"

The rest of the departing officers' conversation was cut off by a loud buzzer that sounded from another door opposite the information screen. A tall gray creature accompanied by yet another peacekeeper strolled out, the former carrying a plastide box full of clothing and other personal possessions.

It was Aerius. And he was completely naked.

The chayat lowered the box to cover his modesty, stared at Abe and Quinn for a second, then turned back to the open door and shouted what sounded like an obscenity in his native tongue.

"And don't look at me like that, you *kalt*!" Aerius said, addressing the police officer.

The officer shook his head and left the prisoner with Abe and Quinn.

"Is that you, Aerius?" Quinn asked.

The chayat let a glimmer of a smile cross his thin, dark-gray lips. "Is your ship nearby? I require a shower."

Aerius left the bathroom on *The Lady Grace* wearing a drab, one-piece jumpsuit and his liquid armor vest. With the floral smell of soap wafting off his gray skin, the alien used a bath towel to dry his bald head and took a seat in the ship's kitchenette area with Abe and Quinn.

"Much improved," Aerius said. "Thank you."

Abe looked across at the alien and cut right to the chase. "Would you mind telling us where you've been this past year?" He pointed at the chayat. "Twelve months and barely a whisper out of you. Then we get your message, come here, and find you in jail! What happened? And when can I get the money back for posting your release?"

Aerius closed his eyes and held up his hands in a conciliatory manner. "I will explain everything." Turning to Quinn, he added, "First, how are you feeling? Have you learned more about the map?"

Quinn nodded. "It comes in bits and pieces, mostly in dreams. Iash didn't just record the location of where to use the Key in his hyper-transmission; he also put some of his memories into that vision I saw."

"Go ahead and tell him," Abe said, even though he had heard the story three times already.

"Aerius, the myths were wrong!" Quinn said excitedly. "Iash didn't *make* the Key—he found it! Found it in some kind of ship that crashed on Shyoph. It's still a little fuzzy. I'm working on the details."

"That is the nature of myths," Aerius said knowingly. "They grow and evolve over time. Who is to say what the original storyteller intended?"

"Yes, it's all very fascinating," Abe said, his tone indicating that he didn't find it fascinating at all. Unable to keep from sitting still, he blurted: "But you have to tell us: Where have you been?"

"First," Aerius said, "do you have anything to eat?"

Abe groaned.

While Quinn got up to prepare a batch of instant noodles for the chayat, Abe recovered himself and shuffled around the kitchen to make a pot of coffee. In a few moments, the three were seated around the table again, steaming cups at each of their elbows and a warm dish piled high with noodles and vegetables in front of Aerius. The smell of spices and soy sauce filled the small living area as the alien began eating in earnest.

"What do you call this?" Aerius asked between ravenous bites.

"Comfort food," Abe said as he brought the cup of coffee to his lips.

"Udon and rehydrated vegetables," Quinn clarified. "Not the healthiest, I know, but…"

"It is delicious," Aerius replied in earnest. "You must teach me how to make it."

Abe and Quinn looked at each other in amused disbelief.

"I have tortured you long enough," Aerius continued. He slurped noodles into his mouth between sentences. "I have found the criminal Nimbus Steele. And Briak Mor."

"Go on," said Abe.

"After retrieving my ship, I started the search on several fronts," Aerius went on, businesslike now that he was dealing with his chayat trade. "I began with the people I know who sell stolen ships. Gabriella Rossi's shuttle was too conspicuous for Nimbus Steele to use for long, so he would have to sell it to someone who would pay cash and not ask a lot of questions. All of my leads turned up empty, except one: a trader off the moon of Pentosh II suggested I try one of his associates on Nyoploris named Choram."

"Just tell me," Abe cut in, "did you see Steele? Did you give him a good whack for me?"

"Let Aerius finish the story," Quinn said.

Aerius went on, "I did not find Steele at once, but Choram *had* bought the ship that Steele took from Gabriella Rossi."

"Great!" Abe said. "Where is he? And where's the Key?"

Aerius shook his head. "There is more, and I'm afraid the news is not good. Choram works for a very exclusive client, and Nimbus Steele wasn't paid in cash. In exchange for the ship, Steele bought protection. Protection from Shotel Zero, the most feared cyber crime lord on the planet."

CHAPTER TWENTY-TWO

Quinn choked on a sip of coffee, cleared his throat and coughed several times. When he got his breath back he said, "That's it then. I guess we'll be going home now."

"Going home?" Abe was aghast. "We're not going anywhere. Who is this person? Where can we find him?"

Quinn looked his great-grandfather full in the eyes. "You've never heard of Shotel Zero?"

Abe looked from Quinn to Aerius. "Should I have?"

"For someone who reads the news every morning, I'm surprised," said Quinn.

"Hundreds of habitable worlds—that we know of—and you expect me to know everything about all of them?" Abe replied.

"Your pop pop—" Aerius still put too much of a pause between the syllables "—is right. I had also not heard of this Shotel Zero before coming to Nyoploris."

"So, *genius*," Abe said to his great-grandson with just the right amount of goading, "you gonna tell us about it or what?"

Quinn smirked. "Iash says, 'To educate another is to touch the divine.' That's a new one, by the way."

With a withering stare from Abe, Quinn cleared his throat again and went on, "Shotel Zero is a hacker. He likes to break into banks and other companies that he and his followers think are 'corrupt.'"

"The name comes from his computer handle," Aerius added, "which, in turn, comes from a word from *your* home world."

"Mars?" Abe said, raising an eyebrow.

"Earth," the chayat replied.

"I've heard that too," Quinn said. "Apparently, *shotel* was a weapon from ancient times with a curved blade. Warriors would use them to hook around an opponent's shield. Shotel Zero took the name because of how easy it is for him to hack around digital defenses."

"Charming." Abe said.

Quinn turned to Aerius. "Back up a bit. How'd you get arrested?"

"Ah, yes," the chayat said. "After tracking down Choram, I inquired as to employment with this Shotel Zero, using the trader from Pentosh as a reference. About eight standard months ago, I began running vehicle CPUs between Choram and one of Shotel's hacker cells in Oaso City. The technicians would wipe the hard drives and install new software so the stolen ships could be sold through one of Shotel's legitimate front businesses. After about six months, Choram saw my value and offered me more work—receiving shipments, going on test flights with important customers.

"I began to infiltrate the organization, finding out what I could while performing my duties admirably. I had just learned about Nimbus Steele, Briak Mor, and the auction when I was arrested during a normal CPU run. Someone informed the police of my route, perhaps someone in Choram's group who was jealous of my rise."

"You said something about an auction," Abe remarked. "What auction?"

"I became close with one of the programmers in Oaso City," Aerius explained. "These people are connected to Shotel Zero's digital network, though he keeps it very compartmentalized. The programmer learned that Shotel is going to auction Briak Mor and give Nimbus Steele a portion of the profits. The auction is being held late tonight at a secure site in Oaso."

Abe couldn't hide the surprise, confusion and outrage from his face. "What a fool! Why would this criminal *sell* the Key?"

"From what I have seen," Aerius said, "Shotel Zero is already an *andrak*—a god—in the digital realm. He does not need the kind of power that Briak Mor can unlock in this reality. But he does need the power it can *buy*. Only about twenty powerful, important people have been invited to the auction. Shotel Zero will have enough leverage over whoever buys the Key to get what he wants from them in the future."

Quinn sighed. "Another dead end," he said.

"Well we've got to try *something*," Abe exclaimed.

"If this auction is so exclusive, there's no way we're getting in without an invitation," Quinn added heatedly.

"Incidentally, I may have a lead on that," said Aerius, his gray face breaking into a rare grin. "But it requires swift action. What time is it?"

Quinn told him, and Aerius stood hurriedly, nothing left of the noodles now except for a few lakes of soy sauce that formed their own geography on the surface of the plate.

"I have to go," the chayat said. "I am already late." He strode toward the side hatch of *The Lady Grace* before Abe or Quinn could even move. "Wait for my signal, and share with Mama Rossi everything I have told you."

"Wait, we—"

Abe was going to say that Mama Rossi had not responded to any of their messages since they had left Mars, but Aerius was already gone.

"Well," Abe said irritably, "what do we do now?"

Star and Sky Transports was located in a four-story, glass-fronted building in the prosperous Borough of Dynetan. Aerius stared up at the gleaming edifice, looking at the vessels on display behind the glass and bathed in the golden light of late afternoon. He took a moment to brace himself, then strode up to the entrance of the building.

A chime sounded as he crossed the threshold, and a robot attendant, humanoid with an oval head, approached from one side. Just the right amount of light reflected off the robot's stainless surface, the SmartTint wall of windows letting in the perfect percentage of sunlight to make the vessels—and everything else—on the showroom floor glow.

"How may I help you, sir?" the robot buzzed.

Before Aerius could answer, a burly Delta Proximan salesman shouted across the desks that had been placed strategically throughout the display floor so as to see everyone who entered the front door. "Aerius? You got out! Jeez, man, I didn't think you'd make it back in time."

"I am here, Gial," Aerius replied, extending his hand.

Gial had the typical red skin and brow ridge of his kind and was nearly as tall as Aerius himself. He wore a cravat and a formal shirt with short sleeves that could barely contain his bulging arms.

In the months that he had gotten to know Gial, Aerius had learned that the Proximan was passionate about weightlifting and bodybuilding. He had come to Nyoploris initially to get muscle band augmentations on his arms and legs. He had also learned that he was good at selling ships and had stayed on planet to pay off his surgery bills by working at Star and Sky Transports and as a weekend bouncer at one of Shotel's clubs.

Gial put an arm around Aerius's shoulder and took him past the gleaming display models. The chayat could feel the power radiating through the bicep that rested on the back of his neck.

"The boss was real worried about you," Gial said quietly. "Knew you wouldn't talk, but you're one of the best couriers he's had in a while. To top it off, he didn't know *who* was gonna demo the VS-7 for Mister Piller today."

"Well," Aerius said, "I remembered the switch for the electromagnetic pulse. It wiped everything in the truck when the police pulled me over. I lost the shipment of CPUs, but the authorities could only arrest me on minor charges. I suppose Choram will not be pleased that I lost his goods."

"If you help close this deal with Mister Piller, I'm sure the boss'll forgive you," Gial said, pointing at the chayat's chest.

"I shall do my best," Aerius said.

Gial led Aerius through the showroom and toward the service area at the back of the building. Through a dynoplas door marked "Bay 3" was a new suborbital transport, hull shining, ready for its first test ride. Aerius took a moment to admire the graceful lines, the chrome accents on the metal skin and the twin engines that could provide more power than anyone needed outside of the Hitar Racing Circuit. Approaching the nose of the small sportster, Aerius could see a large emblem that read "VS-7" in front of the two-person cockpit.

"Oh man, what I wouldn't give..." Gial said as he admired the ship alongside Aerius. "You know, word is Choram had to bribe somebody on Vortas just to get one of the first models that rolled off the assembly line. Mister Piller will literally be one of the first people in the galaxy to own one. Make sure you mention that."

"I will," Aerius said.

"And you read the piloting materials I sent over?"

"Yes, it is very similar to a Vortas Mark Eight. That was my first ship."

Gial nodded his head in appreciation. "That right? Whew, what a beauty!"

They would have gone on like this, talking shop and comparing ships, if not for the arrival of the reception robot. The machine swung its ovoid head to both Aerius and Gial in turn and said, "A Mister Piller has arrived to see you."

Mister Piller, an assumed name that the translators could handle, was from Isos Prime. He had amassed a fortune through a precious metals export business that his family had owned and operated for three generations. On his last visit, Piller had told Aerius that he came to Nyoploris exclusively to buy his ships because he trusted Choram and because Star and Sky Transports was "the best dealership in the galaxy."

Now Piller sat next to Aerius in the well-appointed cockpit of the VS-7, red eyes taking in every luxury of the ship's luscious interior: components molded and fitted to give a sense of gentle fluidity, buttons and dials accented with shimmering chrome that showed nary a fingerprint.

"Well, the designers certainly spared no expense," Piller said, running one green hand over the genetically engineered leather seats; the material had been grown in a lab for the highest levels of buttery softness.

"No expense at all, sir," Aerius said, waiting patiently with hands on his lap. He knew better than to do anything with the ship without Piller's express permission, that a buyer of his caliber liked to call the shots.

"Well, start it up," Piller finally said. "I want to hear these legendary engines that the reviewers keep talking about."

Aerius buckled his restraining harness and did as he was told. He said, "You likely won't hear a thing with the cockpit canopy down, sir." Lifting a hand, Aerius traced an arc in the glass with one finger. "There is a dampening field manufactured *inside* the glass to provide the utmost quiet and comfort."

Piller hummed. "Later then." He paused for a beat. "Let's take her out."

Aerius hit a series of controls on the instrument panel, keeping an eye on Piller in his peripheral vision. Only one button was necessary to open the doors of Bay 3, but the others activated the ship's tracking beacon and sent a signal to *The Lady Grace* on a silent frequency. Luxury indeed! There were a number of covert systems on the VS-7, and Aerius had learned about all of them in the ten minutes it had taken him to read the eight-hundred-page manual.

Piller, though, took no notice of what Aerius was doing because he was too concerned with checking the dimensions of the glove box. Nor did the buyer feel it necessary to put on his own harness.

Good, Aerius thought.

The chayat gripped the quad-handle yoke and eased the VS-7 forward, feeling the immense power that could be fed into the racing engines. Keeping the ship under control would be difficult; the temptation would always be there to go faster. *Nothing this powerful should be legal for suborbital use,* he thought.

Banking the ship right, Aerius brought the VS-7 into the flow of traffic and headed for the open skyway above the crowded metropolis. Spires, antennae, towers and satellite dishes passed below as the ship rose thousands of feet over Dynetan, the townhouses and corporate buildings falling rapidly away. In moments, they were in the open, with only a few other ships riding the high-altitude skyway back to Oaso City.

"Go ahead and open her up," Piller demanded. "I came all this way to see what she could do!"

Aerius obliged, jolting the yoke forward so the g-forces pressed the chayat and his passenger into the yielding yet supportive racing seats. The sheer power of the ship sent a shiver through Aerius's body. He smiled; he was genuinely enjoying this.

Piller whooped.

"I am told," Aerius went on, "that Mister Choram worked very hard to get this model. You will be one of the first people in the galaxy to own the VS-7."

Piller sighed, as if the topic bored him. "Yes, Choram has already boasted to me of how *difficult* it was to acquire. I'm sure he'll be adding that expense to his usual fees when we close the deal tomorrow."

"Will you be buying the ship?" Aerius clarified.

"Humph!" Piller let out a sardonic bark. "If I could have gotten one myself, I wouldn't have gone through Choram. And if I'm not totally broke after my meeting tonight, I shall be back to make the purchase. But enough of this—I want to see what this ship can *really* do!"

Aerius responded by gunning the yoke again, confirming out of his peripheral vision that Piller still wasn't using his harness. The chayat imagined the cerulean fusion burn from the engines as the ship rocketed down the skyway at unsafe suborbital speeds. He needed no such imagination to see the gleeful smile painted on Piller's face as the blue-banded red eyes danced at the sight of the blur outside the cockpit canopy.

A shout of surprise.

One moment the skyway was clear of traffic; then, in a heartbeat, there was suddenly a recreational cruiser with a pointed cockpit and a cylindrical body right in the path of the VS-7. Piller threw his hands out against the canopy, as if the motion would stop the instant liquefaction of his body upon impact. But Aerius steered away just in time, banking hard to the right in a maneuver that sent Piller's head into the canopy with a cringeworthy *thud*.

Abe unleashed a series of curses that were unsuitable for a man half his age as his heart raced from the near impact. From the cockpit of *The Lady Grace*, he and Quinn had barely had enough time to register terror as a fancy suborbital racer bore down on them. Aerius had instructed Abe and Quinn to hone in on the chayat's signal when the racer had blasted out of nowhere. Now they watched the instrument panel as the signal moved away from *The Lady Grace* and turned in a rapid U.

"Was that—?" Quinn began as the communications alert sounded.

Aerius's voice came over the speakers. "My apologies," the chayat said. "Are both of you all right?"

"What do you think you're doing, flying at that speed?" Abe barked while clutching his chest.

"A near miss," Quinn clarified. "No harm done."

"As was my intention," Aerius said. "I apologize that I did not have an opportunity to explain earlier. Time is still against us, though. Please come and pick me up."

The communications link broke as the racer edged closer to *The Lady Grace*.

"We're working for *him* now?" Abe grumbled as Quinn moved the ship into tandem with the racer.

Aerius put the VS-7 on autopilot and unstrapped his harness. Piller was out cold, head lolling to one side. The chayat worked quickly. He leaned over and started searching Piller's patterned overshirt and slacks. In the back pocket of the latter, Aerius found a slim metal case that contained a hexagon-shaped chip. He touched the chip gingerly with one finger, as instructed by the programmer in Oaso City, and saw a series of red numbers flash across the surface: coordinates for the auction.

There was a glint of metal out the corner of his eye. Aerius looked up to see *The Lady Grace* hovering next to the VS-7. The chayat pressed a button on the instrument panel to open the canopy.

"Warning! It is dangerous to open the cockpit while in mid-flight," said an electronic female voice through the speakers. "Please confirm override."

Aerius pushed another button and was immediately buffeted by wind and cold as the canopy lifted. Strangely enough, though, his first thought was about how *clean* the suborbital air felt compared to the constant smell of ozone and electronics down in the cities of Nyoploris. He breathed deep, remembering the forests of his home world, before noticing that Abe was gesticulating wildly from behind the cockpit viewport of *The Lady Grace*.

Aerius held up the metal case to show that he had succeeded, then stooped to enter a few more commands on the instrument panel of the VS-7. In moments, the racer was a hand's breadth away from *The Lady Grace*, which had its side hatch open so that Aerius could jump from one ship to the other.

"I am safely aboard!" Aerius shouted moments later. He turned in time to watch the VS-7 cockpit close and the ship fly away on a predetermined course with the unconscious Mister Piller still aboard.

"Where did you send that ship?" Quinn asked as Aerius moved into the cockpit.

"On a joyride, of course," Aerius replied.

CHAPTER TWENTY-THREE

Though it was technically night on Nyoploris, light pollution from hundreds of neon signs and sky advertisements created a kind of perpetual twilight in Oaso City. Aerius, Abe, and Quinn strode down an alley plastered with ads for the upcoming transdimensional boxing match between Handsome Joe Floyd and Gryyggaxx the Destroyer. Beads from the chayat's tribal war coat chattered in the night air, while the shells running down his back, which had come from some kind of land animal, made a basso *thump* with each step.

"Are you sure this is the right way?" Abe complained as he paused again to hitch up the sash-robe draped over one of his shoulders.

Aerius turned, the light from the signs revealing two laser-thin stripes that he had painted underneath his eyes with red dye. "The coordinates are very specific."

"Well, I still don't understand why we had to play dress-up."

"I am Chief Aerius of the Uonko Tribe of N-31 Alpha," the chayat explained for at least the third time. "You are my retainers."

"I like these robes," Quinn said, stopping to stand proudly for a moment and admire his reflection in a storefront window. "It gives us a chance to learn more about Aerius's home world. As Iash said—"

"Oh, can it!" Abe cut in. "This fabric is unbearable. What *is* this stuff?"

"Fibers woven from the morongo plant," Aerius replied. "Very breathable when the humidity rises in the forest. Unfortunately, a small percentage of offworlders have suffered caustic rashes from wearing the traditional *ib* robe."

Abe looked up in alarm while Quinn said, "I'm glad I decided to keep my pants on after all."

The group passed a parlor selling memory upgrades and subdermal augmentations, components displayed in a streaky shop window on hammered metal pedestals, before coming to the entrance of what appeared to be a squat apartment building. A hexagon was branded on the door.

Aerius shot a meaningful glance at Abe and Quinn. "Remember: Important chiefs of my home world will sometimes take on alien retainers who want to learn the ways of my ancestors. You will not speak unless spoken to. There is no telling what kind of surveillance the auction will have, so make no mention of this from now on."

Abe and Quinn nodded, and Aerius reached for the door handle.

A long corridor greeted them, filled with the sound of pulsing music from somewhere behind the walls and, underneath it, the telltale static of a dampening field. Aerius's electroreceptors prickled slightly at the presence of the field, something he doubted the humans could sense. About thirty feet away, the corridor curved to the right at a ninety-degree angle.

"Keep up," the chayat said, his tone and gait radiating confidence.

Past the turn in the corridor was a guard whose original species was indeterminate based on the number of augmentations on his head alone. He looked up at Aerius, unsurprised that the group was there, and stared at the newcomers through a combination of one natural eye and one multiwave camera array.

"Invitation, please," the guard said.

Aerius handed over the hexagon-shaped chip and watched as the guard inserted it into a cylindrical drive that had been integrated into his right wrist. As the guard did so, Aerius saw that nearly the entire left side of the creature's head had been augmented as well, from advanced sound detection to three memory slots where the ear should have been.

A beep emanated from the guard's wrist drive.

"Through the weapons scanner," the guard said.

The scanner was sunk into the walls and ceiling of the corridor, bands of metal backed by sensitive detection equipment.

"All that tech in his head and he can't even tell if we're carrying LAS-er weapons," Abe said quietly to Quinn.

Aerius shot the two humans a surprised glance, then drew an arm back and slapped Quinn across the face. To Abe, the sound of the impact seemed to echo in the empty corridor. Quinn staggered back a step.

"You have been neglecting your duties, acolyte," Aerius raged. "You were to teach your companion the path of quiet reflection. He will never find anything in the forest if he makes unnatural noise out of turn."

The guard watched all of this with detached curiosity, cocking his head to one side.

Aerius turned back to the guard and said in a more controlled voice, "I apologize for the insolence of my retainers."

The guard straightened and looked Aerius straight in the face. "Encyclopedic recall identifies your species as originating from N-31 Alpha." A pause. "Isn't this man a little old to be undergoing the *nalc* trial?"

Aerius was momentarily stunned by the unexpected use of his native tongue. In the same heartbeat, the guard lowered one hand to a LAS-er pistol that was strapped to his hip.

The movement galvanized Aerius. He regained his composure and said, "The ancestors tell us that we are unworthy to judge who may pass the nalc and who will fail, but that all should be welcome to try."

The guard seemed satisfied with this response. He removed his hand from the weapon and gestured once more toward the corridor. "Through the weapons scanner," he repeated.

"As you wish," Aerius said.

He passed the scanners embedded in the wall and ceiling, followed by Abe and Quinn, without incident.

"Go only to the door at the end of the hall," the guard instructed. "Enjoy the auction."

With that, the guard turned to welcome a Dar'morian woman who had just rounded the corner. Aerius led the others to the indicated room, noting three other doors in the hallway.

The auction room itself was a sparse, square space with about twenty metal chairs and a pedestal at the front of the assembly. Several creatures of various species milled about, some sitting alone, others talking in couples or small groups. The din of conversation filled the air, punctuated only briefly as those assembled glanced at the newcomers before resuming their discourse.

Aerius leaned into Quinn and Abe. "I doubt Shotel will be able to hone in on individual conversation in this room," the chayat whispered. "I apologize for striking you, Quinn, but I did not want to risk injury to your great-grandfather."

Abe let the rage show on his face. "If you ever lay a hand on him again…" he hissed.

"It was necessary," Aerius said. "If you had remained silent, like I asked—"

"It's all right," Quinn said with the right amount of appeasement in his voice. "Let's just get on with it."

They sat in the back row of chairs, closest to the door, while taking stock of their surroundings.

It was impossible to know what kind of infrastructure existed behind the walls of the room, but it was safe to assume that Shotel Zero had had some kind of security measures installed.

The chairs and display pedestal appeared ordinary, and the door through which they had entered was the only way in or out.

Next, they examined the other auction-goers. As expected, there were several humans among the bunch, many with augmentations that made them appear formidable or with alien bodyguards in tow.

In the row of seats directly in front of them was a Drav smeltlord, his leathery skin giving him a reptilian look. Sitting quiet and alone, he wore dark, heavy clothes designed to maintain a set body temperature and ward off the heat of his home world.

Beyond the Drav was a corpulent Cherhovan aristocrat, his roly-poly frame typical of the egg-shaped species. As the aristocrat spoke, he ran one hand over his silk-and-fur-lined waistcoat while gesturing languidly to a four-armed Rauskon.

There was a sound from the back of the room. Aerius, Abe, and Quinn turned to see the Dar'morian woman enter. The Cherhovan noticed as well, because he broke off his conversation with the Rauskon and waddled immediately to greet the well-appointed lady.

"Madam," the aristocrat said, taking the offered pinkie and touching it gently to both of his cheeks. "I'm pleased you could join us. It gladdens me to be in your presence again."

The woman smiled and withdrew her hand into an ornate shawl that covered the shoulders of a couture wrap dress. The smile did not touch the woman's beautiful, almond-shaped eyes. "Barquad," she said in a lyrical voice. "I was hoping you'd be here. It has been too long since our last meeting."

The woman's dress glittered with a sparkling radiance as she allowed Barquad to lead her to a seat.

The final arrival was perhaps the most surprising of all. Moments after the Dar'morian had taken her seat, the door to the room opened for the last time to admit a quintessent priestess from Itvero Beta, followed by four attendants. Everyone in the retinue wore white, bell-shaped garments that covered their entire bodies, except for a rectangular eye slit so the wearer could see where she was going. Apart from the sound of the door opening, they glided into the room soundlessly, each covered in a burlap-like material that was perfectly hemmed so that it brushed the floor but revealed nothing of the feet or wearer.

The entire room had gone quiet, and Quinn whispered, "They look like ghosts. Like caricatures of ghosts."

Aerius remembered the role he was playing and said, "Attend to me now. Notice how the four attendants take up places at the corners of the room. They represent the four elements—soil, space, fluid, and fire—when the priestess is present. The priestess herself represents the fifth element, quintessence."

With the attendants in place around the room, the priestess sat in one of the back rows, her covering making barely a susurrus as she sank into her chair. Conversation resumed cautiously among the other occupants.

Before long, a crackle of static came from somewhere nearby. Everyone turned their attention to the podium at the front of the room, where the holographic display of some beast out of legend appeared.

"That's Shotel's avatar," Quinn hissed.

"I see from the network data that all of the chips I gave out have been redeemed," the beast said in a deep and terrible voice, and out of a mouth that should not have been capable of intelligent speech. "Welcome. You were handpicked for this particular gathering through my research and the application of certain algorithms that I designed to search out the most capable buyers of what I have to offer."

Barquad, the Cherhovan aristocrat, seemed incapable of keeping his seat. "And is what you have to offer the genuine article?"

"Undoubtedly," the avatar replied.

"What certainty do we have?" Barquad pressed.

"If you're interested in certainty," the holographic monster growled, "you should keep to the ledgers in your counting room.

We are dealing here with the stuff of legend, and as far as that goes, I can guarantee the object's authenticity."

"And is it here, in this building?" the Drav smeltlord rumbled.

"No, but I have it in my possession at the origin point of this transmission," Shotel answered. "The winner of the auction will be given coordinates to a mutually agreed-upon rendezvous following receipt of a non-refundable twenty percent deposit. Is that acceptable?"

The beast head paused, seemingly to scan the room.

"Excellent," it went on. "If there are no other questions, we can proceed."

The image of the head was replaced with something Aerius, Abe, and Quinn had all seen before: a nondescript rectangular box. Before their eyes, the holographic box opened to reveal the Key to the Universe.

There was a collective gasp from the assembly, coupled with shuffling and stirring as everyone craned their necks to get a better look at the hologram. The only ones who remained rooted in place were the priestess and her four attendants.

"I hope you all have gotten a good look," said the same voice as before, though the beast avatar did not reappear. "Bidding will start at one million Standard Credits."

"One million!" said Barquad immediately, sending off the opening salvo.

"One-point-one million," said the Dar'morian with a beautiful and devious grin. She inclined her head slightly toward the Cherhovan.

The aristocrat smiled back, pleased that the game was off to its start, and sputtered excitedly: "One-point-two million."

"One-point-three," rumbled the smeltlord.

Those in the room whipped their heads back and forth between the bidders, listening as the price quickly skyrocketed to five million credits.

"Well, now what?" Abe muttered. "I don't have that kind of money. And you already owe me for your release fee."

"We bid to win," Aerius whispered, "and hope we get taken to wherever Shotel and the Key are being kept." The chayat raised his hand and said in a loud voice, "Six-point-two million."

The bidding continued. Several of those who had not entered the fray realized the price had extended beyond their means and remained quiet to watch the spectacle. Soon, there was only Barquad, the Dar'morian, and Aerius bidding against each other as the price passed the three hundred million mark.

"Quiet!" the smeltlord suddenly growled.

All of the bidders looked in the direction of the dark-clad lizard creature, who simply raised his arm and pointed to the priestess from Itvero. Unnoticed by anyone else, the priestess had stood at her seat and appeared to be waiting for the rest of the assembly to notice her.

"What do *you* want?" Barquad sneered.

The priestess waited a beat before turning her eye slit to look at the Cherhovan. "I wish to bid," came a meek voice. "One billion credits."

CHAPTER TWENTY-FOUR

asps arose as the enormous sum was announced. The Drav smeltlord slowly lowered his arm to stare at the priestess; the Dar'morian blinked her beautiful eyes in rapid succession; and Barquad the Cherhovan gaped unabashedly and seemed on the verge of a nervous fit. The attendants at the four corners of the room still had not moved.

"Shall I repeat—" the priestess began.

"How *dare* you!" Barquad interrupted. The aristocrat's nervous excitement had transformed into envious rage, coloring the Cherhovan's face in shades of scarlet. "You mean to lock the rest of us out completely, to stifle our chances of winning."

"That *is* the point of an auction," the smeltlord explained.

"Shut up!" Barquad said to the lizard creature. He turned back to the priestess. "You will rescind your bid so the rest of us have a fighting chance."

The rest of the room erupted into an uproar as the auction-goers shouted their support or disdain for Barquad's order in equal measure.

"Yes, let's restart from the beginning!"

"She has outbid us all fair and square!"

"No priestess has that kind of money. Show us the cash, sweetheart!"

"That's uncalled for! Show some respect!"

Barquad turned in a circle and whistled for silence. Returning his gaze to the priestess, he said, "Will you rescind?"

The full-body garment shook in a definitive negative gesture.

Barquad screamed, his face becoming, if possible, even redder than before, and launched himself at the priestess. Before he could make contact, though, there was a shot from a high-power weapon that struck the Cherhovan square in the chest and sent him flying toward the far wall.

Abe, Quinn, and Aerius flinched, shrinking into themselves and looking around the room for the source of the blast. One of the attendants had lifted an arm—a surprisingly *burly* arm—out of her shroud-like garment and was holding a large LAS-er weapon made of some transparent material.

Before anyone else could react further, four panels folded out of the room's upper corners to reveal security guns that took a bead on the assailant. In a simultaneous flourish, each attendant threw off her covering to reveal that they were actually four Nalaxans, each holding a clear LAS-er weapon. The priestess also disrobed as one of the horned creatures tossed a spare gun in her direction. Underneath the robe was Mama Rossi, who caught the gun in one hand, ducked behind her chair and began firing at the wall-mounted weapons.

Laser fire filled the air, followed by shouts and bedlam. The auction-goers toppled over chairs and one another as they converged on the room's only door, some getting caught in the crossfire and dropping like meteors, others shrieking and pulling up short to crawl into little balls of terror. The four Nalaxans were trying to herd everyone into the center of the room while Mama Rossi took out the slender wall-mounted guns one by one.

As the laser fire ceased, the augmented guard from the security scanner burst through the door with his own weapon held forward. With trained reflexes, the Nalaxans turned as one, firing four precision shots that struck the guard square in the chest. He crumpled, dead, in the doorway. At the front of the room, the holographic representation of the Key flickered atop the podium and went out.

A cacophony of voices filled the room once more as the auction-goers discovered who among them was wounded and dead. Barquad was among the fallen, the first shot fired from the Nalaxan's gun having taken his life. Several of the bodyguards were dead too, having shielded their masters from the wall-mounted weapons. The smeltlord's clothing, meanwhile, was singed in several places, but the lizard creature seemed un-harmed. The Dar'morian woman was likewise uninjured, though she was shaking uncontrollably. Mama Rossi's Nalaxans tried to keep order in the ensuing confusion as the mafiosa stood from behind her chair barricade and waddled over to where Abe, Quinn and Aerius had taken meager shelter behind their own chairs. The whole battle had lasted barely a minute.

"Abe, how nice to see you again," Mama Rossi said. She extended her hand to help the old man up from where he had dropped to the floor during the melee.

Abe slapped the hand away, stood with difficulty, and brushed off the front of his itchy ib robe with as much dignity as he could manage given the situation. "I wish I could say the same," he said with a scoff.

Mama Rossi shrugged, looked over her shoulder to ensure that the Nalaxans had everything in hand and returned her atten-tion to Abe.

"I'm sure you're proud of this little coup, but it doesn't get us any closer to the Key," Abe said. "Why'd you have to go and bid such a ridiculous amount?"

"Because I intended to win," Mama Rossi said. "I'm sure your plan was the same as mine: win the auction, get escorted to the Key, take it by force instead of paying. Am I right?"

"I—" Abe opened and closed his mouth, his thought pattern unseated by how transparent their scheme had been. He started again, "I, that is…" A pause. "How did you get those in here, anyway?" He pointed to the transparent LAS-er weapon.

Mama Rossi rapped her knuckles on the gun. "Made completely out of a high-impact composite free of both plastide and metal. Just to be safe, we disassembled them and sewed the individual components onto the inside of the robes. My dear boys have been putting them back together ever since we got past the security scanner."

"Clever," Abe admitted. "But how did you get here? And why didn't you respond to any of our messages?"

Mama Rossi flashed a smug smile. "Me? The most powerful crime lord in the solar system? Shotel Zero invited me. Unlike you, I suspect. And no one said I had to come as myself. As for your messages, well, I couldn't risk having Shotel's network intercepting them, could I?"

"You have an answer for everything," Abe said.

"I wouldn't be here if I didn't."

Wary of the Nalaxans from his last encounter with them, Aerius swept his eyes around the room, made sure that none of the auction-goers would raise a fuss, and went over to where Quinn—unnoticed by everyone else—was studying the hologram podium.

"Are you hurt?" Aerius asked the young man.

Quinn looked up from an open panel on the side of the podium. "No, are you?"

"I am unharmed." Aerius paused and glanced at the small screen and exposed wires that had been hidden in the podium's innards. "What are you doing?"

"I'm trying to trace the source of the hologram's transmission," Quinn replied, dividing the wires from bundles as thick as his thumb. "It may lead us to Shotel."

"Would Shotel not have safeguarded against such an eventuality?"

Quinn shrugged. "It's a long shot," he admitted. "But it's also possible Shotel didn't feel vulnerable here. There weren't any fellow hackers at the auction, just businesspeople—and I use the term loosely—with lots of money."

"He did not feel threatened, so he may not have scrambled the signal," Aerius finished. "That's chayat thinking. Good. What do you need?"

Quinn extracted the small screen and indicated a set of wires that ran around the display. "Pull these apart. Yes, that's it. Hold that so I can get to the access port."

Aerius did as he was told. Quinn looked surreptitiously at his great-grandfather, then rolled up his right sleeve and pressed a beauty mark midway up his forearm. A spring-loaded hatch popped up to reveal a portable bio-chip.

"*You* have an augmentation?" Aerius asked.

Quinn hushed the chayat. "Not so loud. Pop-pop and my mother would have a fit if they knew. Besides, it's just one data chip, which is useful at school. A lot of students have them."

Aerius watched as Quinn slipped the data chip out of its organoplast sleeve and plugged it into the screen's access port. Coded sets of numbers ran across the display.

"Yes!" Quinn exclaimed.

Abe and Mama Rossi stopped their argument long enough to glance over at the podium.

"What is it?" Mama Rossi asked.

Quinn disconnected the data chip and held it up. "I know where Shotel is transmitting from. And it's a good bet the Key's there too."

"That's wonderful news, dear," Mama Rossi said.

She pointed her transparent weapon in the air and fired three rapid shots. Everyone except the Nalaxans flinched, and some of the remaining auction-goers, like the Dar'morian woman, shrieked in surprise.

"I'd like to have everyone's attention, please," Mama Rossi continued in a firm, polite voice. "You likely all know who I am. Some of us have even done business together before. Mister Mulciberian," she nodded to the smeltlord, "I'm glad to see you were unharmed in the fighting."

"It would take more than those stingers to pierce *my* hide," the Drav muttered.

"Doubtless," Mama Rossi said, turning in a circle to look at the rest of the room's occupants. "Those whom I have treated with in the past can tell you that they have always profited from the experience. My associates," she indicated the Nalaxans, "have currency cards loaded with five hundred thousand credits for each of you. We'll be leaving now, and you may do so after we've gone. Don't follow us, and the money is yours. I'll send the activation code in twenty-four hours."

In the silence that followed, Mulciberian grabbed one of the room's overturned chairs, placed it upright with no little amount of scraping, and pointedly sat down.

"I can live with that," the smeltlord said.

"Good," replied Mama Rossi. "I don't think you would have liked the alternative." She turned to one of the Nalaxans. "Mario, start distributing those cards and let's get out of here."

CHAPTER TWENTY-FIVE

The dream is always the same: the alley of rocks, the clearing, the crater, and the ship from another world.

Iash-Quinn removes the dead pilot and finds the Key to the Universe.

Time melds, bends, jumps as it is wont to do in dreams, and Iash-Quinn is suddenly inside one of the cliffside caverns in the desert canyon. He is sitting cross-legged in the traditional meditative pose. The Key is on the ground in front of him. The Quinn-half knows through dream memory that the Iash-half has been drawn to the Key and wants to interpret its meaning.

With his meditative being, Iash-Quinn raises his consciousness above his body. Above the cave. Above the canyon. Above the continent and above the planet into the reaches of space. This is the Inner Eye of the Cosmos, and he is searching, searching.

A voice intrudes: "Are you sure this is the place—?"

Abe looked out of the cockpit viewport of *The Lady Grace* at a well-appointed row of townhouses in one of Dynetan's most exclusive neighborhoods. The sun had been up for about an hour, but the neighborhood was extremely quiet. When Abe had inquired about this, Aerius had explained that it was the weekend;

he had gotten into the rhythm of Nyoploris during his time on the planet.

"Still," Abe said, "this doesn't look like a hacker's residence. I was expecting, I don't know, a transmission station or something. Are you sure this is the place?"

"Make no mistake," Mama Rossi said from the cockpit's passenger seat. "With the tech Shotel's running, he could reach the planet's outer moon with a transmitter the size of my thumbnail."

Abe was about to respond when he heard Quinn stirring from the midship living quarters. Aerius, who was standing in the cockpit entrance behind the two pilot seats, shifted aside so the young man could come forward.

"Good morning. You dozed off after we left the auction house," Abe said to his great-grandson.

"Sorry," Quinn said. "It makes me tired, my brain working overtime and all."

"Are you still processing the information?" Aerius asked.

Quinn yawned, stretch and rubbed his eyes. "Yeah. It comes mostly in dreams. I'm getting close to something though. Iash was drawn to the Key after he found it. Something about it compelled him, and he wanted to learn its secrets through meditation."

"I wish our problem was solved as easily," Abe said, returning his gaze to the object of their stakeout.

"Does anyone want coffee?" Quinn asked.

The others nodded their assent.

Suddenly, Aerius pointed out the viewport. "Who is that?"

A figure had emerged from the front door of the end townhouse. He wore a leather jacket and looked furtively in both directions before reaching into the jacket's inner pocket to withdraw a self-lighting cigarette. The man pulled the tab at the end and inhaled a lungful of smoke.

"It can't be," Mama Rossi said.

"Nimbus Steele," Abe muttered.

Nimbus Steele took a deep drag of his cigarette and welcomed the momentary release of stress. Even this vice had been denied him the past few days while holed up in this place.

"Don't go outside, Nimbus," he mimicked in a little-girl voice. "No cigarettes, Nimbus."

He took another drag and spit on the stoop of the townhouse. He bet no one had done *that* before, not here in the rarified atmosphere, where the wealthiest citizens of Oaso City lived in their architecturally couture buildings, technology safely hidden behind beautiful infrastructure—form melded gracefully with function.

Like the others in the neighborhood, Shotel's townhouse was tall and narrow, the end unit with a half-sunken garage bay at the base, sloped launch drive, winged dividers between units that held private balconies, and narrow windows set in a façade of warm Elchoir tidal bamboo. There were no wires present, no satellites or transmitters, no security cameras. There was only the building, which 98 percent of the smoggy, technocrowded masses of Nyoploris could never afford.

The cigarette had burned almost to the filter. Nimbus wondered if he had time for another before Shotel got out of the bath, before the genius hacker was ready to apply massive brain- and computing power to the problem of the Key. Nimbus hated all of this skulking around behind monitors and firewalls; he wanted real action.

"How did someone get a gun past the guard?" Nimbus wondered aloud, and not for the first time. He had been trying to reason through the problem since the images of those armed priestesses had come through the security video feed. There wasn't much to go on, especially since the assailants had taken out the cameras.

He sighed. At least the actual Key wasn't at the auction. They would be able to try again, but when? There would only be more delays until Shotel decided the time was right, until the hacker would thaw Nimbus's assets as payment for putting the universe's most legendary artifact into the hands of Shotel Zero.

Resignedly, Nimbus turned to reenter the townhouse when he saw someone on the stoop of the adjacent building. It was a young man, barely in his teens by the look of it. One of the neighbors? To Nimbus he looked oddly familiar, like someone he had met in passing.

Memory on the verge of realigning, Nimbus felt cold metal press into the back of his neck. Out of instinct, he turned slightly to catch a glimpse of the assailant out of his peripheral vision: a short, plump woman with gray-streaked hair pulled up into a bun.

"Hi, Nimbus," said Mama Rossi. "How nice to see you again."

Mama Rossi, Aerius, Abe, and Quinn quietly trundled Nimbus Steele through the front door of the townhouse before any of the *actual* neighbors could see what was going on. They found themselves in a short entranceway that opened into a two-story foyer bathed in light. A simple wrought-metal staircase wound to the upper floors while sunbeams from front and rear windows fell on elegantly molded exotic tiles. The brain strained to define the shape of each ceramic block, which were veined with tones of green and purple. Somewhere from the upper levels came the sound of running water.

"Where's Shotel, and where's the Key?" Mama Rossi asked while Aerius ranged farther into the foyer, his own gun muzzle scanning every corner of the room.

"I—"

"I already regret not killing you at the Adams Café," Mama Rossi said. "Don't give me an excuse to rectify that error."

Nimbus composed himself, straightened and said, "Shotel's in the restroom. The Key is in the basement."

"Lead the way," Mama Rossi said. "I want to be out of here before our hacker's done with his bubble bath."

Nimbus shot Mama Rossi a surprised look that the mafiosa couldn't interpret, as if they had just shared something that Nimbus hadn't expected her to know. Then Nimbus shrugged and made his way toward the stairs that led to the townhouse basement.

One half of the lower level had been converted into a workspace loaded with high-powered computer equipment. The L-shaped workstation featured a series of monitors on its long end, perpendicular to a projected VR display roughly the size of a small coffee table. Littered about were small portable computers—all with blank screens—storage devices, peripherals, and tools for tinkering with hardware. Holo projectors were mounted to the surrounding walls, and the stasis screen on the VR display showed a slowly rotating 3-D model of a primitive-looking hooked weapon with a wooden handle.

Just as he had done upstairs, Aerius scanned every corner of the room before taking up a watchful position at the base of the stairs, gun held at the ready. Abe stayed close to the chayat, glancing back up the stairs every few seconds while Quinn examined the electronic equipment that was scattered about.

"Well, there you have it—the den of the beast," Nimbus said smugly, as if this had been his plan all along.

Mama Rossi prodded him with her weapon. Nimbus grunted.

"Yeah, now where's the Key?" she demanded.

Nimbus shot her a look of boastful superiority. "Oh, around here somewhere. Where did I see Shotel put it last? It may take me a few minutes to find."

Abe pried his attention away from the stairs and stalked over to Nimbus. "We don't have a few minutes, you imbecile."

"Then you better decide quick how you want to pay me for that information," Nimbus replied.

Mama Rossi brought her gun up to Nimbus's forehead. He looked at it cross-eyed as a bead of perspiration ran from his hairline down the strong line of his nose.

"The payment is your life," Mama Rossi said calmly. "I won't ask again."

Nimbus backed away and held up his hands, palms forward. "Okay, okay. Leave me to the wolves, why don't you."

With her gun still trained on him, Mama Rossi watched as Nimbus elbowed roughly past Quinn and opened a drawer on the workstation directly below one of the holo projectors.

"Hey!" Abe protested. "Don't touch my great-grandson!"

Nimbus ignored him, reached into the drawer, and produced the box that held the Key to the Universe.

"Open it, Quinn," Mama Rossi said.

Quinn did as he was told, verified that the Key was inside, and said as much to the others.

Aerius moved away from the stairs and pointed to the other end of the basement.

"There should be another exit on this level," the chayat said. "The garage bay."

"Good," Mama Rossi said. "Let's go. Aerius, keep an eye on our rear. Make sure Mister Steele stays put."

Nimbus advanced toward the group. "You can't just leave me here! I showed you where the Key was. You owe me—"

"Nimbus, who are you talking to?"

All eyes turned toward the stairs, where a small figure had emerged from the upper level. It was a Dar'morian girl, about ten years old, clad in a bathrobe.

CHAPTER TWENTY-SIX

No one could bear to raise their weapons at a defenseless child. Instead, they all just stared at each other waiting for something, *anything*, to break the silent stalemate.

The girl stared back at them. Her almond-shaped eyes were a deep emerald with pupils the shape of hourglasses, set in a heart-shaped face of tanned, healthy skin. Her hair, wet and combed back from her forehead, might have been dark purple, but now it appeared black and shining, like the feathers of a crow. The girl promised—like most Dar'morian females—to be a beautiful woman when she came of age.

The child huddled within her voluminous bathrobe, coiled as if ready to flee. Finally, she said, "Who are these people, Nimbus? And how did they get into my house?"

"They've come to steal the Key, Shotel!" Nimbus blurted. "Stop them!"

The girl let out a breath and, with it, some of her tension. She stepped fully into the townhouse basement. "Unlike you, I know when I'm outnumbered." She glanced at the LAS-er weapons held loosely in uncertain fingers. "And outgunned."

Holding her bathrobe tightly, the girl glided past the astonished onlookers and flopped into the workstation's lone chair, feet barely touching the floor. She spun to face the intruders.

"Well?" the Dar'morian said.

Quinn was the first to speak. "He called you Shotel. But you can't possibly—"

"Can't possibly what?" the girl cut in, eyebrows raised.

"What he means to say," Aerius said, "is that he believes you cannot be the hacker Shotel Zero."

"Believe it," the girl said. "But you might as well call me Mayron for now."

"How…?" Abe began.

The girl sighed, as if she had had to explain the story many times before. "I'm what you might call a prodigy, and I've always loved electronics. I built my first computer at age five."

"And Shotel?" Quinn asked.

"I created the handle Shotel Zero three years later to crack the Winkroot Financial Trust," Mayron said.

"I remember that," Mama Rossi chimed in. "You exposed some of the law firm's more *clandestine* dealings."

"They had to totally restructure," Mayron said. "I was disappointed they survived at all."

"They're lawyers," Mama Rossi replied. "It's what they do."

The girl nodded, as if accepting this as a valid explanation.

"You've been active ever since," Quinn added. "Setting up cells in Oaso City—"

"Not just Oaso," Mayron interrupted.

"And championing whatever hacktivist causes you see fit," Mama Rossi finished. "I must say, your morality seems a bit… flexible."

"This coming from the head of the Martian Mafia," Mayron retorted. When a look of surprise flashed across Mama Rossi's usually stolid features, the girl added, "I did invite you to the auction, after all."

"Touché," the mafiosa said.

"But tell me," Mayron went on, "how did you find me? I can guess how you got in because this idiot," she thumbed a finger at Nimbus, "reeks of cigarettes, even though I told him not to go outside and smoke."

Nimbus frowned and looked away. But Quinn said, "That was me. I traced the transmission source from the hologram podium."

"The hologram podium—" The girl slapped her forehead in a fashion that matched her age and grunted out a rough laugh. "I meant to encrypt it. But with Nimbus *nagging* me all the time, I must have forgotten." Mayron placed her hands in the lap of her fluffy bathrobe. "Well, I can't say I don't deserve this. Go on. Take the Key."

"You're just going to let us have it?" Mama Rossi asked suspiciously.

"Let you?" Mayron laughed again. "I know what I'm buying with it."

The girl snatched up one of the small devices on the desk and quickly pointed it at Abe and Quinn.

"Facial recognition in progress," the device said in a mechanical voice.

"I'm buying my privacy, my identity," Mayron continued. "I give you the Key in exchange for you keeping the secret of who I really am. And if it ever does leak and I have to do extensive cleanup work, I'll know it was you—" she glanced down at the screen "—Abe and Quinn Titterman. Or you Gabriella 'Mama' Rossi. Or you, Aerius, who I know was one of Choram's men. And you have no idea what harm I can do from this little desk. Do you believe me?"

"We believe you," Quinn said.

"Then our transaction is complete," Mayron said. "You can use the exit at the far end of the basement. It goes out to the launch drive."

Sensing that Mayron's dismissal broached no argument, the others turned to leave. Abe, though, remained rooted in place. He stared at the girl with an expression of perplexity on his face. Mayron, who had immediately gone back to tapping away on one of the portable computers while waiting for the interlopers to leave, looked up.

"Yeeees?" she said.

"Maybe I'm an old man who's out of touch with the universe," Abe said, "but I don't understand why you're doing this. Where are your parents?"

A flash of surprise crossed the girl's features. However, it was gone in a heartbeat, replaced by the same steely willfulness that she had demonstrated moments earlier. Putting down the computer, she said, "Look at me, Abe Titterman. Do you know what I am?"

The others had stopped to watch this exchange.

Abe shook his head. "A Dar'morian?" he asked uncertainly.

"A Dar'morian *girl*," Mayron clarified. "You think we live in an enlightened, progressive, pluralistic civilization? Think again. You know what my career options are?" She held up a hand to tick off her choices. "Nurse. Hostess. Wife. The very lucky ones become 'diplomats,' which is a nice way of saying they use their charms to manipulate government officials. I like this path better. As for my parents..."

She reached for a remote and pressed one of its buttons. The holo projectors on the wall immediately crafted an image of feminine childishness: the desk was replaced with dolls, plush animals, and a small table with a play tea set.

"They never come down here—when they're actually home, that is."

Abe felt a hand on his shoulder, turned, and saw that Mama Rossi was standing beside him.

The mafiosa looked past Abe and addressed the girl, "Your secret's safe with us, Shotel. C'mon, Abe."

"One more thing," Mayron said. "Is that *really* the Key to the Universe?"

"Yes," Abe said. "It's really the Key."

Mayron smiled, but Abe couldn't tell from her expression if she believed him or not.

They turned once more to go when Mayron said, "Wait! Where do you think *you're* going?" In a flash, she jumped up from the chair and bounded over to Nimbus Steele. Before he could react, she had slapped something onto his wrist.

"Ow!" Nimbus protested.

"The others may have bought something," she said, "but you still owe me."

Nimbus laughed nervously. "Owe you? What are you talking about?"

"I brought you under my protection in exchange for the Key," Mayron said. "I don't have the Key anymore. Now you have a debt to pay off."

Mama Rossi smirked and ushered everyone else toward the exit.

"Wait!" Nimbus cried, head swiveling between Mayron and the retreating group. He turned back to the girl. "What have you done to me?"

"You likely feel a diode pressing into the underside of your wrist," Mayron replied. "At my command, that bracelet can deliver a precise electrical charge that will stop your heart. You work for me now."

Nimbus had seen the snare now and was frantic. "No!"

Mayron ignored him and went on, "I figure it'll take about twenty years to pay off what you've cost me today. After that, if you cooperate, we can talk about unfreezing your assets. There's also the matter of where to place you. Not with Choram, certainly. Perhaps my cell in Metro-7…"

Nimbus continued protesting while Mayron explained about the bracelet's tracking capabilities and threatened to demonstrate its uses by sending Nimbus into cardiac arrest. After that, the others had passed through the basement door and heard no more of Nimbus's vain attempts at conciliation.

CHAPTER TWENTY-SEVEN

W ithin an hour, *The Lady Grace* was soaring toward the upper atmosphere with the ships of Mama Rossi and Aerius close behind.

Quinn opened a general communications line between the three vessels. "We have our escape vector through the satellites," he announced.

Mama Rossi's voice came through over the speakers as clearly as if she were sitting in the cockpit of *The Lady Grace*. "Good. Set rendezvous coordinates for my compound on Mars. Certain parties will be glad to know that the Key is back in our possession."

"I was planning on going back to Phobos," Abe interjected. "Quinn is *this close* to unraveling this thing."

"No," Mama Rossi said vehemently. "We need to regroup somewhere secure. I've had enough adventures."

Abe could feel his temper rising. "Secure?" he exclaimed. "Your compound was *real* secure last time the Key was there."

"I've ensured that further precautions are in place," Mama Rossi replied. "And anyway, it's safer than your antique shop."

Abe seethed. But before we could argue more, Quinn said, "Standby. We're coming into the satellite cloud."

The young man cut the communications link and checked to ensure the ship was on autopilot. Then he turned to look expectantly at his great-grandfather. "What should we do?"

Abe opened his mouth to deliver a ready retort, to perhaps say something about Mama Rossi's insult, but was stopped by his great-grandson's words. Abe had expected an argument from this quarter as well, had expected sensible Quinn to insist that they head back to the mafiosa's compound to regroup. Instead, Quinn was asking Abe what their next move should be.

"I—that is, are you asking me?" Abe stammered.

Quinn smirked. "Well, we've come this far. And despite the countless Solar laws we've broken, I'm at least a little curious to see what the Key does."

Abe laughed. "That's the spirit! I knew my granddaughter hadn't bred all the adventure out of this family. Your great-grandmother would have been proud."

Quinn laughed as well. "I wish I'd known her," he said.

Abe nodded and squeezed Quinn's shoulder. No further words were needed between them. Quinn checked their progress through the satellite cloud. Floating mechanical objects were all around them now, blotting out everything else in the viewport as the computer guided them on a safe course through the morass.

"There's just one thing, though," Quinn said.

"Hmm?"

"My brain still hasn't finished processing the hyper-transmission. I'm close, but I don't know where to use the Key yet."

"Then we'll figure it out at home," Abe said. "Set a course for Phobos once we get out of here. Mama Rossi can go back to her compound and wait for *us* for once."

The Lady Grace continued to bank and weave through the satellites. Finally, Abe and Quinn began to see patches of star-light among the spinning debris. The clear emptiness of space had never looked so beautiful.

"I still can't believe that little girl was a galactic hacker," Abe said. "From what you've told me, she's done terrible things."

"Terrible maybe by human morality," Quinn said.

Abe huffed. "As if there's any other!"

"That's a bit xenophobic, don't you think?" Quinn said. "What we think of as right or wrong may not apply to other species. Perhaps what we see as immoral is perfectly acceptable to Dar'morians."

"How can you say that?!" Abe exclaimed.

Quinn shrugged. "Well, she did have a point. Unless they come to our solar system, Dar'morian women don't have many options."

"Bah!" Abe grunted. "I'm not getting into a philosophical debate with you."

"Come on," Quinn said. "I know you're not like that. You've got to understand that—"

Before Quinn could finish, a proximity alert blared throughout the cockpit of the ship. Both Abe and Quinn snapped their eyes forward in time to see *The Lady Grace* emerge from the satellite cloud only to be confronted by a colossal warship.

Aerius's voice came over the restored communications link: "SFS *Melee* straight ahead!"

Quinn punched at the controls just in time to bank the ship away from the looming hull of the *Melee*, the unexpected maneuver producing powerful g-forces that pressed Abe and Quinn into their seats. Abe's arm shot out to brace against the instrument panel. Quinn gripped the controls with white-knuckle intensity.

There was a crackle of static as someone cut into the communications link, followed by a visual transmission. Hearts pounding from the near miss, Abe and Quinn glanced at the display and saw a human woman with fair skin and blond hair, one eye hidden behind a hologram that projected from a computer implanted on part of her right cheek and temple.

"Madeline?" Abe heard Aerius say over the link.

Madeline turned to speak to someone off screen, "Our calculations were correct." Turning back to the transmission, she said, "Abe Titterman, Gabriella Rossi, and Agent Aerius—this

is Captain Madeline of the SFS *Melee*. We've been monitoring
your transmissions for some time. We know you have the Key
and are prepared to take it by force. Surrender now!"

"Madeline," Aerius repeated, "what are you doing?"

"As *Mama* Rossi—" Madeline bit off the honorific "—
pointed out during our last encounter, this ship needed a new
captain. And I'm it. The Solar Free Ship *Melee* answers to no
government, no planet. We live in total freedom, taking what we
need when we need it."

"I doubt you *need* the Key," Abe replied sarcastically.

"You're right," Madeline replied with cold indifference,
"we need the Key *and* your great-grandson. You have five seconds to lean to before I disable your ship and send over a
boarding party. One, twwwwooooozzzztttt—"

The frantic voice of Aerius came over the speakers, "I've
locked her out of the communications loop. Run! Now!"

From her place in the cockpit of her cruiser, Gabriella ordered
the Nalaxan pilot to arm the ship's weapons. The SFS *Melee*
loomed in the viewport, a formidable menace that would be
heavily shielded. There was little chance that Gabriella's LAS-er
cannons would have any effect on the battleship, but she hoped
to buy enough time for Abe to activate his FTL drive and get
away. That was the main thing now—protecting the Key. She
wouldn't lose it again.

"There!" the Nalaxan pilot said, pointing to one of the
cockpit instruments.

In the viewport, Gabriella saw the *Melee* unleash a volley of
gunfire into the silent void. *The Lady Grace* zipped out of the
way, but the battleship's cannons were able to track the small
cruiser with little difficulty.

"Target the weapons," Gabriella said with an outward calmness she didn't truly feel.

"They'll be shielded," the Nalaxan pointed out.

"Less shielded than the bridge," Gabriella said. "Just do it!"

As the Nalaxan prepared to fire, Aerius's tracker ship swooped in for a strafing run, the weapons on the underside of the vessel's wings unleashing a rapid barrage on the hull of the *Melee*. There was a series of explosions on the skin of the battleship. But when the fire cleared, it was clear that the attack had done little more than score the side of the *Melee* with a series of black marks.

"She's changing targets," the Nalaxan said. "Now bearing on the other ship."

"He's the bigger threat right now," Gabriella said. "Fire, while they're distracted!"

The Nalaxan activated the targeting controls and fired the canons—just in time to see *The Lady Grace* zip back into the fray.

Shots from the *Melee* rattled the cockpit of *The Lady Grace* as they skirted the hull.

"She's mad!" Abe said. "Get us out of here."

"Working on it," Quinn replied as he toggled the navigation computer.

Abe glanced at the instruments on his side of the cockpit. "Hurry up! They're getting ready to fire again."

"*Working on it*," Quinn repeated with more than a little irritation.

Just then, Mama Rossi swooped in for her own attack on the *Melee*, firing a spread that targeted the weapons of the large vessel. The impacts appeared to cause little damage, and the *Melee* responded in kind, turning its weapons away from *The Lady*

Grace and Aerius to target the mafiosa instead. As Abe and Quinn watched, shots from the *Melee* struck the underside of Mama Rossi's cruiser and sent it spinning away from its intended trajectory.

"No!" Quinn cried, and gripped the controls to swing the ship around.

Abe braced himself again. "What are you doing?!"

Eyes glued to the viewport, Quinn said, "We can't let them get off another shot. They'll destroy Mama Rossi!"

"This is no time for heroics," Abe replied. "We don't have any weapons. The best course is retreat. Mama Rossi would understand that."

But Quinn had stopped listening, concentrating instead on darting in and out, back and forth in the *Melee*'s field of fire, an annoying insect that evaded the swatter time and time again.

Mama Rossi's voice came over the speakers, distorted: "Get out of here, you idiots! We'll cover you."

The command snapped Quinn out of the single-mindedness of his "attack."

"You heard her," Abe said as another volley from the *Melee* passed over their hull.

Quinn nodded and gripped the controls to swing the ship away from the planet. There was a sudden *wooshing* in his ears, but when he turned to ask his great-grandfather if he heard it as well, Quinn's vision began to tunnel. He felt his hands go slack where they held the controls.

"Quinn—?" Abe asked, the name catching in his throat. To Quinn, his great-grandfather's voice seemed to be coming from a great distance.

Then the convulsions began.

Quinn's body slapped back into the seat as *The Lady Grace*, without a pilot, began to drift off course.

CHAPTER TWENTY-EIGHT

The dream is always the same: the alley of rocks, the clearing, the crater, and the ship from another world. The finding of the Key.

Then Iash-Quinn is inside one of the cliffside caverns, meditating. The Key is on the ground in front of him.

With his meditative being, Iash-Quinn raises his consciousness above his body. Above the cave. Above the canyon. Above the continent and above the planet into the reaches of space. This is the Inner Eye of the Cosmos, and he is searching, searching. He has done this countless times, but this time, he turns the Eye back to Shyoph and sees a shimmering line no thicker than the width of a hair. It is a thread, stretching from the Key resting on the rock in front of Iash's body into the reaches of space. If Iash-Quinn had not turned back to the planet, he never would have seen it in the vastness of the void.

The thread. What is the thread? Where does it terminate? Iash-Quinn will have to meditate on this further, and knowing this, he—they—sink deeper into the dream state.

From the bridge of the *Melee*, Madeline watched with both her natural and her computer-enhanced eye as *The Lady Grace* drifted past the floor-to-ceiling viewports. All crewmembers were bent on the attack, waiting eagerly for their captain's next command. Madeline's second, the Rauskon V'lari, stood at the navigation table, checking the locations of the three ships.

"We should finish them," one of the crewmembers said.

Madeline held up a hand. "Wait," she said. "What kind of readings are you getting from that ship?"

"Its engines have powered down," replied V'lari, his tone reflecting a mixture of confusion and suspicion.

"And the Mafia ship?" Madeline asked.

"A holding pattern," said V'lari. "If I didn't know any better, I'd say they were as confused as we are."

"What are you up to?" Madeline muttered. Then, louder, she said, "Stay alert. Keep weapons trained on all three vessels. And prepare a boarding party. If nothing changes, I want to be on Abe Titterman's ship in five minutes!"

"Quinn! Quinn!"

Abe had laid his great-grandson on the floor just outside the cockpit and was shaking the young man furiously. Quinn was breathing, his heart beating, but he simply would not wake up. Someone else was shouting in the background, but Abe was too preoccupied to care. He gripped his great-grandson by the shoulders once more and tried again to rouse him.

"Quinn! Wake up! I can't pilot this thing, you know that! C'mon!"

It was no use, and Abe had to acknowledge that someone was calling his own name with vehement intensity.

"Abe Titterman, you old goat! Answer me!"

The voice belonged to Mama Rossi, and it was coming through the communications system. With reluctance, Abe returned to the cockpit.

"Here," Abe said breathlessly.

"What in the name of all things sacred are you doing?" she shouted.

Abe couldn't even muster the energy to be offended by her tone. "It's Quinn. He's had some kind of seizure."

That stopped her short.

After a moment, she said, in a much quieter tone, "Activate your FTL drive and get out of here."

"I-I don't know how," Abe stammered. "Grace and Quinn were the ones who knew how to fly, not me!"

Neither Abe nor Mama Rossi said anything for a few seconds, the silence on the communications line punctuated occasionally by static. Finally, Abe asked, "What's your status? We saw your ship hit."

"Significant damage," Mama Rossi confirmed. "We've lost everything except limited maneuverability."

Aerius chimed in: "What happened? Why haven't they finished us?"

"I don't know," Mama Rossi said to the chayat, "but can you pull up a schematic of Abe's ship?"

"I do not know," Aerius said. "If I had the model number—"

"All of this talking isn't helping Quinn!" Abe shouted as he fell back into his cockpit chair with Quinn still prone on the floor.

He felt his full age then, a defeated old man. How could he have been so impetuous, so reckless? It was ironic to say that he should have known better, at his age. But then, it was Grace who had always been his foil—her caution when he wanted to rush in, her confidence when he was uncertain, her reassurance when he was anxious. She had been his counterbalance. With that force gone, he had no sense of equilibrium.

Grace would have known what to do in this situation. A lifetime together, and she knew him better than he knew himself. But Grace was gone, and Abe was on the verge of losing Quinn now as well.

Abe stared out the cockpit viewport, the satellite-ridden atmosphere of Nyoploris hanging there like an infected cell. The *Melee* was out there too, no doubt preparing to board Abe's ship.

"Having trouble?"

"Curses, yes!" Abe replied. Then he froze, realizing he didn't know who had asked the question. The voice was quite close, separate from the communications link. He spun in his chair, half expecting to see a stowaway in the ship's living area.

"Standby, you two," Abe said to Mama Rossi and Aerius. To the quiet ship, he asked, "Who said that?"

"I did," the voice said. "Over here."

Abe stood and followed the voice to the midship kitchen, where he had left the box with the Key inside.

"Keep talking," he said.

"The box, Abe."

And Abe realized that the voice belonged to Mayron, the hacker child they had left back on the planet.

"Mayron?" Abe asked as he lifted the box lid, feeling foolish the entire time.

"That's me," the girl said, her voice coming from a small transmitter on the inside lid of the box. "Did you think I'd let the most precious treasure in all the universe go without having some way of tracking its whereabouts? Even *that* information could one day prove valuable. And there's nothing I like more than valuable information."

Abe held the box up to the light to examine the transmitter, which was no bigger than his smallest fingernail. "What is this?" he asked.

"I call it a Spy Dot," Mayron replied. "Not very creative, I know. But it has listening, audio, and tracking capabilities. Once I come up with a better name, I'll have one of my cells begin manufacturing them for sale. They'll help me phase out my partnership with that idiot Choram."

Abe didn't know what to say. Fortunately, Mayron got right down to business.

"I've been monitoring your progress, and from the sound of things, it doesn't look like you have much time," she went on. "I'm willing to make a deal with you—"

"I am *not* giving you the Key," Abe said. "Especially not if Quinn is—"

"I'm not asking for the Key," Mayron replied hastily. "It's just... I want you to take me with you. I want to see what it opens."

To hear a statement of such childlike wonder come from the infamous hacker gave Abe pause. She had seemed so hardened down on the planet.

"And you can get us out of here in exchange for that?" he said. "*Alive?*"

"Undoubtedly," Mayron replied.

Abe's response was swift: "Do it."

"Very well," Mayron said. "Listen carefully..."

CHAPTER TWENTY-NINE

Madeline looked at the ship's clock display, then at V'lari. As if anticipating this, the Rauskon said, "The boarding party is ready."

"Good," Madeline replied. "We've waited long enough."

With a signal to the bridge communications officer, a line was opened between the *Melee* and her opponents.

"This is Captain Madeline. Prepare to be boarded."

"Captain," Abe's voice replied over the link. "I'm glad you called. I'd like to discuss the terms of your unconditional surrender."

Madeline laughed. "That's very amusing. You don't even have any weapons on that ship. And your companions can barely make a dent in my shielding, as you've already seen."

"Do you surrender?" Abe pressed.

"No," Madeline said with a smile.

"Very well," Abe said resignedly, just seconds before something large collided with the hull of the *Melee*.

Abe watched through the viewport as a colossal, blocky satellite used its correctional jets to gain speed and smash into the side of the battleship, metal wrenching silently as debris simultaneously cut into the hull and exploded in all directions.

"Abe!" Mayron said. "Pay attention."

Abe tore his gaze away from the viewport and stared from the controls of *The Lady Grace* to the Key box from which Mayron's voice still emanated.

"I've pulled up a full cockpit schematic on your ship's model," Mayron was saying. "I'll walk you through how to fly it. You'll need to get out of here quickly; there's a lot more where that satellite came from."

As she said this, two more satellites flew past the viewport, large bullets that collided with the side of the *Melee* in similarly spectacular fashion. The crew of the battleship, it seemed, was finally coming to the realization that they were under attack; they trained their weapons on the next set of incoming projectiles, albeit too late to fire.

"You can hack into all of these?" Abe asked incredulously.

"Satellite controls and medical devices have some of the most unprotected software in the galaxy," Mayron said confidently. "But in about two seconds, there's going to be more debris than you or anyone else can handle. Look straight down at the main cockpit display. You'll see something that reads propulsion control. Access it."

Abe did as he was told, pressing buttons in the brief sequences that Mayron ordered. *This isn't so hard*, he thought. *Maybe I'll take flight lessons for my 109th birthday.*

"Where did that satellite come from?" It was Mama Rossi on their communications link. "Abe, answer me!"

"Get out of here," Abe said. "We'll rendezvous on Phobos three days from now."

"I *can't*," Mama Rossi cried.

Abe's hands froze over the controls, but only for a second.

"Mayron," Abe said to the Key box, "Mama Rossi is still out there."

"You're going to have to leave her," Mayron replied.

Abe edged his voice in steel. "She'll die."

220 · PATRICK SCALISI

"If you want to get out of here alive with the Key, you'll do—"

"I won't accept that," Abe said with the same mettle.

"You're in a *recreational vehicle*," Mayron shot back. "You have no weapons, no tools. You don't even have a suspension field!"

"No, but Aerius does."

A pause. As Abe watched, more and more satellites slammed into the *Melee*'s hull and engines. The stream was constant now, the *Melee*'s weapons unable to keep pace with the bombardment. As the battleship tried to turn, it became apparent that it was having difficulty maneuvering.

"Mayron—quickly, what happens next?" Abe asked.

"The satellites I've dislodged will create a cascading chain reaction," the girl said. "You've got about thirty seconds!"

A new status screen appeared on the display console of *The Lady Grace*. With a series of computer animations, it showed the position of all ships in orbit, along with a large mass of objects converging on their location. The satellites would damage or destroy everything in their path.

Abe took a second to examine the display, looking for a clear area safe from the juggernaut that was bearing down on them. The display was divided into grids, and in the upper corner was a space that would escape the impending onslaught. He noted the coordinates and opened a communications line to Aerius, all the while thinking: *This is easy! I* will *take flight lessons when I get home!*

"Aerius, when I give the word, you need to tow Mama Rossi's ship with your suspension field to the coordinates I've just sent," Abe commanded. "You don't want to be in the way of what's coming."

"I am locking on now," Aerius replied.

"Good" came Abe's nearly breathless reply. "Three, two—go!"

Outside the cockpit viewport, Abe watched as the chayat's ship swung into view, weaving away from a shuttle that had launched from the *Melee*, and nabbing Mama Rossi's cruiser with its suspension field. Abe let out a triumphant "Yes!" before Mayron's voice brought him back to the present.

"Abe! Get out of there! Get out of there now!" the girl cried.

Abe fell hurriedly back into his chair and punched the combination of commands that Mayron had given him earlier.

"That last satellite caused only superficial damage," reported one of the *Melee* bridge crew.

"It's a distraction!" Madeline said. "I don't know how they did it, and I don't care. Target all weapons on any incoming projectiles. And protect our shuttle—I want to be on board Abe Titterman's ship in three minutes!"

"The tracker ship's making a move!" V'lari announced from his station near the navigation table.

"Attacking our shuttle?" Madeline asked.

"No, picking up Gabriella Rossi's ship," V'lari replied without lifting his gaze from the computerized display of the conflict. "Looks like they're moving off."

Madeline grunted. "Let them go. It's the Key we want."

A communications line from the boarding shuttle sounded on the *Melee* bridge: "Come in, bridge! Are you seeing this?" the commander of the boarding party asked in a harried voice.

Madeline started to reply, "Don't worry about the chayat and Mama Rossi. We have—"

But before she could finish, the entire bridge crew heard the commander of the boarding party cry, "Get out of here now! Go! Go!"

222 · PATRICK SCALISI

Madeline looked confusedly at V'lari as frightened murmurs filled the bridge.

"What is he—?" she began.

"Look!" someone shouted.

The murmurs erupted into full-on panic as the discipline
that Commander H had once so carefully cultivated broke and
crew members left their stations to flee the bridge, bottlenecking
at the door as they pushed, shoved, and hit each other to get free.
Madeline had just enough time to look up at the rain of metal
bearing down on them through the floor-to-ceiling viewports
before the deadly collisions began.

CHAPTER THIRTY

*T*he dream is always the same: the alley of rocks, the clearing, the crater and the ship from another world. The finding of the Key.

Then Iash-Quinn is inside one of the cliffside caverns, meditating. The Key is on the ground in front of him.

Using the Inner Eye of the Cosmos, Iash-Quinn raises his consciousness above the cave. Above the canyon. Above the continent and above the planet into the reaches of space. He turns the Eye back to Shyoph and sees a shimmering line no thicker than the width of a hair. It is a thread, stretching from the Key into the reaches of space.

What is the thread? Where does it terminate? Iash-Quinn sinks further into the dream state. With astral hands, he plucks the thread, watches as the vibration moves up the length of the line and disappears in the distance. He does it again, but this time he uses the Inner Eye to race along with the vibration, flying faster than the speed of thought through galaxies and systems both inhabited and barren. Racing along, he finally sees where the thread terminates. And with complete awareness, he awakens from the dream at last.

Abe was dozing in a chair in the midship living quarters of *The Lady Grace* when Quinn's eyes finally fluttered open. There was no gasp on the part of his great-grandson, no bolting upright as he came back to consciousness. Instead, Abe registered a slight change in the air that he had grown accustomed to throughout the length of his twenty-four-hour vigil.

In the cockpit, Mayron was piloting the ship to Mars, the no-color light of hyperspace illuminating her young face with a harsh glow. The hacker had made arrangements for Abe to secretly pick her up in the immediate aftermath of the battle with the SFS *Melee*, using her abilities to guide *The Lady Grace* in and out of the deteriorating satellite soup without being detected.

As the subtle shift brought Abe out of his snooze, he looked down at Quinn to see his great-grandson's eyes open and staring at the ceiling. Abe started.

"Quinn?" he asked tentatively.

The eyes moved to focus on the old man's seamed and weary face.

"Quinn!" Abe exclaimed.

He threw himself down onto his great-grandson, hugging the young man as tears of relief glittered at the corners of his eyes. The scene had been all too reminiscent of his last days with Grace, except these past hours had been filled with overwhelming guilt as Abe considered again and again how he had put Quinn in mortal peril. With Grace, Abe had felt powerless, but not guilty—never guilty—about the long and full years they had spent together. But with Quinn, Abe still had time on the clock, still had years to see his great-grandson develop into a successful young man.

Then why are you so focused on the past, silly? said a competing voice inside Abe's head that sounded uncannily like his late wife. *It's time to look ahead.*

Quinn mumbled something.

"Say again?" Abe said in a cracked voice.

"You're crushing me," Quinn repeated.

"Sorry." Abe pulled back, wiping the moisture from his eyes.

"Is that Quinn?" Mayron asked from the cockpit.

"Yes," Abe called back.

"Told you," the girl said smugly.

Quinn looked at his great-grandfather quizzically. "What's that supposed to mean?"

"Mayron made a bet that you'd wake up before we got home," Abe said. "Since your vitals were stable, we decided to head back to Mars for proper medical treatment. Our young friend said you might be in some kind of 'processing hibernation' while your brain worked out the rest of the hyper-transmission."

"The hyper-transmission!" Quinn exclaimed.

"Yes, that's what I said," Abe replied.

"No, I mean—that is…"

"You're babbling."

"I know where to use the Key!" Quinn sputtered.

Abe blinked, unable to reply, while Mayron turned in her seat to stare at them both.

Quinn's need for medical treatment now seemingly moot, *The Lady Grace* changed course to rendezvous with Aerius. Within hours, they had arrived in orbit around Alpha Centauri Bb, less than five light-years from the solar system.

Alpha Centauri was not habitable, but it had served as a crossroads of sorts in the early days of interstellar flight, with several orbiting platforms and whole societies to support the technicians who had initially helped humanity reach beyond its home system. With the advent of better FTL drives, especially with technology adopted from Vortas, the platforms at Alpha

Centauri had been more or less retired, with only occasional squatters or smugglers using them.

Mayron located Aerius's tracker ship at once, and the two vessels docked together with a series of clicks and hisses. Mama Rossi greeted them at the hatch.

"Didn't expect to see you here," said Abe as they boarded Aerius's ship.

"I left my ship with Mario," said Mama Rossi, taking Abe aside. "He'll work on getting the battle damage fixed and returning the shuttle to Mars." She hesitated before saying anything further, as if debating with herself how best to phrase the words she wanted to say. Finally, she went on, "I understand I have you and Mayron to thank for saving my bacon back there, for telling Aerius to haul me out with his suspension field."

"That's right," Abe said tentatively, unsure of where the conversation was heading.

"You shouldn't have risked the Key like that," Mama Rossi scolded.

"Well excuse me," Abe retorted. "I thought my great-grandson was dying and I didn't want any more deaths on my conscience."

The mafiosa shook her head. "What I mean—that is…"

Abe raised an eyebrow.

"*I'mtryingtothankyou*," Mama Rossi said in a rush. "There."

Now it was Abe's turn to be speechless.

Having gotten her stride, Mama Rossi went on. "I just wanted to let you know that I'm grateful. You had the Key; you didn't have to save us too. We can head back to Phobos if you want. It's your choice."

Abe nodded, realizing what it must have taken for the mafiosa to make such an admission. He said, "Forget it. I won't mention it if you won't."

"I'd appreciate that," Mama Rossi said. "I do have a reputation to maintain, after all."

Quinn, Mayron, and Aerius were crowded around the tracker ship's cockpit when Abe and Mama Rossi made their way forward. Quinn was in the midst of a technical discussion with Aerius.

"—if we hook it into your sensor system," the young man was saying.

"Yes, that could work," Aerius replied. "But I have something better. I call it 'The Sovlax.'"

"What's that?" said Quinn.

Mayron, too, wrinkled her brow in confusion. "A sovlax is a small animal. People keep them as pets. They can be trained to do tricks and play fetch."

"Sounds like a dog," Quinn said. "I don't see how that will help."

Aerius looked at them amusedly. "Let me show you."

The chayat unfolded his lanky body and went over to a storage locker built into one wall of the cockpit. From the well-ordered shelves, he produced a cylindrical container with a transparent door and several cable jacks of various size and configuration embedded on its surface. Returning to his seat, Aerius removed a cable that he kept stored inside the container, unrolled it, and located the necessary port on the ship's control panel. After hooking the other end into the ship, Aerius triggered a series of commands, whereupon several indicator lights on the cylinder illuminated red, then yellow, then green.

"Place the Key inside, if you will," Aerius said.

Quinn removed the Key from the velvet-like interior of its storage box and nestled it into the device that Aerius had called The Sovlax. As he did this, Mayron examined the container more closely.

"Oh, that's *clever*," Mayron said, half to herself. "And I don't say that often."

"What is?" Mama Rossi asked.

"Aerius has modified a standard 3-D topography unit so that it can be tied into a sensor computer to extrapolate data. It can 'play fetch.'" The hacker turned to look at Aerius, who was absorbed in his work. "Are all chayats this ingenious? I may have to hire a few when this is over."

"You're not the only one," Mama Rossi agreed.

Aerius, who had largely been ignoring their compliments, said, "I am getting something now. You were right, Quinn. The Key is transmitting some kind of weak signal. We never would have seen it otherwise."

Aerius brought up a map of their current location, as well as the surrounding systems. A thin red line, like the thread of Quinn's dream, stretched from Alpha Centauri Bb into the expanse of space.

"It'll lead to these coordinates," Quinn said as he punched in a series of numbers on the control panel.

Mayron stood on her tiptoes to get a better look. "But that's nowhere," she said. "There's nothing there."

"That we know of," Abe pointed out. "Space is big, after all."

Mayron rolled her eyes. "You sound just like my teachers…" Her voice trailed off as she left the cockpit.

"Did she just…?" Mama Rossi said.

Abe sighed. "Now I remember why I avoid *some* of my preteen great-grandchildren."

"In any case," Mama Rossi continued, "we've come this far because of you two. What's our next move?"

Abe and Quinn exchanged glances; no words were needed between them.

"Get a good night's sleep everyone," Abe said. "Tomorrow we go for it."

CHAPTER THIRTY-ONE

The news people called it the "Disaster at Nyoploris," which Abe particularly liked because it sounded like the title to one of his favorite holo-serials. The cascading storm of space debris that Mayron had initiated to assault the *Melee* had destroyed 30 percent of the satellites in orbit around the planet. Technicians had to work day and night with their navigational computer algorithms to get the rest into line, while companies from around the planet scrambled to deal with outages and coverage breaks. The insurance claims alone were staggering.

The *Melee*, meanwhile, had not been destroyed—it had been designed for interstellar combat, after all—but it had been completely disabled, the crew dazed and dealing with triage when Nyoploris Extraorbital Patrol arrived. The infamous pirate captain, Madeline Cytherean, was taken into custody, her reign of terror over the sector finally at an end.

Abe read these and other headlines over the Solar Network as *The Lady Grace* zoomed toward its destination the following day. As he closed the news display that overlaid the general shipboard functions, Abe looked out the viewport and tried to imagine their eventual destination.

Grace had suggested they take up amateur stellar cartography after Abe retired from Intergalactic Curios, and the little-explored Delphoid Expanse would have been their first stop once their recreational ship arrived.

"Now I'm doing enough exploring for both of us," Abe murmured. He was surprised to find that the thought comforted rather than saddened him.

"Did you say something?" Mama Rossi asked from the other cockpit chair where she was piloting the ship.

"Just thinking aloud," Abe replied.

Mayron chose that moment to wander into the cockpit. "What'd you think we'll find at this mysterious destination where nothing supposedly exists?"

Abe shrugged. "Who knows? We haven't exactly been operating with all the facts."

Mayron looked over her shoulder to where Quinn and Aerius were seated together in the ship's midsection with The Sovlax.

"Do you really think Iash *mystically* puzzled this all out and gave the knowledge to your great-grandson?" she said quietly so those outside the cockpit wouldn't overhear.

"Well, if you believe Quinn—and I do—then you have to accept that Iash somehow figured out that the Key was transmitting some kind of signal and used what we might call transcendental meditation to trace it across the stars," Abe replied.

Mayron scowled. "Not everything has to have a supernatural explanation, you know. Iash was Shyophian, right? Well, Shyophians have evolved to detect invisible forces like electrical and magnetic fields, different spectra of light. It helps them predict storms in the desert."

Mama Rossi placed a hand on the young Dar'morian's shoulder. "Then again," the mafiosa said, "not everything has to have a *rational* explanation either."

Mayron spun. "Don't tell me you buy into this *flemag*, Mama," the girl said. She had taken to using Rossi's honorific over the past day.

The mafiosa shrugged. "In the past year, I've been to a restaurant that can predict the future and the home world of a long-dead philosopher whose instructions have crossed the centuries. All I'm saying is to keep an open mind. And watch your mouth."

Just then, Aerius looked up from where The Sovlax was connected to the ship's computer. "We are nearing our destination," the chayat said.

"Get ready to cut the FTL drive," added Quinn.

Mama Rossi acknowledged and hit the appropriate sequence on the instrument panel. Everyone took their seats. In moments, they were all looking at the black void again, stars sparkling in the distance, the area completely… *empty*.

Mayron, despite her cynicism, excitedly scanned the skies for any break in the darkness. "What's out there?" she said.

"Any idea what we're looking for, Quinn?" Abe asked.

The young man blew out his cheeks. "I couldn't even guess. We're in uncharted territory now. Even Iash never got this far."

"The signal is the strongest it has yet been," Aerius announced.

"But there's—" Mayron began.

Those in the cockpit gasped simultaneously. Out of seeming nothingness, a small planetoid had drifted into the ship's line of sight. From orbit, the sphere appeared barren, barely more than a dead moon.

Mayron reached over Abe's shoulder to punch something on the control panel. After a moment's examination, she said, "You're not going to believe this, but I think we could breathe down there."

"Going would be undoubtedly dangerous," Aerius chimed in.

"Well, we didn't exactly come here to eat pizzelle and drink coffee," Mama Rossi said. "Let's check it out."

Upon landing, Aerius insisted on leaving the ship first to ensure that the instruments weren't mistaken. After taking his first few lungfuls of air without incident, he signaled to the others, who piled onto the planetoid's bleak surface.

At ground level, their destination was little different than it had appeared from space. Bare rock and dust stretched in all directions. Nothing grew. Nothing moved. There were no smells or sounds, just the absolute silence of an isolation chamber. Or a tomb.

Aerius pointed one way that seemed no different than any other. "The readings from The Sovlax said we should go in this direction," said the chayat, who had removed the Key from his custom tracking device and given it back to Quinn.

The group began walking, amazed both by the uniform sameness of the terrain and the clarity of the heavens overhead. To the naked eye, it appeared as if the planetoid had no atmosphere with which to block out the stars. Yet everyone was able to breathe and move easily, as if the air and gravity had been taken directly from their homeworlds.

"Look!" Mayron shouted.

Something on the horizon was distinctly different from the flatness of the world around them. As the group got closer, they noticed that it was actually three *somethings* rising from the terrain.

"What in heavens?" Abe muttered.

Aerius consulted a handheld instrument. "According to the last readings from The Sovlax, the signal stops just ahead."

In moments, the group stood before three identical columns that Quinn estimated were at least fifteen feet tall and about five feet to a side.

"What is this?" Mama Rossi asked.

—*Welcome, travelers.*—

The voice had no visible source but seemed to come from everywhere.

"Who said that?" said Abe as he and the others turned in a circle.

—We are the voice of the columns that stand before you.—

The group turned as one to stare at the featureless columns.

—We are called the Pillars of Creation, and we welcome you to our observatory.—

"Are you the makers of the Key to the Universe?" Quinn asked.

—Is that what it's being called this millennium?—

Abe urged his great-grandson on with a gesture, and Quinn held up the Key.

—The Key to the Universe. Briak Mor. Ho-Shalem. And dozens of other names since the dawn of time. Yes, we are the makers, and you no doubt have many questions.—

Excited murmurs broke out as the travelers exchanged congratulations and excited comments. Quinn's heart raced. Aerius bent briefly to one knee.

"What happens now?" asked Mayron, face flushed with anticipation.

"We wouldn't be here if not for these two," said Mama Rossi as she indicated Abe and Quinn. "Go on."

Abe gave Quinn a nod of encouragement. Quinn smiled in reply and turned back to the Pillars.

"Why did you make the Key?" the young man asked.

—To share our knowledge.—

Quinn waited a beat to see if more information was forthcoming. When it appeared that the Pillars would say no more, he frowned and went on.

"And who are you exactly? What do you do here?"

—We are the Pillars of Creation. We have watched over all sentient life since the first spark. We will continue to watch until the final flame gutters into nothingness.—

"So it's true that the Key can grant unlimited knowledge?"

—Yes.—

A thought crossed Abe's mind. He put a hand on Quinn's shoulder and stepped even with the young man.

"Has anyone returned with the Key before?" Abe asked.

—Yes, some. We were just one when life began. Now we are three.—

Abe wasn't sure what that meant. The Pillars continued.

—When last we were visited, the Key was sent back out into the universe to be found again. The last individual who came closest to solving the puzzle was the one you call Iash.—

Quinn smiled excitedly and said, "We wouldn't have made it here without his help. He left all his knowledge in a hyper-transmission."

—We know.—

Now Mama Rossi stepped forward. "If you know everything," she said, "are there any limits on what we may ask?"

—You are welcome to all we have learned.—

"We can ask about how to hack into any computer network anywhere?" Mayron said.

—Yes.—

"About how to make terrible weapons capable of destroying whole civilizations?" asked Mama Rossi.

—Yes.—

"About the meaning of life?" Abe said.

—Yes.—

They looked at each other in stunned silence. The implications were staggering. What could they not learn that would change life in the cosmos irrevocably? That could eliminate any kind of hardship or stop any kind of threat? That could destroy anyone who disputed the direction in which *they* cared to take the future of sentient life in the universe? That—

Quinn shook his head. It was too much. To even consider a fraction of what the Pillars knew made his mind reel and his stomach nauseous. And, of course...

"What is the cost of this knowledge?" Quinn asked.

The Pillars repeated their previous answer.

—*You are welcome to all we have learned.*—

"But to leave with this knowledge—" Aerius began.

—*You may not leave.*—

Abe started. "What?"

—*To partake in this knowledge, you must stay here. Forever.*—

CHAPTER THIRTY-TWO

The proclamation was shocking. After a moment's pause, everyone began speaking at once. Quinn tried to shout above the debate to regain some kind of order. When the arguments had mostly stopped, he turned back to the Pillars.

"Why must we stay here forever?" he asked.

—*Ultimate understanding precludes the ability to interfere in galactic affairs. To receive this boon, you must therefore stay here.*—

"There is no food here," Aerius pointed out. "No water. Nothing of substance to sustain us."

—*That will not be necessary. You will become like us. Watchers. Beyond physical need.*—

"I say no," Mayron said at once. "I'm not staying on this rock forever, even if it means I won't learn 'the meaning of life.'"

—*Of course, you may choose to leave now without the knowledge.*—

"Now just wait a minute," said Abe. "You may have made up your mind, but the rest of us haven't. I'm one-hundred-eight years old. The idea of staying here at this stage has its merits."

"You'd really consider it, Pop-pop?" said Quinn.

"I said the idea had merit," Abe clarified. "I didn't say I'd made a decision."

"I can't say it sounds very appealing," said Mama Rossi with a scowl.

"Sounds more like a prison sentence if you ask me," Mayron rejoined.

"This is obviously a serious decision," said Quinn, addressing the Pillars again. "We need time to talk it over."

—*Time means little to us.*—

"Clearly," said Abe.

—*The one who brought the Key must choose.*—

Even though the Pillars didn't have fingers with which to point, everyone knew they were talking about Quinn.

"Great," said Mayron dramatically. "My fate's in the hands of this guy."

Quinn walked over to the hacker, his eyes practically glowing. "Aren't you just the least bit curious?"

"Sure," said Mayron. "But what's the use of ultimate knowledge if you can't do anything with it?"

"I'm with Mayron on this one," said Mama Rossi.

"What about knowledge for knowledge's sake?" asked Abe. "'I think, therefore I am.'"

"The drive to learn is what makes us who we are," added Quinn.

Mama Rossi turned to Aerius. "And what do you think of all this?" she said to the chayat, who had remained mostly silent throughout the debate.

Aerius hesitated. "I… I do not know. To be at the place where Briak Mor originated—some of my people's greatest thinkers worked their whole lives for this. Who am I to turn down such a gift?"

Mayron balked. But Aerius held up a conciliatory hand, all six fingers splayed.

"And yet," the chayat went on, "to never see my home or my family again…" He trailed off. "I can see the argument both ways."

"Still," said Mama Rossi, "it seems the decision's up to Quinn."

"That's not fair!" cried Mayron.

238 · PATRICK SCALISI

"You're right—it isn't," said Mama Rossi. "But that's the situation we're in, whether we like it or not."

Quinn looked around the group, his anxiety rising. Mayron pouted. Mama Rossi stood with arms crossed. Aerius was as unreadable as ever.

Abe, seeing his great-grandson's distress, said, "I'll support whatever choice you make."

Quinn turned away from the others to face the Pillars. Unlimited knowledge. It was too tempting. The chance to have every question answered, to learn every mystery in the universe, to watch civilization unfold as new things were learned, new advances made. To see the future not just of humanity, but of all sentient life—and all sentient life yet to come—spread out like an unending road that stretched beyond even the farthest horizon.

And he wouldn't be alone! True, he would never see his mother or the rest of his family in the flesh again, but he would have his great-grandfather, his pop-pop. Together, they would watch over the Tittermans from afar. And Aerius would be there too! Aerius, with whom he had lately become so close. They would all share it together, this one ultimate adventure.

Quinn shot a look over his shoulder at Mayron. She was so young, with her whole life ahead of her. Did he have the right to take that from her? Mama Rossi didn't seem quite as opposed, and they would both thank him when they realized the width and breadth of the gift he had given them.

Had *forced* upon them…

"No," Quinn said quietly, barely loud enough for the others to hear. Then louder, "No, it's too much. While any of us could make our own choice, I can't make it for the others. I say no."

Turning back to the Pillars, Quinn continued, "I'm sorry, but we can't stay. To learn on one's own, to discover, to be in the world are more important than being given something I'm not sure we've earned. I can't speak for Mayron or Aerius, but we humans must use the time we're *given*. And that time isn't meant to last forever."

"Well said!" exclaimed Abe.

Mayron heaved a sigh of relief. Even Mama Rossi looked reassured.

—Of course, you are free to go. Know that once you leave this place, your memory of the Key and its function will begin to fade. You will take it with you, to be found by others, to perpetuate its own myth, but you will not recall its significance.—

Quinn held up the Key again. "Thank you."

The Pillars lapsed into silence then, their secrets locked deep within their stony cores. There was nothing left to say or do.

As they began walking back to the ship, Abe caught up to his great-grandson and asked, "Are you all right?"

Quinn shrugged, his shoulder slumped in defeat. "I guess."

"There was no right or wrong decision, Quinn," Abe reassured him. "You weighed the choice with wisdom, and that's all that counts."

Quinn sighed. "It's not that. It's… Well, I just can't help but think that this whole thing was for nothing."

Abe laughed. "Nothing? I got to go on an adventure with my great-grandson. One to rival the holo-serials, even! And that's worth more to me than knowledge or treasure or power." He paused. "Well, maybe not *all* treasure. I mean, can you really put a price on the lost jewels of King Qsobo? Or—or a first edition of *The Essential Teachings of Iash*?" He poked Quinn in the ribs.

Quinn's disappointment warred with the smile that came to his face unbidden. He laughed in spite of himself.

CHAPTER THIRTY-THREE

Quinn's spirits began to buoy as *The Lady Grace* left the planetoid and sped toward home.

"It's hard to believe I got captured by a madman and tortured over this," he said while staring at the Key. "What do you think Peter Halloran would have done if he had learned the truth about the Key? About what he would have had to sacrifice?"

Aerius shrugged, a human expression he had picked up since falling in with Quinn and Abe. "The Halloran human was blinded by avarice and anger. He would have no doubt lashed out at the Pillars with violence."

Quinn chuckled. "I would have liked to see him try. Who knows what those things were capable of!"

With the ship's FTL drive engaged, Abe, Mama Rossi, and Mayron joined the others in the midship living area.

"I don't know about you," said Abe, picking up the conversation, "but I'd like to see the look on Nimbus Steele's face when you tell him about the Key. Mayron, would you mind recording it on a holo-scan for me?"

"It'll cost you," Mayron replied. "And more than just keeping my identity secret."

"About that," Mama Rossi said. "How would you like to bury Shotel Zero and come work for the Martian Mafia? We could use someone of your skills as I move the organization into its next phase."

"I'm listening," Mayron said.

"We can go over all the details back on Mars," the mafiosa went on. "But there is one thing you should know up front."

The Dar'morian girl raised one perfectly arched eyebrow. "What's that?"

"Your name, dear," Mama Rossi said. "'Mayron.' It simply doesn't fit into the corporate culture. I'm thinking… Isabella."

Mayron made a face as if she had swallowed something particularly sour. "*Isabella*? What kind of name is that?"

Aerius turned back to Abe and Quinn as the hacker and the mafiosa continued their discussion.

"What will you do now, Quinn and Abe Titterman?" the chayat asked.

"I think it's about time I took flight lessons," said Abe. Turning to Quinn, he added, "Tell your mother that's what I want for my one-hundred-and-ninth birthday."

Quinn's face brightened even more. "I'll let her know," he said. "Maybe you can practice with me."

"And you?" Aerius said to Quinn.

The younger Titterman thought for a moment. "I don't know. School will be starting again soon. Maybe I'll take some business electives this year." He looked at his great-grandfather. "After all, someone's gonna need to take over the family business on Phobos."

"Right they do!" Abe said, clapping his great-grandson on the back. "Let's have no more talk about the, well, about the, uh… the *thing*."

Quinn looked at his great-grandfather quizzically. "What thing?"

"The thing," Abe said. He gestured with one hand toward the Key, hoping to pull the word for it out of thin air. "You know, the thing. The *whatsyacallit*."

Quinn looked at the Key and frowned. "It's starting."

By the time they got back to Mars, no one was talking about the Key anymore. In fact, Quinn accidentally left it in the ship when they disembarked and had to go back for it when they were halfway across the compound. With each passing hour, it became less and less prominent in their minds.

On the evening of their return, Mama Rossi arranged for a farewell dinner that her subordinate, Mario, got from the Adams Café. The meal consisted of family-style pasta for the humans, udon and vegetables for Aerius, and a Dar'morian *wrex* flank steak for Mayron. After dinner, in the privacy of her office, Mama Rossi confided her secret to Mayron. The mafiosa explaining that she was a Solar Government agent installed to dull the power of the Martian Mafia from within and eventually transition it to legitimate business dealings. Mayron, Mama Rossi assured her, would likely be the youngest-ever employee of the Solar Government, and the hacker decided that it was time to hang up the mantle of Shotel Zero once and for all. Together, they decided on an appropriate demise for the legendary cyber criminal: death by electrocution while building a custom supercomputer to simultaneously crack the defenses of the Nyoploris Reserve Bank and the Takar Gambling Syndicate. Mama Rossi would arrange to have Solar Agents visit Mayron's parents and explain that she had been selected to attend a special school for highly intelligent young women on Mars.

It was not without a few tears that Aerius parted ways with the group the following day. Even Abe shook the alien's hand— a gesture whose significance was no doubt lost on the chayat— and thanked him for helping keep his great-grandson safe. Aerius told the others that he would return to his home planet for a while before continuing his work as a tracker. In the wide universe, he never crossed paths with the Tittermans again.

Some weeks later, Quinn was arranging the day's schedule at Intergalactic Curios on his last day before returning to school. He had just about finished uploading the appointments to the shop's computer when Abe came down from his apartment above the store.

"Good morning," said Quinn.

"Good morning," Abe replied. "What do we have on the docket today?"

"Missus Finegraft will be in momentarily to pick up the pieces she needs to complete her Quemos stalactite set."

Abe rolled his eyes. "Are these the ones from the caves on the southwest continent?"

"Yep," said Quinn. "And she confided in me that she'll be starting on the southern hemisphere next."

"Tell your mother I'm keeping you here just to deal with the customers," said Abe with a grunt.

"Come now, Pop-pop," Quinn replied. "Iash says, 'Service comes at the expense of our egos—but we gain much more in return.'"

Abe opened his mouth to continue the debate when a ship landed outside the front door. Moments later, two people entered the shop, the older of the duo supported on the arm of the younger.

As they made their way toward the front counter, Abe said quietly, "I think you can handle this transaction."

Quinn flashed a smile and said genially, "Missus Finegraft, how nice to see you again."

The old woman detached herself from her escort and placed both hands on the counter. A nebulous cloud of thinning permed hair surrounded her head, and costume jewelry made from cheap plastide adorned her ears, neck, and six out of ten fingers.

"Mister Quinn," Finegraft said, "we spoke on the comm. This is my niece, Alice, who's helping me today." She gestured to the younger woman, who was about Quinn's age and very

pretty. "I've come for the last of the Beng Cave System stalactites."

"Yes, we have them boxed up and ready to go. It's that one,
Pop-pop," Quinn said, pointing to one of several boxes that had
been stored behind the counter for imminent delivery.

Abe placed the box on the counter and was about to retreat
behind Quinn again when Missus Finegraft crooked a finger at
him.

"Abe, my dear," the old woman went on, "now that I've
completed the Beng Cave System, I want to talk to you about
the Martash complex in the southern hemisphere. You've done
very well for me all these years. I'll have a diamond dripping
from every cave on the planet when we're through."

Abe revealed his salesman smile. "Quinn can take down
whatever you need."

Quinn shot a sidelong glance at his great-grandfather. "Yes,
but you should listen too since I'll be going back to school tomorrow."

"Is that when your classes begin?" Alice said. "Mine start in
another week. I wish it were sooner."

"Alice is at the Grotzinger Academy," Missus Finegraft
said with pride. "She's absolutely in love with learning. Probably wouldn't take a summer vacation if we let her."

"Not when there's so much to do, Aunt Arian," said Alice.
"Wasn't it Iash who said, 'Like a garden in the oasis, never allow your mind to go fallow'?"

Quinn could only stare at the young woman.

Abe, though, grunted and said, "Oh, you two will get along
famously."

Over the next several moments, Quinn took down a detailed
list of the pieces Missus Finegraft wanted to acquire. Abe assured her that finding the stalactites would take several weeks
but certainly no more than three months. They exchanged pleas-
antries and the two women were about to leave when Alice

pointed to an object resting on the counter that had seemingly been put there as an afterthought.

"What is that?" she asked. "It's beautiful."

Quinn followed her gaze and cocked his head as he examined the object. Made of a burnished gold material, the object was about six inches long, with a cylindrical shaft two-thirds of its length that attached to a four-sided handle. Two square-like teeth jutted up from the end of the shaft, and another halfway down. The handle was carved with intricate patterns and strange symbols. A ringed planet formed a kind of pommel at the end.

"I… don't think it's anything," Quinn said haltingly.

Abe saw what they were looking at and added, "We think it came in one of our consignment lots. It's not worth anything, if that's what you're asking."

"Oh," said Alice, disappointed.

"Until next time, Misters Titterman," said Finegraft, and they turned to go.

Quinn watched as they left and prepared to board their ship. He looked from the object to Alice, torn with indecision.

"What?" said Abe, noticing his great-grandson's uncertainty.

"You said it's not worth anything, right?" said Quinn.

"That hunk of junk?" said Abe with a scowl. "Nah!"

"*She* seemed to like it."

Abe handed the object to Quinn. "Well, what are you waiting for?"

Quinn took the thing with a smile and sprinted after Alice.

The Key was ready for its next adventure.

Selections from the Encyclopedia Galactica

 The author is proud to present these entries from the *Encyclopedia Galactica* that are pertinent to this text.

Ad-unt Elnor: Galaxy-wide religious group dedicated to stopping the wonton spread of technology (though this does not prevent them from using starships to travel between worlds for the purpose of preaching their faith).

Aetherstone: A type of stone found exclusively on certain asteroids that can be crafted into building materials and dyed in any color. Named for "aether," a primitive term for outer space, the search for aetherstone has launched mining operations in the Solar Asteroid Belt and in similar extrasolar locations.

AugmentCon: Short for Augmentation Holdings Consolidated, this medical, pharmaceutical, and biotech company based on Nyoploris specializes in biological augmentation.

Chayat culture: Select phrases native to the culture and languages of N-31 Alpha.

- ***andrak:*** a god or godlike being
- ***Briak Mor:*** The N-31 Alpha word for the Key to the Universe
- ***ib:*** Ceremonial robe made from fibers of the morongo plant
- ***kalt***: Insult meaning "dishonorable one"

- ***laqhon:*** Period of penance for a serious transgression of the chayat code
- ***morongo:*** Plant used to make fibers for ceremonial dress
- ***nalc:*** path of acolyte training for offworlders who have been paired with a powerful chief to learn the "ways of the ancestors"
- ***umkala:*** burrowing animal that is prone to bite individuals who stumble upon its nest. Umkala bites are rarely fatal since the antitoxin is widely known, but the wounds are nonetheless painful.

Currency: The Solar Government issues paper money in the form of "solar notes" that is accepted throughout the solar system and at other intergalactic hotspots (like the Adams Café). Intergalactic transactions generally occur with electronic funds, often called credits, that can be converted to local currency.

Currency is sometimes used in idioms. For example, "It isn't worth a wooden Galavan spot-coin" refers to the much-forged currency of the planet Galavan that is rarely accepted as legal tender. The phrase means, "It isn't worth anything."

Dynoplas: Special kind of plastic used for a variety of building purposes that is stronger than most metals.

Elchoir tidal bamboo: Fast-growing plant from the water world Elchoir whose wood is often used for decorative facades or panels.

Faster-than-light (FTL): Generally, any engine that is capable of traveling faster than light in hyperspace. Used for interstellar travel. (See also: hyperspace; hyperspeed; Whyte Industries Limited)

Floyd's Register of Starships: Database of all star-faring vessels that includes such data as date and point of origin, owner, schematics, etc.

Fungus flu: Common name for Influenza T-Type 37. Generally found on worlds that have undergone the terraforming process. Symptoms include fever, vomiting, and chest congestion. The most severe symptoms typically clear in twenty-four to forty-eight hours, with chest congestion lasting up to a week. Fungus flu is usually harmful only to elderly or infant patients, or patients with compromised immune systems.

Fusion drive: Preferred engine for sub-hyperspeed travel.

Golden Age of Missionaries: A period shortly after the solar system joined the intergalactic community that was marked by the spread of ideas between planets, especially schools of religion and philosophy. (See also: Iash)

Holo-serials: Serialized holographic entertainment, usually adventure stories, whose popularity waxes and wanes. Classic serials from about a hundred years ago marked the golden age of holo-serial entertainment. There have been a few revivals. Among the most seminal titles are *Queen Belle of the Stars*, *Disaster at Kreyanos, Starchasers* and *Galaxy Rebels*.

Hover propulsor: Engine that allows an object—such as the Adams Café—to remain at a fixed point in space without having to orbit a spatial body like a planet or moon.

Hyperspace: Spatial state of being outside of normal space-time bonds achieved by using a FTL engine. Hyperspace is characterized by a "no-color brightness" in which the visual sensation of travel is nullified. (See also: faster-than-light (FTL); hyperspeed)

Hyperspeed: Synonym for FTL travel. (SEE ALSO: faster-than-light (FTL); hyperspace)

Hypersteel: Next-generation metal alloy.

Iash: Shyophian philosopher whose teachings spread extensively during the Golden Age of Missionaries. The seminal work of Iashian teachings, which has been translated into 1.34 million languages, is called *The Essential Teachings of Iash*. Iash is particularly known for his adages, which often contain important teachings presented in simple language. A few of his most famous sayings are as follows:

- "A gracious host is always punctual, even if his company is not."
- "It is the capacity to wage peace, not war, that determines the *civility* of a civilization."
- "A dead man's purse is as worthless to him as his body."
- "A *broq* holds the sweetest fruit." (Looks can be deceiving.)
- "A well-rounded individual is never prevented from rolling forward."
- "Choose your battles wisely, because even the smallest rat is deadly in large numbers."
- "Forgiveness is more precious than gold and just as hard to come by."
- "Invention is an imperfect process."
- "To educate another man is to touch the divine."
- "Service comes at the expense of our egos—but we gain much more in return."
- "Like a garden in the oasis, never allow your mind to go fallow."

(See also: Golden Age of Missionaries)

Ion drive: Engine used for sub-hyperspeed travel; largely replaced by more efficient fusion engines. (See also: fusion drive)

LAS-er systems: Galactic-wide manufacturer of energy beam weapons in a variety of sizes and configurations, from personal protection to military applications. LAS stands for "Light-Activated Shooters."

- **cannon:** Large-caliber model with mostly military applications. "Cannon" is generally a catchall term for any large LAS-er weapon that is mounted on the hull of a ship. Many different models exist.
- **Derringer 2:** Small, personal model that can fit in one's pocket or purse; "Fashionable among protection-minded ladies."
- **Eagle Sight:** Military-grade pistol favored as a high-end sidearm for officers
- **pistol:** Typical, standard-issue sidearm for personal use
- **rifle:** Larger weapon, generally for military and hunting purposes

Martian Mafia: Organized crime syndicate based on Mars and currently headed by Gabriella "Mama" Rossi. Rossi is known to be a staunch traditionalist and makes all of her associates take Italian names—regardless of their species or planet of origin.

Martian Rosea: Skin ailment particular to Mars that is mostly observed in young people in their teens and early twenties. If not treated properly, Martin Rosea can leave pockmarked scarring. The disease is thought to stem from the unique differences between Martian soil and the soil of humanity's homeworld, Earth.

Martian stone: A sturdy red rock sourced from Mars that is used for building.

Organoplast: Sterile, biological membrane used for a variety of purposes in body augmentation.

Plastide: Next-generation plastic used for countless purposes, including everything from cargo manifest printouts to costume jewelry.

Secession Wars: Series of civil conflicts in which the inner planets of the Terran Solar System tried to break away from the outer planets and form their own government. The end of the Secession Wars brought about the reunification of the Solar Government. (See also: Solar Government)

Solar Government: Bureaucratic body that oversees the governance of all planets and settlements in the Terran Solar System. Each planet has its own local government run by a governor. The Solar Government itself is run by a president, who is elected to a ten-year term. Senators and judges are elected for five-year terms. (See also: Secession Wars)

Solar Network: Interplanetary computer network connecting the planets of the Terran Solar System.

Suspension field: Technology aboard a starship that can be used to tow or hold objects in space.

Viewport: Windows or portholes on a starship, generally.

Whyte Industries Limited: Based at the Vortas shipyards, Whyte Industries is the leading manufacturer of FTL engines. One example is the Pulsar Class, which is a standard FTL drive available for personal and small commercial applications. (See also: faster-than-light (FTL); hyperspace; hyperspeed)

ACKNOWLEDGEMENTS

My name appears on the cover of this book, but I am hardly the only person to have worked on it. As such, I'd like to publicly acknowledge the following individuals.

First, a tremendous thank you to Emma Nelson and Hannah Smith at Owl Hollow Press, who decided to take a chance on *The Key to the Universe* and saw the book's potential, even in its raw form. From the first time we spoke, I was so pleased to hear that our visions for this tale aligned. It has been a pleasure working with you to get the book on shelves.

Thanks to OHP's editor, Olivia Swenson. Working with you felt like a true collaboration. I was so pleased to have your patient and knowledgeable help in making this book the very best it could be.

Thank you to Cherry Weiner for your guidance on certain rights matters and to Tim Waggoner for introducing us.

Thank you to Lauren Brown, who fearlessly answered my call for a beta reader when the book was still in an unpolished state. Your insights and feedback were invaluable.

Thank you to my family for your constant love and support, especially my mother who fostered my ambition to write from childhood.

Finally, thank you to Crystal Cassetori, who shared in my frustration, joy, anxiety, and excitement every step of the way. I love you.

Deepest apologies if I've forgotten anyone. Any errors or omissions are solely my own.

Patrick Scalisi is an award-winning journalist and communications professional. He has published countless short stories
and the book *The Horse Thieves and Other Tales of the New
West*.

When he's not writing, Patrick enjoys art, gaming, storytelling,
and pop culture. He loves watching way more movies than are
good for him, reading more books than he has shelves for, and
playing the collectible card game *Magic: The Gathering*.

Patrick lives in Connecticut and can be found online at
patrickscalisi.com.

#TheKeytotheUniverse